Further Mysteries by Elizabeth Gunn

The Jake Hines Series
TRIPLE PLAY
PAR FOUR
FIVE CARD STUD
SIX POUND WALLEYE
SEVENTH INNING STRETCH
CRAZY EIGHTS
McCAFFERTY'S NINE *
THE TEN MILE TRIALS *
ELEVEN LITTLE PIGGIES *

The Sarah Burke Series
COOL IN TUCSON *
NEW RIVER BLUES *
KISSING ARIZONA *
THE MAGIC LINE *
RED MAN DOWN *

* *available from Severn House*

NOONTIME FOLLIES

NOONTIME FOLLIES

Elizabeth Gunn

Severn House Large Print
London & New York

This first large print edition published 2016
in Great Britain and the USA by
SEVERN HOUSE PUBLISHERS LTD of
19 Cedar Road, Sutton, Surrey, England, SM2 5DA.
First world regular print edition published 2015 by
Severn House Publishers Ltd., London and New York.

British Library Cataloguing in Publication Data

Gunn, Elizabeth, 1927- author.
Noontime follies. – (The Jake Hines series)
1. Hines, Jake (Fictitious character)–Fiction.
2. Murder–Investigation–Fiction. 3. Police–
Minnesota–Fiction. 4. Offenses against property–
Fiction. 5. Chemical industry–Fiction. 6. Green
movement–Fiction. 7. Detective and mystery stories.
8. Large type books.
I. Title II. Series
813.6-dc23

ISBN-13: 9780727870865

Typeset by Palimpsest Book Production Ltd.,
Falkirk, Stirlingshire, Scotland.
Printed and bound in Great Britain by
T J International, Padstow, Cornwall.

One

I was brought into the world one crisp October evening, late in the twentieth century, by a janitor who fished me out of a motel dumpster in Red Wing, Minnesota. I was probably a couple of hours old, naked in a stiff breeze off the Mississippi and almost too cold to cry.

Smart money, if there had been any around, would not have bet on a bright future for this shriveled brown-skinned castoff with the puzzling face. But I caught a few lucky breaks – the Minnesota welfare system kept me from starving, and I was helped along the way by a great caregiver and a couple of talented teachers. So now, in my late thirties, contrary to reasonable expectations, I'm not in jail or living under a bridge. In fact, I'm a husband and father, with all the markers: the mortgage, the car seat, the worried frown from always being late. My name is Jake Hines, and I'm a cop.

I run the detective division of the Rutherford, Minnesota Police Department. It's a good job, usually – challenging enough to keep my synapses firing but not so alarming I can't sleep nights. My chief is a reasonable man, I've got smart detectives on my team, and I make a living wage – or it will be a living wage as soon as I conquer my ingrained tendency to spend next year's money last week.

As a lucky stiff damn well ought to, I stay pretty contented. Except once in a while . . . like last Monday morning, on a beautiful day in the first week of October. I was interrupted on my way to my on-duty parking spot by a string of squad cars pulling out of the station. The drivers were all in fresh blue uniforms, sporting that bring-it-on gleam cops have at the start of a shift. Watching them, I began to ask myself: why did I work my butt off to get a desk job?

I used to be one of those carefree street cops, I remembered. Look at them now, getting ready to drive around all day in perfect golden sunshine, waving to shopkeepers and being admired by nubile young women. Meanwhile, I would be crouched in my chair under a blue energy-saver bulb, fretting about cold cases and struggling with next month's schedules. Oh, and come to think of it, I was slated for a budget meeting in half an hour – really, all that was missing from this day was an impacted molar.

Habit and a lack of alternatives propelled me through the tall front doors of Government Center and up into the processed air on the second floor. At least, I was glad to see, the People Crimes section looked orderly and quiet – six full-time detectives tapping on keyboards, describing the spousal abuse, gang rumbles and sexual assaults of a typical weekend in the heartland. All depraved crimes to be sure, but nothing major was going on or I'd have heard about it.

Property Crimes section, of course, showed the

usual bustle – a dozen busy detectives chasing missing bikes and power tools, outboard motors and electronics. In line with national trends, auto thefts were way down in Minnesota – a thirty percent drop in the number of vehicles stolen over the last five years. Interestingly, the value of the vehicles stolen was down by even more – fifty percent. Newer cars are harder to steal, thanks to smart keys and electronic tracking devices. Druggies have to make their nut some way, though, so the theft of electronic gizmos was growing by leaps and bounds.

Property Crimes is essentially an arms race: whenever the mopes invent a new wrinkle, we find the ways and means to match. This year new versions of easily portable electronic gadgets were coming off the assembly line at dizzying speed, so naturally more hoodlums were swiping them. But improved communications with the sheriff's department, better tracking devices and neighborhood watch groups were all helping us. So surely Kevin Evjan, the headman of Property Crimes, was not watching me unlock my door and then following me into my office to talk about the same old, same old, was he?

He was focused on something, though – beady-eyed with determination and carrying two pages of handwritten notes. I got ready to fend him off.

Kevin's Irish–Norwegian good looks and roguish charm enabled a colorful social life, which given any encouragement he would gladly describe in vivid detail, especially on a

Monday morning when his weekend adventures were fresh in his mind. His sexual adventures could be mildly amusing, but mostly I tolerated his stories because it seemed to me that high self-esteem was what kept his boat afloat in the Property Crimes swamp – he seldom complained and rarely asked for help. I started in Property Crimes, so I know what a soul-sucker it can be. As he plunked his long, handsome body into my visitor's chair, I reminded myself how lucky I was to have a Property Crimes headman whose bubble never seemed to burst.

But I didn't have time for any of his raunchy monologues right then. Any minute, my phone would ring and the chief's secretary would summon me to his office. There are hard realities that can be mitigated in this building, but Lulu's summonses are not among them.

'Hey there,' I said, hanging up my jacket, not meeting Kevin's eyes. I still had work to do for the meeting.

Undeterred, Kevin settled the crease in his pants, inspected the shine in his loafers approvingly and said, 'Something weird is going on.'

'Can it wait a couple of hours? I need to get ready for a meeting.' On Monday mornings the chief liked to go over plans and schedules for the week and month ahead. Most of our plans are reduced to rubble by noon on Tuesday, but we keep trying because our job description says we never quit.

'The details can wait, sure. I just want to let you know I'm going to need a consult today. I'm dealing with a rash of break-ins like nothing I've ever seen before, and before it goes any further we need to decide on a policy. Or strategy?' He did a large shrug and turned his hands up. '*Attitude*, maybe.'

'Attitude, that's a good one. Go away now and I'll give you all the attitude you can handle by ten o'clock.'

'Deal.' He folded his notes along a precise center crease and stood up. As he went out the door, he said over his shoulder, 'Be ready to think outside the box.'

Well, there now, I had my instructions.

Outside the box or in it, I didn't have time to worry about him right then. I did anyway, a couple of times, nagged by the realization that Kevin Evjan rarely confessed to uncertainty. But my curiosity had to wait while Chief McCafferty and I addressed personnel issues and, oh, God, money.

Without much argument, we agreed on a maternity leave, two commendations for extra effort, and one promotion. Then we got to the hard part, the budget for the upcoming year, and Frank began to lay out some big uncertainties.

'I don't see any goddamn way,' he said, 'to make a credible budget for a city that seems to be growing in its sleep.'

A big, broad-chested man with a rich baritone voice, Frank McCafferty could rattle the windows with his protests when anxiety gripped him. Budget season was always a fraught time for him because the city of Rutherford was a lot like me – its needs invariably exceeded its means.

The air grew bluer as he reviewed the challenges.

'Every damn meeting I go to – and do I ever have a day without one now? – we're talking about a ribbon cutting for a remodeled building, or green-lighting another New Science start-up – experimental hemp, herbicide-resistant wheat.' He waved his arms around. 'Does it seem like there's no crop left in Minnesota that we're not experimenting with?'

'Science is changing things fast, all right.'

'Some of these plants I can't even pronounce – what the hell is quinoa?' He said it *queen-oh-ah*.

'I think they say it keen-wah,' I said. 'Ancient grain. Gluten-free.' I read that on the package and it was all I knew.

'What the fuck's wrong with gluten all of a sudden?'

'Don't know. If Trudy says eat it, I eat it.' The one useful piece of advice I carried away from Boy Scout camp was never argue with the cook.

'Well, sure. But my point is we've been getting along fine without all these bright ideas. But now it seems to me we have a dozen busy scientists working on some version of them in a shiny new lab in downtown Rutherford.'

'I should have bought one of those empty buildings downtown when they were all on the market so cheap.' Except for having zero credit left anywhere in the world, that would have been a good idea. 'That empty block on South Broadway's filling up fast now.'

'Why not, when there's tax-increment financing? Hell's bells, did you see the story on the front page yesterday? A six-story building going in where that closed hardware store's been standing empty for four years.'

'Why do you find that alarming?'

'Well, is anybody thinking about how many more cops it's going to take to police all this? A whole new subdivision's being bladed off out west of Granite Avenue, where there's never been anything but corn.'

'Well, that's where they put the new co-op building for small start-ups, isn't it? That place they call Three to Get Ready.'

'Funny damn name for a building. But I guess it means just what it says, huh?'

'Yeah, the city got a federal grant to build offices where people with new product designs get three years of cheap office rents courtesy of the Commerce Department while they try to make their idea fly.'

'Such a sensible idea to come from the Feds.'

'Hold your breath while they screw it up, right? But what have you got against it? Isn't recovery good news?'

'Sure, but every time I ask for a raise in my budget the city fathers start crying that the recession isn't over yet. What have we got here, hard times or runaway growth?'

'Depends what you do for a living, I guess.'

'Well, in what I do for a living, I need a plan I can stick to! Every year for the last five we've slid a little farther behind in equipment and personnel because they won't give me money enough to keep up. Tell me the truth, Jake: how many cold cases have your part-timers got now?'

'About the usual,' I said. 'We're working on it.' Better be careful of that one. Today he wanted me to support his argument, say we had too many cold cases. But if I got into details he'd remember them, and by the middle of the week he'd be in my office saying, *Tell me again about that McCoy case; can't we bear down a little harder and get that cleaned up?*

He hates unsolved felonies. I agree we could use a couple or three more detectives, but sometimes I remind him that while everybody loves stories about DNA identifications, most cold cases are cold because nothing is cooking on their trail.

We finally settled on a request for five new detectives, three for Property and two for People, and a part-time steno to take some of the load off LeeAnn before her desk collapses. We figured ask for five and you might get three, and we could live with two if we had to. It was the best we could do because Frank knew he had to put more uniforms on the street – he had twenty more street miles to patrol than this time last year, and the equivalent of a village coming soon to downtown.

After an hour of talk we ended up with almost exactly the budget I would have predicted before we started. On budget issues, Frank is like a big, well-trained hunting dog – he's very capable but he needs to be stroked occasionally to stay motivated.

By ten o'clock I was glad to get back to Kevin's problem. Property Crimes might not be pretty but usually it was reassuringly matter-of-fact. A normal conversation in Property Crimes involved (a) what's missing, (b) who probably took it, and (c) whether or not there was a chance in hell we could catch the bugger.

Usually the answer to (c) is probably not. But we always tried, and we made sure the injured party knew exactly how hard we tried. Least we can do, I figured, especially when we couldn't do anything else. Filling out insurance claim forms has to be one of the least gratifying activities known to man, so we tried to compensate by giving good search reports. Rutherford's recovery rate might not be any better than average, but we made our clients feel cared for. So what did we need this attitude business for?

But Kevin was clutching his handwritten notes, looking ready to make the sale.

'Looks like you added a page,' I said.

'Two, actually,' he said. 'Tom Sjelstrom brought in his report.'

'OK.' I turned over my wastebasket, empty because all the paper that belonged in it was still on my desk. Propping my feet on the metal can, I settled my tush in my chair. 'Pour it on me.'

'Fourteen break-ins in the last five business days,' he said, 'mostly downtown. Offices, not stores. And not one item taken from the lot.'

'What?'

'My guys have searched, with the help of the owners. They can't find anything missing. These are all small business offices and labs, mostly start-ups burning through government and foundation grant money. Small staffs and they know their equipment. It's all still there.'

'Fourteen, no shit? But you said break-ins – what was broken?'

'Actually, hardly anything. In almost every instance they jimmied a lock on a door or a window. Quite sophisticated work – very few marks. When it was possible, they even re-set the lock when they left.'

'So how do you know they were break-ins? Were they trashed?'

'No. Neat as a pin.'

'Well, then—'

'The intruder left a message.'

'The same message every time?'

'Close to the same. Adjusted here and there to fit the jobs being performed.'

'Which are what?'

'Mostly experimental stuff – one's doing studies on molecular structures, half a dozen are working on genetically altered crops. It involves complicated computer modeling and they have small farms or grow plots out in the country. Two are labs – one biochemistry and neuro . . . *something* – they explained what they were doing but Tom couldn't understand it so he wrote down "science."'

'Ah, science. That'll narrow it down.'

'Right.' Kevin gave me a level look, which I read as *snarky's not going to help*. 'Two of the break-ins were in small investment houses specializing in taking start-ups public. One is a two-person office that specializes in finding grants – a small start-up lives or dies by its grants, they say. The biggest company that's been broken into so far is Minnaska.'

'Huh. Nothing experimental about them, is there? Everybody's favorite weed killer for the last twenty years.'

'Yeah. But their big hot success is with GMOs. You know what that means, right? Genetically modified— OK, don't get insulted, I just want to be sure we're on the same page. Their store on the Beltway didn't get hit – this is the lab downtown. The biggest lab of this lot' – he waved his papers – 'by far, with what looks like a fair-sized admin office at one end, full of suits.'

'You went to look?'

'I did. Mac and Bernie took the call, came back and said, "Better go see, Kevin, must be some big new hummer of a crop in the pipeline."'

'So you went and saw what?'

'Busy scientists in blue lab coats and gloves. You want attitude, Jake, these guys have got it up the ying-yang. They talk in code and look as if it's very satisfying to know how the world's going to end.'

'They told you that?'

'Of course not. They said they're working on improvements to their existing products. But they had a kind of a clever look when they said that. Like maybe it's an improvement to an existing product and maybe their geniuses have discovered something so life-altering it's going to blow our minds right off to the moon.'

'Good to know you hit it off with these people,' I said. 'What else?'

'The office suits look like very successful bankers. Their eyes start to glaze when they have to talk about anything but money, but they stayed focused long enough to tell us they're helping to find the money for the improvements. That's their job, they say – to help.'

'Sounds like a swell bunch of guys. And the B-and-E experts left them a message?'

'Yes. On a kind of a scroll. Good typing paper laid end to end and glued together. Written in neat cursive with a black Sharpie. The one at Minnaska's the longest of all the messages – it was laid out across four lab benches. It says' – he read from his notes – '"GMOs are not real food! GMOs must be labeled so people who want safe food supplies can avoid them." The rest of the message reads the same for everybody. "We are peaceful Friends of the Earth, who urgently want to remind you that Mother Nature will not be defied. Please stop making war on Gaia. If you do not desist, retribution will be swift and sure, and it is coming SOON!"'

'Is it signed?'

'No. No signature on any of the messages. The one at that little start-up out west of town, the one that calls itself SmartSeeds? Their message says, "God gave seeds all the smarts he meant them to have."'

'Ah. So the basic argument seems to be with too much science.'

'Or changes to the natural order. Something like that.'

'But we don't know whether we're looking at one wingnut or fifty.'

'No. Although common sense says it takes more than one person to get in and out of this many locked spaces in five days. Or nights, actually; it's all getting done at night.'

'And you've been investigating these complaints for five days? Why haven't I heard anything about it? And why no stories in the media?'

'Seven days. These invaders don't seem to like weekend work. I didn't put out the story because I couldn't decide what to call it. The first call came in on Tuesday of last week from the people working on plastic substitutes for frac sand – that stuff we had the commotion about last year, remember?'

'God, yes. Not likely to forget that for a while.'

'The fight's still going on, too. Listen, Jake, before you settle too deep into that wingnut characterization, I should warn you there's a large protest movement against genetically altered foods that's growing fast. And many of them are very solid people of the intellectual persuasion.'

'Oh, I know that. But this is the first I've heard of threats to do bodily harm. "Retribution will be swift and sure" – that's a threat! Which brings me to the attitude part.' I put my feet down and sat up. 'We're cops. We don't do attitude, we do law. Don't be distracted by the fact that nothing was stolen. Trespassing is against the law and if we catch them at it we'll nail them for it.'

'Well, sure. That's only a misdemeanor, though.'

'True. But threats are something else again, and in my book that line about swift and sure retribution constitutes assault. We're not going to be hamstrung by the notion that the message was supposedly written by conscientious people who believe they're working for the greater good. Doesn't that also describe terrorists?'

Kevin opened his baby blues a little wider. 'In a way, I suppose it does. I never thought of it that way.'

'The plague of our times – self-satisfied scoff-laws. A lot of those people murdering children in Syria put out statements that sound like they're doing social work. Here we have blameless tenants going about their business, and they're getting invaded and threatened? We're not going to put up with that. I want you to copy every report of these break-ins to People Crimes – you haven't yet, have you?'

'No. But we will; I see where you're going.'

'Damn right. Get a list of recent start-ups from the Chamber of Commerce and give it to Dispatch with a BOLO, see if we can get some extra drive-bys of these new small firms that are being targeted. Make it clear to everybody that the entire investigative division is working on this case. We don't countenance threats and we're going to put a stop to them.' I was beginning to sound a lot like Frank McCafferty, I thought contentedly.

'Good. That was what I was hoping you'd say. Fingerprints, handwriting studies, the whole nine yards?'

'Yes. Collect all of those messages, get them dusted for prints and, oh, hell, ask your techies to see if they can lift some DNA off those scrolls before they get dusted. We can't justify ordering any tests yet, but let's file some DNA evidence in case these outlaws of the intellectual persuasion decide which kind of retribution they'd like to try. And see to it that all media get the story right away. Who's on the info line today – is it Melissa?'

'Yup. Lissome Melissa.' There went Kevin's never-fail balloon again. He just had to let me know he'd been there. He's one of those guys for whom sex is not quite pleasurable enough until he's bragged about it.

'Tell her we want to play it as big as we can, get stories out to the effect that the chief says breaking and entering is no prank. We're taking these threats seriously and we're asking everybody to phone or email any information, anything they saw or heard that might have a bearing on the case.' I blinked at him a few times and said, 'That enough attitude for you for now?'

'Perfect. I'm on it.' He strode out at a brisk cadence left over from his time in the National Guard. He enjoys interacting with the media, and loves it when they quote him.

I tackled my desk, which grows paper like ditches grow goldenrod. In half an hour I was getting glimpses of wood-grain laminate. By 11:30 a.m. I was sitting at a clean desk answering emails, thinking about what else we ought to do to strike fear into the hearts of would-be eco-terrorists.

But apparently we'd done enough already, or maybe the terrorists thought they had. There were no more reports of break-ins on Tuesday or

Wednesday. No more scolding manifestos left on desks.

'See,' I told Kevin on Friday, 'we just had to take a firm stance with these people, show them we're not going to tolerate vigilante justice.'

'Uh-huh,' he said. He's cynical about all righteous speeches except the ones he makes himself. But he agreed we should keep beating our own drum since it seemed to be working. He got Melissa to put out a follow-up story about how vigorously we were pursuing every lead. Without actually lying, she managed to suggest that we expected to have the trespassers in custody soon.

Despite the fact that we still had no idea who left the messages, Kevin and I went home for the weekend feeling pretty satisfied with our job performance. This glow of hubris lasted until shortly after noon on the following Monday, when my chief of People Crimes section stuck his long, sad face through my door.

Two

Actually, Ray Bailey was quite a happy man these days, having recently married the woman of his dreams after years of tireless wooing. But not even happiness can change the fact that the men of his family are born with faces so grim they can wreck a party just by showing up.

He was never anybody's dream date, and now

in his forties he was freckled, gnarled and balding. But he was also driven and relentless, able and willing to work twenty-four hours straight in a blizzard if that's what the job required. Also, his grim demeanor allowed him to hold the attention of his scrappy crew without raising his voice. So while he was never my favorite guy to have a beer with, when events started circling the drain in People Crimes, Ray Bailey was my guy.

He said he had just sent two detectives to the headquarters of a firm called SmartSeeds.

'Oh? That's one of the places that got broken into recently, isn't it?'

'Yes. The one that got the message about what God wants.'

'Did they get another message today?'

'Maybe. An architect in a nearby office came over to visit a few minutes ago and found one of the two scientists who own the place slumped over his desk, non-responsive. He called nine-one-one. The leader of the EMT squad that answered is a guy named Scotty Antrim that I used to play hockey with. You know him?'

'Don't think so.'

'Very good head. Soon as he got a look he called me and said, "I can't see any reason why he should be, but this person is 10-72 for sure, a couple of hours at least." Asked me if I wanted to skip the trip to the ER and just call the coroner. And you know what a fanatic Pokey is about keeping dead bodies out of the hospital.'

'Uh-huh.' The coroner was quirky like a fox. 'He says they wash off too much.'

'Yeah. So I told Scotty, "Sure, we'll take it from here," and I called Pokey. Bo and Clint are on their way to meet him out there.'

'Out where? Oh, that's right – SmartSeeds is one of the tenants in that new co-op on the west side, isn't it?'

Ray nodded, standing a little sideways in front of my desk, looking into the corner of the room. When he's thinking hard he often stands like that, moving his lips occasionally like he's talking to himself – you wonder sometimes if he's forgotten you're in the room with him. He's not much of a talker but if you stick with him you find out he is a better-than-average thinker.

'So,' I said, 'for now we're treating it as an unexplained death, right?'

'Have to.' A tight little shrug. 'A dead body with no apparent injuries? No way to call it anything yet.'

'Has Property Crimes sent you their incident report on that firm? I told Kevin to copy everything to you.'

'Oh? I'll go pull it up.' He was back in two minutes with a mostly clean sheet of paper. 'First part seems to be a copy of a website. All it says is SmartSeeds, and then two names and a founding date. See?'

He showed me. The names were Nathan Gold and Daniel Brennan. The firm name was followed by a phone number, and each partner had an email address. The bottom line of that segment read, 'Mission statement to follow.' It was followed by a one-paragraph report of the discovery of the break-in: the front door locked as usual when the office manager arrived in the morning, but then she found the message scroll declaring God's intention for seeds arranged across the desk of the partner, Daniel Brennan, whose brass name sign said, 'President.'

'This is all we've got? Who did the interview? There must be more profile than this somewhere, or why would the holy messengers bother breaking in?'

'That's what you're calling them?' Ray grinned, a rare flash of amusement in his dour face. I noticed for the first time that he had white, even teeth. 'The Case of the Holy Messengers – I like it.'

'Ray, please, forget I said that, it's just something that lodged in my head. We don't want to make something weird out of what's probably just a heart attack.'

'For sure.' His face settled back into its usual gloomy expression. 'But I think it's important to remember that the people who did the break-ins were there to leave messages. Maybe extremists. Terrorists?'

'Well, let's not get terrorized just yet. Have you told Kevin about this?'

'Haven't had time.'

'Let's get him in here now.' I pushed the button and put the phone on speaker. Kevin said, 'Evjan.' America has tweaked his name till it sounds like that pricey French drinking water, the 'j' rendered as 'i,' and he's developed a crisp way of saying it that somehow removes any lingering aura of Norwegian farmers in four-buckle overshoes.

I asked him to come over to my office and bring everything he had on SmartSeeds.

In thirty seconds he was in my doorway carrying a single sheet of paper that looked suspiciously like a duplicate of Ray's.

The air in my office changed as it always does when Kevin and Ray see they are slated to work together for a while. I used to think they were like oil and water, hard to mix. Lately I've decided they're more like soap and dirt, unalterably opposed. There were two chairs in front of my desk, but nobody sat down while Ray repeated his news about the call from the emergency squad.

Kevin was profoundly shocked to hear about a death at SmartSeeds. His mouth fell open for a couple of seconds and when he closed it he looked up at the ceiling and said, 'Oh, shit.' Not finding any help in the overhead light, he stared over at me accusingly. 'So much for that firm stance, huh, Jake? *Damn.*'

'We don't know it's homicide,' I said. 'Let's not get all excited till we hear Pokey's report.'

Kevin said, 'Which one is it?'

'Which one what? Oh, the deceased?' I looked at Ray. He shook his head. 'We don't know that yet either. What I want to ask you is don't you have anything more in your records about this firm? Looks like what you're carrying there is the same stuff Ray's got.'

'Fourteen goddamn break-ins in five days, Jake, remember? We've been running a fucking *marathon* over there.' Kevin the suave, who had more than once stated his opinion that an adequate vocabulary did not need any help from obscenity, was sweating and swearing. 'I remember the SmartSeeds report came in the same day as Minnaska's, and guess which one got more attention?'

'OK, I understand Minnaska's a powerhouse, but still—'

'Those weren't the only ones that day either; there was at least one other. I can't— I'd have to review my records to tell you the name, but I know there was a third one and it also had a lot more going for it. In fact, SmartSeeds was the smallest of all the firms that reported break-ins. And it seemed to have so little going on – I mean, two scientists with no prizes to quote and they didn't even have clearly stated goals. We were all thinking how did these guys ever raise their grant money?'

He was so deep into defense posture that a sneaky suspicion began to form in my mind. 'Kevin, you did send somebody from your section to actually interview these people, didn't you?'

'Of course!' He rose up on the balls of his feet, adding another inch to the two he already topped me by, and glowered down at my tie tack as if its plain dull gold owed him an apology. 'It was a scramble, but I pulled somebody off one of the teams and sent . . . let me think.'

'That's another thing,' I said while he thought. 'Don't you have a form for these reports, and aren't they supposed to be signed? What I've got here looks like a copy of a website.'

'Frosty! Of course. Let me find him, see what

else he's got.' He flew out the door and made a lot of noise across the hall for a couple of minutes. Ray stood stiffly across the room from me, looking like a sad statue. Then the noise stopped and two sets of footsteps came back across the hall.

'Jake, you remember Forrest Amundson, don't you?' I did. Bland and blond, about my age, with very pale blue eyes. Frosty was a nickname he got in high school basketball, where he gained a reputation as a cool hand with a lay-up. He had not impressed anybody in the Rutherford PD as noticeably frosty, I was guessing; he was in my testing class when I got my first detective rating and I heard he'd flunked. He had been working graveyard in the northeast section ever since – it had taken him a long time to try again. 'He recently passed all his tests,' Kevin said, 'and joined our team.' Forrest was carrying his own chair, so finally we all sat down.

'It *is* a copy of their website,' Forrest said. 'It's all I could come up with to put in the slot. I wasn't able to get an interview with either partner.'

I gave him my not-mad-yet-but-gravely-concerned look. 'How come?'

'Neither one was ever in the office when I went there. Everything I got on the SmartSeeds break-in was from an office manager named Marilyn that first day. Talking to her was a pleasure, as far as that goes. She's built like a' – he outlined a female shape, grinning happily – 'and she's very friendly and tries to be helpful. But she didn't seem to know much about the product or what their plans are,' he said, getting serious when he saw me frown.

'What's Marilyn's last name?' I said.

'Hmm? I forget. Didn't I put that in the report? Sorry! She's kind of a distracting gal!' He grinned again, then looked uneasy when he saw none of us thought he was funny.

'In what way is she distracting, Forrest?' Kevin asked him, trying to reclaim a little gravitas for his side of the hall.

'Well, like I said, she's very' – he cleared his throat, looked in vain for an understanding face, and finished – 'feminine. Wears these clingy blouses – wow.'

Kevin, now almost as grim as Ray, said, 'Didn't she give you any information about the partners? There's nothing on this report.'

'Well, yeah, anecdotal stuff. Let's see . . . she said the president – what's his name? Brennan, that's right – is a hard-charging guy of about forty-five, with about a zillion friends on Facebook and LinkedIn and Twitter, always on the phone or his email when he's there, which isn't often. She's been told he mostly arranges meetings with money people, explaining the SmartSeeds story.'

'That's what she called it, the "SmartSeeds story"?'

'Yes. And she said the other partner, Nathan Gold, is a somewhat younger scientist, "kind of quiet, like he's deep in thought all the time." Said he has a couple of young assistants working part-time, mostly to help with the computer work, but they weren't around that day. The second time I went back she explained that Gold was the one doing all the testing, so he was often out in the field. She couldn't show me where he works – it was locked up and she doesn't have the key. It's a back room full of high-powered computers and reports full of, what does she call them? Algo-something.'

'Algorithms?'

'Yeah, that. She said she called Doctor Gold when she found the break-in, but he wasn't much concerned. They just have a conventional household lock on the front door because there's nothing in the front room but a couple of desks and some chairs. Well, and a standard computer, not a new one. The important computers that they keep the crop records on are all in the second room, behind a metal door with a heavy deadbolt lock on an electronic switch that only the partners carry an opener for, she said. So that's where all the value is, and Doctor Gold said as long as that was safe he didn't give a rip what the message said. "Just some nut," he said. But when she said she was a little spooked working alone in an office that had just been broken into, he said, "Well, then, call the police." So she did.'

'Next time, Forrest,' I said, 'put all those details in the case notes.'

'Even when it's all just who's not there and how nobody cares?'

'Oh, yes. All those facts matter to us, understand?'

'OK.'

'But you didn't get any reaction from either partner?'

'No. I went back twice, but I never found either one of them in. And we had so many other interviews . . .' He looked at Kevin for confirmation.

Kevin said, 'I finally told him: if they don't care, we've got bigger fish to fry. Because the bespoke suits at Minnaska were really on my case.' His face grew haunted. 'Jesus, wait'll they hear about this.'

'Kevin, whatever it is, we didn't do it, remember? Don't let anybody lay the guilt on you – you know better than that.'

'I did know better than that,' Kevin said, 'till I met those more-pinstriped-than-thou boys from Minnaska.' He shuddered. 'Wait till you meet them, Jake, they've got this sort of a Master of the Universe *gloss*—'

'Kevin,' I said, 'look at me.' When he quit flailing around and met my eyes, I said, 'Fuck 'em. You hear me? Fuck the suits and get back to work. Think licenses, permits, patent applications. Think about what SmartSeeds is growing out there in those fields – find out where the damn fields are, first. You don't know, do you? Well, then. When you've got something useful, come back and see me. Go help him, Forrest,' I said. Good old Jake Hines, all heart. 'Earn your pay today, help your boss.'

When they were gone, Ray Bailey relaxed a little and quit looking like he had been assigned to stand all day demonstrating the Mountain Position. In fact, he said, 'Aren't we jumping the gun a little here?'

'Maybe,' I said, 'but I had to give him

something difficult to do before he got so psyched by the suits he went into total brain freeze. What's your take on Minnaska, by the way? You heard any rumors about a super crop on the way?'

'No. But I don't do the Friday night bar crawl much since I got married. I'm way behind on my schmoozing. Even when I did make the rounds, the guys I hang with mostly stick to stuff like, "How about them Vikings?"'

'Yeah, well, since you brought it up, how about them? You enjoy handing half a billion tax dollars to the Wilf brothers for their new stadium?'

'Don't start,' Ray said. 'I do not have time to get into a rage today.'

'I thought you were a fan.'

'Of football, you bet. That Adrian Peterson, I could watch him run all day. But smooth-talking New Jersey carpetbaggers coming out here to steal money from schoolboards? Syphon off tax dollars we need to fix roads and bridges? Hell, I've seen some pot-holes on the southeast side of town big enough to bury Mark and Zygi both, which come to think of it is not a bad idea.' He shook himself. 'You see, you did get me started. I gotta go make a bunch of calls.'

He went out, checking his notes. I did what nobody else in the building seemed to be doing at that moment – answered my ringing phone.

Three

I'm not a farmer. But I live in the country, so the first thing I do every day is check the weather. My job is forty miles from my door, my wife's job is about the same distance in the opposite direction, and I now have a toddler to drop off at day care. Bad weather mornings, I might have balky motors to start, a driveway to clear – in the winter maybe even chains to put on. Some days, I've done a pretty good day's work before I even reach my desk.

On the first Tuesday in October, though, we had clear blue sky going up to forever, and the TV news said to expect crisp morning temps rising to high sixties by afternoon. Trudy blew me a kiss as she pulled out of the yard on her way to South Saint Paul, where she's a criminalist at the Minnesota Bureau of Criminal Apprehension. She does DNA studies at the state crime lab and loves her job.

While she was bopping up the highway thinking about nothing more serious than the structure of the human cell, I tackled the hard stuff: got my toddler son suited up and started the wrestling match required to get him into his car seat.

At about a year and a half, Benny seemed to notice that he was never out of sight of the adults in his life, and decided he was due for a change. Since then, every chance he got, he's tried to run away. He has no fixed goals, he just flings himself away from us, heedless of ditches and traffic and thorns. Small miracles have been required every day just to keep him alive. Trudy had begun to dream about a Velcro strip we might use to paste him to the refrigerator when we needed to catch a break.

Once body-blocked into place and lashed down securely, though, Ben got fairly contented in the pickup, waving and babbling at the sights. They were glorious that morning, bright sunshine gleaming through golden aspen and red oak leaves. You only get a couple of weeks, usually, after the leaves turn, before an early storm reduces this serene perfection to a cleanup job. I try to get outside and enjoy it while I can.

Ben liked it too. One of his few words – besides 'No!' which I believe he mastered the first time he heard it – was 'flower,' which he used for anything bright and pretty. It sounded much like 'floor,' when he said it, and that morning he yelled 'floor' at all the brightest trees on the way to town. He found several maples on South Center Street worth hollering 'floor' at, and one or two struggling aspens on the grittier street leading to his day-care provider. When I parked at the curb in front of her house, though, he forgot about bright-colored leaves and switched to his other favorite almost-word, 'Mags-EE,' which was as close as he could come to 'Maxine.'

Not many parents are lucky enough to have day-care arrangements like ours. Maxine Daly, Ben's nanny five days a week, was once my foster mother, the best one I ever had. She has one green eye and one brown, a wardrobe tastefully assembled from the best things she can find at Goodwill, and an offbeat sense of humor which she sorely needs. Her house is small and clean, with all the bare necessities and no extras, and I'm always happy when I'm in it.

I lost her when I was nine, owing to her late lamented husband's unquenchable thirst for beer. One of the times he swiped the state support money to go drinking, a well-meaning neighbor noticed we had no heat and reported Maxine for child abuse. The welfare lady found us hungry as well as cold, and took me away kicking and screaming. For the rest of my childhood, I got better amenities but a lot less affection – sometimes none, because for several years I was a snotty kid looking for a fight. A talented teacher in middle school persuaded me to try using my brain, and the good grades that followed that effort enabled a career in law enforcement.

Finding Maxine again after many years took all my smart-cop moves and, when none of those worked, another stroke of fantastic luck. I knocked on her shabby door on an errand, to pick up another cop's child for him, and there she was, the caregiver as usual. Since then there's one thing I know for sure – I am never going to lose her again.

Trudy, at first, was polite but puzzled by my attachment to this shabby woman. After Ben was born and she saw how he thrived in Maxine's care, she understood why I valued her. She quit being polite then, and began freely dumping all her anxieties about child care onto Maxine's patient ears. Maxine told me once that working mothers suffer more than stay-at-home ones because of guilt. To me, what Trudy went through with Ben during his infancy just looked like my perfectionist mate doing what criminalists do best – fussing over details.

I dropped my wriggling son into Maxine's arms and took off fast, barely on time for work, as usual. And for the first couple of minutes in the truck by myself, in the sudden glorious silence, my brain seemed to stretch and expand back to its original size. Toddlers are never quiet except when they sleep. Awake, they suck up all the energy in whatever space they occupy.

But now I had ten beautiful minutes of travel time in which to think. For about two traitorous seconds my brain shrank away from thinking about the dead body on the slab in the morgue – it seemed like such a waste of this perfect morning. Then reality snapped into place and I began to make mental lists.

The dead man, we had learned yesterday, was the younger of the partners. His name was Nathan Gold. As soon as the death was confirmed, Ray sent Clint to notify Gold's wife at the children's clinic where she worked. Rosie Doyle met him there and went in with him because, due to gender bias which nobody would express, we all thought she could help if the wife grew hysterical.

'Awkward, on the job like that,' I'd said.

'What else can we do, though?' Ray had said. 'That's where she is, and we can't wait till she leaves work – what if she hears it from somebody else?'

Ray had called me at home later to report that they had stayed with her till she'd arranged to have the balance of her appointments cancelled, and reached a family member who'd come to the clinic and gone home with her.

Bo had stayed at SmartSeeds to talk to the office manager and the people in the neighboring firm who had discovered the body. All these people would be coming in to the station today and tomorrow for more complete interviews.

The rest of the family, if any were local, should be found and notified today. I must update the chief, and the information officer of the day, who would need to give the media a lot more than the bare notice of death we'd fed them yesterday. Gold's partner in the tiny firm – had we found him yet? He was a high priority, and he would probably be very concerned. He could certainly tell us more about the dead man than we knew now, including what their relationship had been like. He might lie about that, of course, but sometimes you can learn a great deal from watching a man lie.

Ray had assigned Bo to the autopsy, which was set for this afternoon. Since he had no apparent injuries, most of our next moves would be dictated by what Pokey had to say after today's autopsy.

I needed to get Kevin's complete list of the firms that had been broken into, I reminded myself – we'd no doubt be getting anxious calls from some of them now.

I hope Kevin's found some more skinny on SmartSeeds, I was thinking. And did anybody say where that office manager was when the neighbors discovered the body? Then: God, there's so much to do today. I stifled that anxiety – having too much to do is par for the course on the day after an unexplained death. But in a couple of minutes I'd gone from not wanting to think about the dead man to not wanting to think about anything else.

I took the stairs to my office two at a time. From my door I could see Ray's team mustering around the big table in the People Crimes section. As soon as I got my lights on and dumped my briefcase, I walked down the hall to join them.

Ray was saying, 'You've each got a fact sheet that shows the little we know so far. I'm starting the recorder now, so be advised, everything we say will be in the case notes. I want to hear first from the team that answered the call to the dead body at SmartSeeds – well, Bo's already gone to the autopsy, hasn't he? So, Clint, you start.'

'If we hadn't been told the man was dead I would have thought we got called to watch a guy sleep sitting up,' Clint said. A good-natured street cop for ten years before he came inside, he's kind of a Goldilocks guy – medium coloring, nothing striking, and his voice and manner are soothingly warm enough, cool enough; just right for quieting things down. People trust him instinctively and they're not wrong – he's a helper. 'He had a drop of what looked like blood on the back of his right arm, just below the edge of his short-sleeved shirt. And a little darkening around it, like a light bruise. Otherwise, no scars showing. And the area around him was neat, no signs of a struggle.

'The only odd thing – Bo noticed it first – was that although the office was cool, he seemed to have been sweating. His shirt collar and underarms were dark with stain. It must have been some time earlier, though – we had gloves on, of course, but I touched the back of my wrist to his collar, and it was dry. So maybe he did something vigorous before he came inside.

'The office manager came in while we were there. Marilyn DiSilvio – she's worked for the company for a little over a year. She was surprised to find us all there, of course, and she was shocked, almost hysterical for a few minutes, when we told her the boss was dead. After she calmed down, though, she tried to help as much as she could, beginning with a clear timeline of how the day had progressed.

'She had opened the office at eight o'clock as usual, she said, and was typing some letters when Doctor Gold arrived. He was a little out of sorts because he woke up late and didn't get any breakfast, just grabbed a shower and ran out to check his fields, she said. She asked him if he wanted her to run out and get him something but he said no, he had a couple of trail-mix bars in his desk – he'd eat those. But he did ask her to do some other errands, take the packages from his car to the post office and pick up supplies at a couple of stores.

'She said these were not unusual requests – she

had done these same chores for him many times. The packages were to go to a lab they used regularly; the supplies were items he used all the time. She gave me a list of where she went and the items she mailed and picked up . . .' Clint started to hand it over, then took it back and said, 'LeeAnn's helping me get all this stuff in the case file—'

'Fine, show me later,' Ray said. 'What else?'

'She left a little after nine, and got back just at noon. There was nobody else in the office when she left, and as far as she remembers only the usual cars around. The complex has about a dozen offices but it's not full. She gave me the names of the other tenants – six in all. We didn't get to all of them yesterday afternoon, but I talked at length with the man who called us – Brad Polk, the senior member of a firm of three architects in the double suite of offices next door to SmartSeeds. Senior but still quite young, I would judge, although he's starting to get gray, like that news guy on TV.'

'Anderson Cooper?'

'No, the Mexican guy with a streak—'

'Miguel Almaguer?'

'Yeah, him. They're all young out there, just getting started, but this Polk seems like a very steady type. They have a funny name for the firm: Aardvark. He explained they have no money for advertising so they gave it a name that's almost certain to get it listed first in any directory.'

'That's pretty lame,' I said. 'Are they gooney?'

'No, very serious guys and the drawings in

their office look pretty elegant, actually. They may not be advertising geniuses – you can't be good at everything – but they struck me as hard-working, serious guys. Anyway, after Polk told us all he knew, he let us talk to Travis . . . uh' – he consulted his notes – 'Diebencorn; can't remember that name. He's the junior member of the firm, the one who actually found the body. Travis seemed pretty spooked; he was very tense – he kept looking over his shoulder, and once when somebody slammed a door he jumped a foot.'

'Did you read that as possible guilt?'

'Um . . . no. Far as I could tell it was just the usual reaction of civilians to dead bodies. Besides this, Travis is quite young, in his early twenties. Brad said something about the ink not being dry yet on his architect's license.

'He said it was the first time he'd ever seen a dead person. He didn't know how to tell for sure, so he ran and found Brad to help him decide. Brad said, "Nothing to decide, just call nine-one-one." And Travis said, "Will you do it?" So that's when Brad called it in.

'Diebencorn said he had just come over to chat and maybe talk Doctor Gold into going out to lunch. Said they dropped into each other's offices like that every now and then if they had time. Those two firms moved into the complex on the same day and became friends during the hubbub of getting settled. They're still friendlier with each other than with anybody else out there, he said.

'Diebencorn said, "I thought I knew him fairly

well. I had no idea there was anything wrong with him; he seemed like a healthy guy." Both architects went back to their own offices and watched from there until they saw the squad cars arrive. Then they came over to say they were the ones who'd placed the call.

'After they'd told the police all they knew, they left again and tried to get back to work, but they said they were having trouble concentrating. The squads had told them that detectives would be along soon, so they were waiting to talk to us. They came right over again. Diebencorn told us he was the one who found the body, but after he said that he let Polk do most of the talking – he's kind of shy, and the rest of the architects in the office seem to treat him like a younger brother.

'Our guys had the place taped off, of course, but one after another, people came up to the tape from all the other offices to see what was going on.

'I asked Diebencorn if he'd seen anybody unusual around the SmartSeeds office before he went over there. He said no. But it's a complex where people come and go all day; after Polk thought about it a minute he remembered he'd heard voices in the parking lot earlier – one of them could have been Gold's but he wasn't sure. A car door slammed and somebody apologized, but he had no idea why or if that had any connection to SmartSeeds.

'That's about it,' Clint said, thumbing through his notes. 'I talked to the other people in the complex but nobody else was as well acquainted with the two guys from SmartSeeds. The co-op seems to be a friendly, laid-back place, though, and they were all, you know, kind of agitated by having something happen to one of them and having police around.'

'OK,' Ray said. 'The rest of the Doctor Gold story is going to come from the autopsy. Now tell us about how you found and notified the wife.'

'The office manager, Marilyn, helped with that – told us how to find the wife. After she quit crying, Marilyn was very sensible and helpful, got us all the information we needed about the family and the partner.

'The wife's name is also Doctor Gold, Doctor Naomi Gold,' Clint said. 'She's a pediatrician at the Burns and Neighbors clinic. A very intelligent, organized lady, about thirty-five, I'd say, used to being in charge. She wasn't going to talk to us at first, told her desk person to have us make an appointment. We had to badger the desk lady to get into one of her waiting rooms. When the doc finally heard our message she was shocked, of course. But she held herself together, asked us politely to wait a couple of minutes while she got her assistant to start cancelling appointments. Had her mother called right away too. Mama showed up within half an hour, and if we thought Naomi had poise, it didn't take long to see that Mama wrote the book, right?'

Rosie nodded. 'Naomi's mom is a class act. She talks like Katherine Hepburn – must have grown up in New England someplace.' Just nodding agreement had dislodged a comb and set all her wiry red curls bouncing around her head. Rosie is *not* a class act but is shrewd and lively and fun to watch when she is not being so disruptive. When she is I want to stuff her in a drawer.

Clint turned a page in his notes. 'Naomi stated that there was no sign of any trouble when her husband left the house yesterday morning. He hasn't been ill, she said he's never ill, and she hasn't seen recent signs of unusual stress. She claims he's been working very hard but that was standard behavior for him. She didn't actually see him eat breakfast, but she assumed he ate his usual – fruit and cereal and yogurt – and took along some energy bars to keep handy in the car. Again, just usual behavior for him.

'She begged off a longer interview yesterday, said she had many phone calls to make, but that she could probably manage one today. I left my card and she's going to call me when she can talk.'

Ray, nodding, said, 'Rosie, your take?'

'The doctor's pretty glacial,' Rosie said. 'I don't think I was looking at heart-shattering grief.'

'Well, doctors are trained to control their emotions,' Clint said.

'So are cops,' Rosie said, 'but I think if you walked up to Jake right now and told him Trudy was dead, he'd show more distress than that doctor did.'

'OK,' I said, hurrying right along so I could stop imagining what she had just said, 'Clint admires the doctor for her self-restraint, and you find her poise off-putting. In fact, you dislike her so much you're ready to pin this crime on her. If it is a crime.' I looked around. 'But we still don't know, do we?'

'Not for sure, till Bo gets back from the autopsy,' Ray said. 'But Pokey told me yesterday afternoon that we'd better start turning over rocks because he'd talked to Nathan Gold's family physician, who told him the man was healthy as a horse when he had his last check-up six months ago. He suggested Pokey come take a look at his records, said death from natural causes was highly unlikely for this unusually vigorous man. Pokey told him he has no time to look at records today but invited him to drop in at the autopsy. The family doc said he'd do that if he could find the time.'

'Docs are good at being the busiest.' I looked around the table. 'Anybody found the partner yet?'

'Yes,' Ray said, 'that office manager notified him right away, and he was on his way back from Fairbanks when I talked to him. Alaska, yes. If you like emotion, Rosie, you should have talked to the partner.' Ray looked at the ceiling light and shook his head.

Rosie smiled at Ray the way she does when she thinks he's being more than usually judgmental. 'What did he say?'

'What didn't he?' Ray flared his nostrils. 'A man of absolute integrity is gone. Doctor Gold had great scientific talent and a consummate work ethic. We won't see his like again anytime soon. Um . . . Brennan's lost a treasured friend as well as an irreplaceable partner. There was more but I didn't have the recorder turned on and couldn't get it all down.'

'So Brennan doesn't keep it all inside,' I said. 'That's not a crime. What was he doing in Alaska – do you know?'

'Raising money, I suppose. That seems to be what he does.'

'Oh? What a handy talent to have.'

'And he's been living off it for years, apparently,' Ray said. 'I had Winnie do a little search on him and she tells me – well, you tell him, Winnie.'

'This is his third start-up that I found so far.' She looked up over her half-glasses, prim in her severe blue suit. Her name is really Amy, but when she started with the department the chief had a hard time pronouncing her last name, Nguyen. He settled on 'Win,' and by the time he figured out whether that was her first or last name we were all calling her Winnie. 'The first company he created was sold two years after its patent was filed, before it produced any product for sale. The second one was incorporated the following year, lost its funding after about two-and-a-half years and was disbanded six months later. SmartSeeds has been in existence about nine months. He has four earlier records of employment with other firms. All short, and the most recent dates back more than ten years.'

'Hell you say. I think we should scrutinize that career path rather carefully.'

'We plan to,' Ray said. 'Winnie's going to

phone the personnel managers of all the firms listed in Brennan's résumé.'

'Good. What else have we got on Gold?'

Ray looked down the table at his newest hire. 'Tell us what you've got, Abeo,' he said. I watched, not quite believing my eyes, as Abeo Okafor slid her reading glasses down from the shining black crinkle of hair that crowns her dome of a forehead and read from a couple of pages.

'How'd you pick her?' I had asked Ray when he first told me about this Nigerian woman he wanted to bring on board.

'Easiest call I ever made,' Ray said. 'I picked out the highest grade on every test and they all turned out to be her.'

So my mind had formed a picture of a studious African woman and I guess I imagined a kind of female Ghandi – a tiny, dark-skinned female with thick glasses, wrapped in bright-patterned cloth. This was nonsense, of course, since I knew very well she'd been a street cop wrapped in a blue Rutherford PD uniform for the last five years. But for some reason I had never encountered her on the job, so when I met her my shocked brain pushed 'studious' aside quickly to make room for 'tall.' Before I could take in anything else about her, I had to get used to the fact that Abeo was the tallest woman I'd ever met.

Because she loomed above me, it was a while before I noticed how elegant she was. She wore very plain clothes, mostly white, gray and black, simply cut fine wool pieces that draped her long limbs and trailed behind when she walked. Her statuesque look was emphasized by a few large pieces of jewelry hammered out of copper or silver. Usually the most serious person on the crew, her occasional gleaming smile tended to stop traffic on the second floor. All I knew about her so far was that her parents had brought her from Nigeria as a child, with the help of a church group, and she'd been a citizen since her teens. Ray thought she showed promise of becoming a very solid performer.

From where I sat I could see that the text she was holding was a jumble of different fonts and print styles, clearly downloads of various records she'd found online.

'Doctor Gold graduated from MIT twelve years ago,' Abeo said. Her accent was standard heartland, with better-than-average diction and a noticeable lack of slang. 'Summa cum laude, by the way.'

'In what?'

'Double major in biochemistry and computer science. Got his PhD at UC Davis, defended a dissertation about, as near as I can tell, the side effects of certain gene transfers. I've got a friend who's a biology teacher at the U in Minneapolis,' she told Ray, 'who I'm sure can help me sort out his academic records more precisely.'

'Good.' Ray met my eyes and nodded, his expression saying, *See what I mean?*

'I haven't found all of Gold's work history yet,' Abeo said. 'Looks like he got recruited by Brennan to help start SmartSeeds the year before last. There was a small item in the local paper about his moving here from New Jersey, where he had been teaching and leading field experiments at Rutgers. He seems to have studied and worked all his adult life for just what he's been doing here – experimental plant science.'

'Anybody found more family?'

'Lots,' Rosie said. 'Naomi's mother gave me a list. Two children, one in a local school, the other pre-school. She asked me to hold off contacting his parents and three siblings until she could notify them herself. They're all scientists, living all over the world, and this is going to be very hard for them, she says. They all loved Nathan.'

'She's going to let you know when she's reached them?'

'And give me numbers for everybody. Then I'll call them all.'

'And Winnie's going after contacts here in town, the chamber of commerce and whatever clubs he belonged to,' Ray said. 'And religious affiliations. The Golds belong to a Reform synagogue which we're told Nathan attended regularly. He also joined an amateur ice hockey team last year. Andy's been a goalie for the Wolverines for years; he doesn't remember Nathan but knows most of the guys on those teams, so I asked him to schmooze around and see what they say about Nathan.'

Andy Pittman, the size of a small Zamboni and Ray's most seasoned street cop, sat across the table, nodding like a wise old sage. He's only in his mid-forties, but because of his size and the hard beats he's walked, he projects an air of vast experience and insight. Not all of that is Alpha Dog bullshit: Andy really is a good man to have with you in a bar fight.

'OK,' I said, 'everybody's tasked, right? I'd better go update the chief. Please keep me informed, Ray, and don't forget to check with Kevin's crew as the day goes along. Nothing much is growing in the fields now, of course, but they're checking roots and collecting the skinny on the greenhouses they keep in some of the small plots. If it turns out somebody did kill the beloved Nathan Gold, sounds like it almost has to be because of his crops.'

I found Chief McCafferty in his office, between meetings but reading through a pile of reports. Bringing him up to speed on the Nathan Gold case didn't take long – I just handed him a list of questions.

'That's just the start,' I said. 'The list keeps growing.'

He listened patiently while I told him about the work underway. His questions, when they came, were mostly about the break-ins at the science-oriented firms. He was particularly concerned about the message left for Minnaska – it turned out Kevin had been in his office before me and shared his anxieties about the suits.

The chief, as he'd told me yesterday morning, had been spending a lot of time in meetings with promoters, new money guys pushing start-ups that were mostly names and ideas with very little product attached. In the privacy of his office he'd told me he thought most of them were dubious upstarts, maybe not outright charlatans but certainly on the take for Uncle Sugar's money. So far his public utterances had been confined to pleading with everybody not to let redevelopment outpace the forces of law and order.

Now his cheeks were aflame because he'd heard about the long warning scroll that had been left at Minnaska, one of the few developers that had actual stores and product lines, and it had raised his blood pressure a couple of notches.

'People getting threatened in legitimate business offices – we just can't have that here, Jake,' he said. 'That doesn't fit with Minnesota Nice.'

'That's what I told Kevin,' I said. 'So we put out a couple of stories about how the whole police force was looking for the people who were doing these break-ins, and we thought at the end of last week we'd scared them off.'

'But now here's this dead scientist—'

'But we don't know yet that there's any connection. The autopsy may tell us he died of natural causes and that'll be the end of that worry.'

'It bothers me, though, that we still don't know who's been making these threats. Somebody knows – it may be a whole group, huh? Can't we get a handle on that? Seems like we need a couple of guys to hang out in some bars and find out what people are saying. Isn't that kind of Bo's specialty?'

'Chief, I don't think concerned environmentalists hang out in bars much. And I'm sorry Kevin came in here crying to you about this; I'm going to put a brick alongside his ear for that.'

'No, he didn't do that, Jake, don't get on his

case. I heard somebody talking in the hall and asked him about it. And I certainly didn't mean to mess up the chain of command – I'm just concerned, you know, because Minnaska's no fly-by-night. It's a big, important company. We really can't afford to get on the wrong side of those folks – the chamber worked really hard to get them to move their lab here.'

'We'll do everything to show concern,' I said. 'We've got all our people working on this case now. But you know, we thought we had the office invaders on the run till we got the report on Gold yesterday morning. And maybe we still do. If the autopsy indicates that Gold's death is not suspicious, we're just looking for busybodies who want attention for their message.'

'Uh-huh. Keep me in the loop on this, will you? I'll be getting calls soon – I can feel them coming. An experimental scientist dead at his desk – shit, does that sound like some B movie or what?'

I wanted to tell him I didn't think Hollywood made B movies any more, but his cheeks were really pretty red, so I let it go.

'It's going to spook the hell out of everybody,' McCafferty said. He fixed me with his neon-blue stare and said again, 'I need to know everything ASAP.'

'You will,' I said. 'I guarantee it.'

I got out of his office then, glad to get away from his worried face, and walked over to Kevin's beehive. He was behind his desk, talking fast to half-a-dozen investigators, all of them standing around his desk looking at the ceiling light as if they might be thinking of shooting the damn thing out.

Property Crimes detectives are used to dealing with hysteria. Every day they confront indignant citizens, often weeping housewives who are shocked, *shocked* to learn that there are people *right here in Rutherford* who would come into a person's house and take their stuff.

Kevin's guys stayed calm through long days of listening to those lamentations because they knew they could count on a headman who was steady as a rock. Just write 'em up, Kevin would say, tell them we'll check the pawnshops and get back to them. *Kevin doesn't sweat the small stuff*, they would brag to their girlfriends and wives. *He knows how to deal with people and he's always on top of the world no matter which way it turns.*

But today their boss was sweating and swearing, looking apprehensive, acting like a client. All because, apparently, some nutcase had left notes in people's offices. Their faces were all saying, *What the fuck?*

'Makes you think about getting back out in a squad,' I heard Arne Asleson mutter.

I was standing just outside Kevin's door, listening as he told his team they didn't have any more time to dick around. He needed the location of every experimental farm plot SmartSeeds had within twenty miles of Rutherford, and the names of the products they had spread there this year – seeds, pesticide, fertilizer, whatever, and he needed them *today.*

Something stirred the hairs on the back of my

neck. I turned to find Ray Bailey standing behind me, breathing.

I said, 'You looking for me?'

'For Kevin. Came over to ask him what he's got on grow plots. Sounds like he's just getting started.'

'We're all just getting started,' I said. 'Why doesn't somebody just ask that office manager? She probably knows more about the grow fields than anybody else in town right now. What did Clint call her?

'Uh . . . Marilyn Di-something. I didn't get the spelling, and I'd like to know more about her – where she came from, how she got that job. Oh, hi, Kevin.'

Standing in the doorway to his office as his whole crew bolted out around him, he said, 'Why are you both standing in the hall? Come in.'

'We were just talking about the office manager at SmartSeeds,' I said, walking in. 'We're not sure how she spells her name and we need to find out when she can come in and talk to us. Is Frosty around? I'd like to talk to him.'

'No, I sent him out on a stolen car complaint. Can you beat this? Guy started his car in his own driveway then remembered he meant to take along a tool he was returning to a buddy. So he left the car running while he ran back in the house to look for it. Came out carrying the router and his car was gone.'

'Amazing,' I said. 'Can you get Frosty on the phone?'

'Of course,' Kevin said. He dialed, waited, tried it again but got no answer. 'He probably turned the damn thing off by accident,' Kevin said. 'He's not the sharpest knife in the drawer, is he? They said he passed all the tests, but I'm beginning to wonder . . . so I decided to have him cover incoming traffic and free up some of my more experienced guys to work on the SmartSeeds case. What do you want to ask him?'

'That office manager's cell phone number and last name,' Ray said, 'and anything else he knows about her.'

'If it's not in the report, he doesn't know it,' Kevin said. 'He swore he gave me everything he knew.' He blinked at Ray. 'Why don't you just call SmartSeeds and ask Marilyn whatever you want to know?'

'I tried that,' Ray said. 'I got a recording saying the office is closed and I should leave a message.'

'Since when?' Kevin looked angry again. 'I talked to her first thing this morning, to confirm that I was sending a team out to talk to her. Shit, I better call Grif and get them to head back.' He picked up the phone, thought a minute, and began dialing. 'Are you sure you dialed the right number? I can't believe she . . . Oh, Marilyn? This is Kevin Ev— Oh, you do? You're pretty clever about voices, are you? Oh, I bet you say that to all the detectives in your life.' He chuckled comfortably and asked her if any of his guys had arrived yet.

Ray and I walked away and left Kevin having a fine time on the phone. 'She left that message,' Ray said, 'I didn't make it up.'

'I know. Make a note of it, will you? Marilyn seems to have a free rein out there. Should we find out why that is?' As we approached his section I asked him, 'When's that Brennan guy due back?'

'He couldn't give me an ETA. He was outside a small rural village north of Fairbanks when I talked to him, and he said he'd have to let me know what flight he could get. Since then I haven't heard squat.'

I stood with Ray in the hall, listening as all the detectives in his section answered ringing phones. 'The word is out about the break-ins and the messages on the desks,' he said. 'We're all getting calls.'

'Has Clint heard back from Gold's wife yet?'

'No. But he seems to be sure he will. Clint is pretty impressed by the lady doctor.'

'Uh-huh. Rosie's reaction was interesting, wasn't it? What'd she call her? Glacial?'

'Yes. But then, compared to Rosie,' Ray said, 'almost everybody is.'

'We need to get Mrs Gold in here and have a proper interview,' I said. 'Tell Clint we need to see her today.'

I turned to walk back to my office, and for a few seconds I didn't quite register what I saw at the end of the hall. A man was standing at the window of the reception desk, wearing hiking boots and rugged all-weather clothing, looking as if he'd just stepped out of the pages of an L.L. Bean catalog. Over his shoulder, I heard Patty, inside the window, say, 'He doesn't seem to be at his desk right now. Hang on, I'll page him.'

Her voice on the PA system asked Ray Bailey to pick up a phone. After a few seconds I heard

Ray, behind me at his desk, say his name. I was halfway between them, hearing both sides. Patty's voice, quieter, no longer on the intercom, told Ray that Mr Brennan was waiting for him at reception. Then Ray's footsteps sounded behind me in the hall. His visitor turned and watched the two of us coming toward him, uncertain which one to smile at. He was a big man with a handsome, weathered face and close-cut brown hair lightly sprinkled with gray.

I turned into my office and, as Ray passed my open door, I said softly, 'Bring him in here, will you?'

Ray said, 'OK,' without turning his head. He walked steadily toward the window, his face expressionless, his eyes fixed on the ruggedly attractive man who was now the sole proprietor of SmartSeeds.

Four

Ray brought the big man in, stood rigidly erect beside my desk and said, 'Daniel Brennan, president of SmartSeeds.' To Brennan, he said, 'Lieutenant Hines, chief of the detective division.'

Brennan said, 'Dan.'

I said, 'Jake.'

He put out a big hard hand and we shook.

'I'm sorry I didn't keep you informed about my progress,' he told Ray as he settled in his chair. ‘I was pretty far out in the boonies and it took some ingenuity and the kindness of a lot of strangers to get here as fast as I did.’

‘We’d like to record this conversation, Dan,’ I said, turning on my desk machine without waiting for his approval. ‘There’s a lot we need to ask in a hurry and this’ll save some time.’

Brennan did a nod/shrug that indicated, *Sure, what the hell*, and went right on with what he was saying: ‘Luckily, people who work in Northern Alaska accept abrupt changes of plan as just part of everyday life.’ He unzipped a canvas vest made up of many zippered pockets, revealing a denim shirt with more pockets. He was festooned all over with pens, pencils, an iPad Mini and a GPS. A smart phone, Leatherman and metal tape measure were clipped on his belt. The man was a walking outdoor office. ‘Tell me,’ he said, ‘what happened to Nate?’

We went over the discovery of his partner’s dead body with him in detail, explaining that there were no signs to tell us how he died or why. ‘We’re waiting for autopsy results,’ Ray said, ‘hoping they’ll tell us something definite.’

I watched him closely as we talked. He registered shock and then devastation, tears welling up in his eyes. Eventually both eyes brimmed over and two fat drops snaked slowly down his cheeks. When they reached his chin and were about to drop off, he felt them and brushed them away with no hint of embarrassment.

We finished the little we had to tell him and he sat still for most of a minute, blinking at the wall behind my head. 'I guess,' he finally said, 'I travelled all those miles thinking this story would turn out to be a mistake.' His voice broke and he waited, swallowing, and we waited with him until he could talk again.

Looking at Ray, he said, 'I knew you told me that two experienced people had pronounced him dead, but . . . Nate was . . . so *vital*, you know?' His hands had commenced wringing each other and he watched them as if he wondered why they wouldn't stop. 'All the way across Canada on that plane my brain kept seeing this . . . kind of like a *movie* . . .' He had to wait longer this time. His lips moved a couple of times but no sound came out. Then, suddenly, he said in a rush, 'This movie where Nathan Gold sits up and says, "Where am I?" and then wants to know why everybody's staring at him.'

He sat watching his dry-washing hands, his shoulders heaving.

When he'd been silent for some time, Ray said, 'We're very sorry for your loss.' It was the right thing to say, but it sounded so hollow it made me twist in my seat.

I said, 'Do you think you could answer some questions now?'

He sat up, took a deep breath. 'Sure. What do you want to know?'

'How long have you known Doctor Gold?'

'Uhh . . . let's see. It'll be three years at the beginning of March.'

'You got together to start a company?'

'Yes. I had an idea I thought was exciting and I was looking for somebody to help me prove it.

I'm not . . . I'm a big-picture guy; I don't have the technical skills or the patience for lab work. I went to a symposium for botanists at Rutgers and there he was, the person on the panel saying all the most sensible things. I stalked him after the meeting till we got a chance to talk, and' – a little bark of a laugh was followed by an amazed-looking shrug – 'we've been talking ever since. He's the most—'

Brought up short by what he had just started to say, he stopped talking and sat with his mouth open, looking ashamed. After an aching silence he went on, talking just above a whisper so I held my breath to hear, 'He was the most intelligent man it's ever been my privilege to know.' He swallowed again, rallied after some more breathing, and said in a normal voice, 'It's tragic that he's gone. For his family, for me, for science, it's an awful tragedy.'

'Do you know anything about his life before you met?'

'Quite a bit. It's a little hard to believe because it's all so good. He knocked everybody's socks off in college and grad school. Went directly into university programs of experiments and teaching, married a brilliant woman with her own career. By the time I met him he was helping her raise two beautiful children. He's had the life we all hope for.'

'Wow. What did you have to offer this paradigm to get him on board?'

'Blood, sweat, toil and tears.' The short bark of laughter sounded again. 'Nate was the real deal, a scientist who thought the search for truth beat any other game in town.' Brennan cleared his throat, showed us an ironic tweak of an eyebrow, and added, 'Of course, if our product proves out there'll be plenty of money, too. But he was willing to draw a modest salary and wait.'

'I suppose having a wife who's a physician makes that easier.'

'Yeah, well, Naomi was making twice as much money where she was, at the University Medical Center in Newark. That was the big problem – Naomi. I almost didn't get him because the move entailed a real sacrifice for her.'

'And you?' I thought there had to be a flaw somewhere in this elegant do-gooder's facade. 'This isn't your first start-up, is it? Does the search for funding ever get old?'

'Oh, well . . .' He stretched and re-crossed his legs. 'I guess I better give you a little history.' He tucked his fists in his armpits and began what I could see was the Standard Story. 'Fifteen years ago I got a small grant, put that on top of a little inheritance of my own and leased a run-down farm in Iowa. Set up a bare-bones lab with two partners. We ran in an extra power line, built a high-powered computer system. A few miles out of a small town, nobody paying any attention to us, we worked seven days a week for three years. Crossed a hardy strain of winter wheat with several fast-growing warm-weather varieties and – well, we got lucky. I admit it was partly luck, but I take credit for the good guess about which variety to concentrate on the third year. By the fourth year we were showing solid promise of a crop that could grow fast enough to exploit the northern creep of global warming that we know is taking place in Canada and Alaska. Three to five days a year more growing time, two years out of three for the last ten years and for the forseeable future, it's just waiting for somebody to cash in. We didn't have the means to finish the field tests and take it to market so we sold out to a big seed company. I got enough to live on for twenty years if I'm careful, so all the money I raise can go into SmartSeeds. Is that what you wanted to know?'

'Um, yes,' I said, thinking how convenient it is that dark-skinned people with my complexion don't blush. But I still had questions. 'There was another company between that one and this one, though, right?'

'Two, actually.' He didn't look embarrassed, just smiled in a way that suggested Ray and I were grown-ups who knew about mistakes. 'If you count the book.' We waited while he did some humorous shrugging. 'I was a proven success now, you see, so naturally I wrote a book on how to bootstrap a small start-up along to success. Hired a programmer and self-published it, waited for some more money to roll in.'

His smile was surprisingly sunny. 'There were several thousand other good how-to books self-published that year. Mine dropped into the pool without much of a splash. I heard from a few old schoolmates, and I still get a check from Amazon every so often, for seven or eight dollars.'

He scratched his ear while we waited. 'Then I

got a call from one of my old partners. He was at liberty after a little debacle of his own. We found a guy who'd invented a glass-making process that imbedded solar cells. No more big ugly panels on roofs, just harvest your solar heat and air conditioning off your skylights.'

Feeling a need to encourage, I said, 'That sounds reasonable.'

'It is. It will be. Ours almost worked, but there were a few glitches. Before we could get them ironed out our inventor found his wife in bed with a neighbor who had a steady job. She wanted a divorce and he went completely insane. Everything went to hell and my partner and I were lucky to get out before we got sued.'

'But somehow you were able to raise enough money to start SmartSeeds.'

'Not as easy this time. My reputation as a boy genius had lost some of its luster. I knew the science had to be solid. Also I needed a partner whose reputation was shiny enough to cover up some of the tarnish on mine. Once I found Nathan Gold I figured I could sell the project, and I did.'

'Your website says, 'Mission statement to follow,' but so far we haven't found one. What is your mission?'

'We're going to develop seeds that can predict the weather.'

I gave him the level gaze I copied from Kevin Spacey in *LA Confidential*. 'And these seeds will share that information with county extension agents everywhere?'

He had a warm chuckle like the fond uncle

I've always wanted. 'In a way.' He turned a little in his chair and looked into the corner for a few seconds, getting ready, I sensed, to give the talk he usually supported with PowerPoint and a laser beam.

'We all know about global warming now. Nobody serious is debating that any more. If it was just a matter of certain latitudes getting a little warmer all the time, we could all go to work designing plants that thrive in warmer weather and wowie zowie, watch world hunger disappear. But the problem, at least in the near term, is not just warmer weather, it's disrupted weather – seasons more unpredictable all the time. Minnesota winters with no snow, followed by a pasting like the one we got last year. Late springs, early frosts, months so wet you get mold growing, followed by months of total drought.'

'Ray and I are both married to passionate gardeners,' I said. 'We know.'

'Good. But what plant scientists have been aware of for a long time is that certain weeds seem to be developing mechanisms to deal with these sudden changes in the weather. Dry summer followed by early frost, fire followed by flood, they can hunker down in something like hibernation mode and wait for the next good growing days.'

'Haven't weeds always done that?'

'To some extent, but the reaction time is getting faster and more efficient. So, for instance, cheat grass, Fendler's water leaf and many thistles all went through the thousand-year flood in Boulder a couple of years back.

A lot of big trees died; rivers actually changed their courses. But as soon as the water went back in its new banks those alpha weeds, especially cheatgrass, came roaring back, stronger than ever because for almost a month they'd had the ground to themselves. Fendler's waterleaf, which had been a mountain plant in that part of Colorado, came right downtown and invaded people's lawns.'

'And you're thinking about copying that?'

'Indeed we are. Find the genes that have evolved to germinate earlier and grow faster, and transplant them—' He looked at me almost placidly. 'I know. You're thinking this company should be named the Lala Land Express. But the truth is lots of people are working on some aspect of this idea.'

He cleared his throat and thought a while. His face was totally serene as he tried to think of the best way to explain this to non-scientists. 'Admittedly, most of the people thinking about weeds are trying to figure the best way to kill them. But we see it as a two-way street. Now that we can read them, plants at the genetic level are like a big shopping mall, and everybody's scrambling to find the bargains. It's a marathon and the big companies have most of the advantage. But occasionally a small and very nimble company will sprint ahead.

'And until this week, with Nathan Gold on my team, I felt sure I had one of those. Quick-witted, intuitive, an incredibly hard worker, he gave this company an edge. From the day I persuaded him to join me till now, I've never had a moment's doubt. SmartSeeds, I was ready to bet with everything I had, would come up with a winner within five years – ten at the most.'

He pondered, blinking at the wall for a while, then came back to us with a sad stare. 'Now there's only me and a couple of clever postdocs who've been helping Nate. He took those helpers into the field with him – they're current with the crops but basically they're flunkies. Mostly he had them doing the hackwork, yards of record-keeping on computers – he said neither one of them was ready for original work.'

Brennan shook his head. 'So I don't know where we are. Have to see.' He took a deep breath and changed gears. 'How soon will you know what he died from?'

'Maybe this afternoon, when we get the results from the autopsy. Or maybe not. If the coroner still can't decide what killed him we'll be waiting for the lab in St Paul to figure it out.'

He raised his eyebrows, not understanding, and I explained the help we have available from the Bureau of Criminal Apprehension. 'Even then, if we know what substance or process caused his death, will we know where it came from, and how it got into him? I can't answer that yet.'

Ray said, watching Brennan's face, 'Has he been using any dangerous chemicals out there in his fields?'

'Dangerous chemicals?' He looked alarmed. 'Didn't I explain to you we're working with genetic modifications?'

He and Ray breathed on each other for a few seconds, before Ray said, 'I'm sorry, I'm afraid

I don't know much about botany. I just thought . . . some of the stuff that's in fertilizer . . . isn't it all kind of . . . tricky?'

Brennan gazed at him across the gulf of misunderstanding he now saw yawning between them, and said quietly, 'We do use some fertilizer occasionally, but Nathan was scrupulously careful with it, and we rotate the products to avoid overexposure to crops or humans. I think we can safely rule out chemical accidents.' He turned back to me and said, 'I have about a thousand things I should be checking on. Can I go out to my office now and keep in touch with you by phone? I'm actually only a couple of miles away and I'll come back whenever you say it's important that I be here.'

'I still have many questions for you, but they can wait. Ray, how about you?'

'Same here.' He handed Brennan his card. 'But if you get any insights after you talk to your people, will you call me right away?'

'Absolutely.' Brennan gave each of us another bone-jarring handshake, thanked us for all our hard work and charged out the door. Ray and I sat quietly, listening to the rhythmic clicking of his clip-on office gear as he strode down the hall.

'Well, damn,' I said when his footsteps had started down the stairs. 'I was all set to put him down as the snake-oil salesman with intentions to rape and plunder before he walked in here. Now I don't think he is, do you?'

'No,' Ray said. 'Just crazy.' He snorted a rare, just-barely laugh. 'Thistletaters, Jesus. Soy nettles?'

'Oh, I don't think we can write off genetic modification, Ray. He might have a lot of searching ahead for the right ways and means, but I've been reading a lot of articles that claim gene slicing and dicing is here to stay.'

'Maybe so,' Ray said. 'But from weeds? Come on. Spotted knapbeans? Mustard oats?'

It's so rare to see Ray Bailey having light-hearted fun that I was reluctant to interrupt. But luckily I didn't have to; the big hand on my desk clock moved forward one mark and the little ding sounded for the hour.

'Aha,' Ray said, 'time for the noontime follies.'

I picked a brown bag off the console behind me and carried it into the break room. Ray went down to his desk and got his lunch too. As soon as he opened his bag I smelled the dill pickle and my stomach growled.

Kevin had given that name to our midday meal when he'd walked past the break room one day, on his way to lunch with a pretty girl, and seen the two of us hunched in there, gnawing on home-made sandwiches.

'Ah, look here,' he'd said, bursting into window-rattling guffaws, 'isn't this a pretty sight? The noontime follies of the married men.'

He'd hit a nerve and the name had stuck. Ray and I both have house and car loans so big we can't even think about going out to eat. Our wives try to compensate by packing lunches better than anything we could get in a restaurant, and we award ourselves little treats to have while we eat. Ray unwrapped great juicy slices of dill pickle with his fat ham sandwich and tucked into it while he leafed through an old copy of *Sports Illustrated*.

I had a plain tuna sandwich but Trudy had sent a big chunk of frosted carrot cake along with it. As usual, I traded Ray half my cake for one of his pickles, because Trudy's the best baker in the world and his wife's mother makes Polish pickles. Trading groceries is as far as lunchtime conviviality goes, though; Ray declared early on that if I kept talking about the cases we were working on he was going to go eat his lunch in the sheriff's break room, which is conveniently just across a landing on the other side of the building. So now I keep a book of crosswords in the cupboard above the sink and increase my word power while I eat.

But as soon as we'd finished, I said, 'Let's go in my office and decide what's next for the mad scientist.'

We sat on opposite sides of my cluttered desk, making a list of everything we wanted to know about Dan Brennan. Starting with the banal stuff – besides the usual records search, Ray would detail someone to hack into his email, Facebook and Twitter accounts. To the delight of detectives everywhere, even seasoned felons turn into hapless blabbermouths when they sign on to social media.

Also, one of his detectives would sniff out romantic attachments, if any. It seemed odd, when I thought about it, that Brennan had not mentioned his family life, and we hadn't thought to ask about it. Is he perhaps gay? (My notes read, *Put Winnie on this*. Winnie's personality is a curious mix of ferocious physicality – she runs marathons and swims like a seal – coupled with a remarkable ability to sit still and focus. On records searches, personal and otherwise, she is a ferret.)

In my notebook, the enterprising scientist who'd described his hard-working life to us descended into slimy pits of lust and greed. The hunting lists of Rutherford detectives would shock a sociopath – in our speculations, blameless fellow citizens morph into Upper Midwest versions of Caligula. The Frank McCafferty manual reads, 'Look for everything possible, then start crossing things off. Don't let anybody off easy.'

Before one o'clock, we had reached consensus around a folder we would label, *Brennan Background.* It read more like, 'Humor the bastard while we figure out how he killed his partner.' I didn't, in fact, have much faith in this vision of Brennan red in tooth and claw, but the searches were all good standard practice for where we were in the investigation, which was, basically, nowhere.

We split up then and went back to our own work. I said I wanted to talk to Naomi Gold and I wanted to do so today, so would he please nag Clint till he got her in here? Ray said he was going to do that and then surf everything he could find on genetically modified plants while he waited for Bo to get back from the autopsy. I tried looking up methods of gene transfer and stared at phrases like *restriction enzymes* and *gel electrophoresis* until I was ready to admit I didn't really understand what I was reading.

So I decided to call my wife. Days when I have too many ideas and suspect they are all bad, I enjoy the convenience of knowing one smart criminologist at BCA who always takes my calls.

Trudy had a batch of DNA coming out of the cooker shortly and couldn't take the time to hear about our dead scientist and his clever seeds. 'OK,' I said, 'but can you give me the name of a biologist I could talk to?'

'Save the whole subject for tonight,' she said. 'I don't have any brain cells to spare for your problems right now.' She said she had a complicated report to write and might be a little late getting home.

I told her I'd make dinner. Side pork and hominy, I suggested, quick and easy.

She said, 'That sounds good. Maybe we can get Ben to try hominy one kernel at a time.'

'If he doesn't seem interested at first, I'll throw some on the floor. Then I guarantee he'll go for it.'

She giggled; a delightful sound, said she must go and added that she loved me. Such a pleasure, I thought as I hung up, to know one smart scientist who seems to think I'm worth talking to.

But even at the risk of condescension, I was beginning to wish I knew one biology nerd who'd give me a short course in the pros and cons of genetic modification. In all these years of police work there must be some science teacher I'd rescued from danger? I didn't meet many professors in my line of work, but surely down the years some student chemist had maybe asked me for a little help with a speeding ticket?

Not that I'd ever . . . I twitch and scratch when I think, so I suppose that's what I was doing when a light tap sounded on the frame of my open door. Kevin was standing there, smiling like a kindly uncle. By his side was a handsome woman in a well-cut black skirt, topped by a white blouse of some crinkly material that molded its snowy folds to her lovely figure. She carried a large handbag made of soft leather, with many tassels and zippers. Her lipstick matched her fingernails and she had a lot of shiny brown hair.

'Jake,' he said, 'this is Marilyn DiSilvio.'

Her smile actually outshone Kevin's; together, they were lighting up my office and parts of the hall. I shook her hand and thanked her for coming in. She said, 'Oh, well, it's a pleasure to come in here and see where all our protection comes from. What would we ever do without you?'

'Ah, well,' I said. 'We do what we can.' I copied that one from Chief McCafferty, who's a stone expert at delivering banal responses to inane remarks.

It seemed to work for Marilyn; she went right on: 'Kevin said he needed some help finding our grow fields, so I said I could come in and help him with that.'

'She's saving us hours of searching,' Kevin said. 'It's going to make a big difference.'

'Well now,' I said. 'That is good news.'

'It's the least I can do,' she said. 'And as I'm here I asked Kevin if I could take a minute of your time to get acquainted, because I want to tell you how much we appreciate all the hard work you're doing for SmartSeeds – my goodness.' She smiled at each of us in turn.

I asked her to sit. Kevin helped her, politely and with no touching, into my guest chair and then pulled up the spare for himself. Marilyn was good at gracious femininity, a strong, capable woman who looked quite able to go find her own chair or even build one if necessary, but was also able to send body language saying she liked being fussed over. Nothing coy with eyelashes or any of that, just a quick glance and a satisfied look about the shoulders – she was very good at the boy-girl thing.

I said, 'It's a hard time for you and your, um, the crew . . . Do you still have the assistants? Are they staying on?'

'Yes, Fritz and Stevie are still with us. In fact, Mr Brennan's got them busier than ever, drawing up charts and making these very complex comparison graphs.' She shrugged. 'Assessing where we are, I guess, and how far along we've come. With the' – she turned her hands up – 'crops. Product.' A little chuckle. 'I never know what to call something while it's still just a concept. I finally asked the guys, "What *should* I call it?" and Stevie said, "Oh, just call it the Smarty."'

Kevin said, 'How does Stevie think you're doing with the Smarty?'

'Oh, both the guys are very optimistic. And Nate was, too. He never had the least doubt they were on to something wonderful.'

'Everybody tells us he was very talented.'

'Yes. And just a demon for hard work! Fritz

said to me once, "Boy, I could kill myself keeping up with that guy! He just never wants to quit work. He gets on the trail of an idea, he never thinks about getting tired or hungry." And that's so true, that's just how he was.'

'So . . . would you call him a hard taskmaster?'

'Who, Nate? Oh, no – you mean like a slave-driver? No. He could seem to be . . . a little *self-involved* sometimes – off in his own world if he was thinking hard. But he was never cruel. You just had to ask, if you needed something, and he was the most generous guy in the world.'

There it was again – everybody loved Nathan Gold.

'And you work in a pretty informal place, don't you? Pop in and out of each other's offices, have a visit with the neighbors?'

'Well, not so much really. That co-op is a nest of hard-working strivers, you know; they pretty much beaver away all day. The colonel's about the only one who drifts in and out.' She chuckled. 'He's a country boy so he likes to pass the time of day, kind of gossip over the back fence, as they say.'

'The colonel?

'Oh, that's what they all call Travis Diebencorn. It strikes all his partners funny that he goes up in the north woods on weekends and drills with those paramilitary guys who patrol the border.'

'Travis is part of that?' I hadn't heard about that before – had anybody? I looked at Kevin, who was watching me as keenly as if he was the scientist and I was the lab rat with a particularly interesting tumor. 'That seems so out of character – isn't he the one you told Clint was just so friendly?'

'Yes, well,' she tossed her bright hair and laughed, 'he certainly is friendly. I think the weekends in the woods are kind of like an extension of Boy Scout camp for him. But what do I know? Maybe there is a terrible threat from terrorists. It all seems kind of remote to me right now.'

'You must have a lot on your mind,' I said. 'It's very good of you to come in. And since you're here . . . I've been wondering about the day of Nathan's death. The timeline?'

'What about it?'

'Would you tell me again what time you left the office to run errands?'

'Let's see.' She consulted the ceiling. 'I believe it was shortly after nine.'

'And you had to go to the post office? And where else?'

'Two or three shops out on the east side of town. It was nothing unusual. Places where he often ordered supplies.'

'And you usually picked them up?'

'Yes, almost always.'

'Just for the record, could you tell us exactly which places you went that day, and what you picked up?'

'Um . . . not right this minute. I'm pretty sure, though, that I gave that information to one of your detectives, that first day after . . . when they found Nate.'

'That's right – now that you mention it I

remember Clint told us that. So it'll be in the case notes.'

'The errands took me more time than usual that morning, I remember, because there was a long line of people mailing packages at the post office.'

'Good – that's another detail I'll be sure to list. Clint said you were very good at keeping track of things and I see now that you are, aren't you?'

'Well, I should be – that's my job!' A little self-effacing laugh, and then she said, very seriously, 'Naturally, I want to help in any way I can.' She leaned forward and looked straight into my eyes. 'We all do, believe me. It's so hard . . . every day we're all feeling bad that Nate is gone, and wishing there was something . . . I asked Naomi what we could do to help, and she looked so sad when she said, "Nothing. I have to do this by myself."'

She looked at the floor for a few seconds, swallowed hard, and said in a choked voice, 'It just about tore me up to hear her say that.'

'Please be assured,' I said, 'that we will spare no effort to find out what caused his death.'

'I will certainly tell Mr Brennan you said that. Thank you so much.'

Kevin stood up then and said they wouldn't keep me any longer – they were on their way to talk to LeeAnn. 'Marilyn wants to show her the best way to organize the list of grow plots. And then we'll just go down the hall to say hello to Ray.' After that astonishing news he thanked me for my time. I smiled up at them both, thinking how well we were all behaving, and that standing in my doorway they looked like the kind of tall, attractive couple you'd see in a glossy magazine ad.

And evidently LeeAnn thought so too, because I heard her, at her desk in the hall, ask them, 'Do you mind standing still for me for one second? I just got this new smart phone and I'd like to try out the camera.' I saw the flash and heard her, as she thanked them, say, 'You're probably going to be the best-looking couple this camera ever records!'

As I listened to Marilyn's laughing disclaimer – 'Oh, heavens, I'm sure not' – I could not help wondering whether Marilyn had been aware that when she'd leaned over like that to tell me how bad she felt about Nate's death, a generous view of cleavage had showed above the top button of her blouse.

I heard their short conversation about the list, and then their cheerful trip down the hall into Ray's office where, predictably, the conversation got quieter. On the return trip they encountered Clint, who greeted Marilyn like a favorite neighbor who's been too long away. Kevin said something that made them all laugh as the three of them strolled back up the hall toward the stairs. Then Kevin led Marilyn to the elevator there, saying, 'Here, now, why should you wear yourself out on that long staircase when you have so much important work to do?'

Our floor got very quiet for a few minutes after she was gone, with a feeling like the day after the fair. I got some emails answered and returned a couple of phone calls, and then Clint stuck his head in my door and said, 'Doctor Gold says she's got a little time she could spare right now. She can be here in fifteen minutes – would that be OK?'

I said, 'You bet. Tell Ray.' I cleared my desk and we collected chairs. When the elevator bell rang and Clint brought her in and introduced her to us, he had a look like the one parents give their offspring when the new neighbors' children come over for the first time: *Play nice*.

Five

Naomi Gold had been winnowing the means of simple elegance, probably, since she went back to her practice after her first child was born. She had it in her DNA now: the neatly parted hair, small earrings, power pantsuit and burnished low-heel shoes – I looked at her and thought, *I bet she can get dressed as fast as I can.*

I thanked her for coming in. I said I knew she must be busy.

'Yes,' she said. 'So many phone calls . . . so much grief.' She lifted a hand and held it over a vaguely defined space between us for a few seconds, put it back in her lap and said quietly, 'And my children are . . . very distressed.'

'I'm sure they are. We're very sorry for your loss.' I watched her wince as I said the cliché. I was thinking, *Just the children?* 'Clint said he gave you a card from Victims' Services, but probably in all the confusion . . .' I eased a card in front of her. 'If you call this number the department will help you in any way they can.' Victims' Services is a good example of the chief's statement that we do what we can. For poor people suddenly confronted with greater needs than ever, small, practical boosts with information and transportation can make a huge difference. For people of means like Naomi Gold, the offer sometimes earns a look of disbelief, like, *How can you imagine that you could possibly help me, you clown?* If Naomi was thinking that, she didn't let it show.

'What would really help,' she watched me out of opaque dark eyes, 'is if we could get his body soon. His family . . . Some of them are coming from far away, and of course they want to have a funeral. When do you think that can happen?'

'Well, you're a doctor so I don't have to explain to you the formalities that surround an unexplained death.'

'No, you don't. How soon is the autopsy?'

'It's today, actually.' Normally I'd choke myself before I discussed an autopsy with a grieving widow. But this grieving widow had brought it up herself and had the manner of a county prosecutor, so I stuck with the truth. 'How soon we can release the body after that depends on what the coroner decides. I promise you'll know more as soon as we do. Now,' I switched quickly to interrogation mode, since seizing the initiative from the doctor was evidently no easy feat, 'I have some questions for you.'

Hands quiet in her lap, she said, 'Of course.'

'The morning of your husband's death, was there anything different, any reason you were concerned about him? I know my detectives asked you this, but I'd like to go over the details again. Was he unusually tense, or worried about anything? Did he mention any discomfort?'

She was still for a few seconds, staring straight ahead as if trying to remember. Then she said simply, 'No. It was just a morning like any other.'

'Could you describe it?'

'We both had routines. He always did yoga for fifteen minutes, then took a shower and had breakfast and went to work. I went out for the two-mile run near the house that I do every morning if it's not raining or snowing. So I wasn't there when he left but I asked Mother and she said he left at the usual time, ten minutes to seven.'

'Really? He was that precise?'

'In everything he did, yes. He liked organization in life, rigor in thinking. In every job he ever had, including study, he quickly established a routine and then stuck to it. He said it expedited his work if he didn't have to think about the schedule.'

'Did that mesh all right with the rest of your lives?'

'Well, doctors are pretty regimented, too. Especially in the big bureaucratic systems I usually work in. I wasn't quite as much of a slave to routine as Nate, but close.'

'Your children have always gone to day care?'

'When they were pre-school I always had a nanny and still employ one part-time, though my mother lives with us here and helps with the children as well. Workdays I see them for a few minutes in the morning then not again till dinner. Nate never joined the family till dinnertime.'

'So, breakfast. Did he always eat the same thing?'

'Pretty much, yes. I guess I should clarify – after our children were born we virtually always ate dinner together because we wanted to establish that family pattern. But for breakfast and lunch we took care of ourselves and kept separate schedules. I know he liked yogurt and wheat germ and fruit for breakfast, and I presume that's what he ate the morning he died.'

'He hasn't been ill?'

'No. In fact almost never, since I've known him.'

'Which is how long?'

'I met him at the beginning of a school year, a little more than fifteen years ago. We moved in together just before Christmas, and were married the following June.' A little shrug. 'Between us we've got a lot of degrees. Events in our life together tended to be arranged around semesters.'

'The move to Minnesota – that was his idea?'

'Yes. He met Dan Brennan at a symposium. Brennan had some ideas about genetic modification of seeds, a strategy to enable them to thrive during global warming. That was a particular interest of Nate's so they hit it off, kept emailing and meeting up. They got this idea about starting their seed experiments in an ideal growth environment in the Midwest, and moving gradually to colder and hotter environments. Before long,' she gave a small, rueful laugh, 'they were asking me how I'd like to raise my children – how did they put it? In a basically rural setting with good schools and great medical facilities all around.'

'How did you like it?'

'I didn't want any part of it. I was very well situated in my own career and had the services I needed for my children. I accepted the idea gradually over about six months of talking and a couple of visits. Actually the move was never what I'd have chosen on my own, but I went along with it because Nate was so excited. I had always felt that he had a superior imagination and temperament for science, and wished he could find a better outlet than teaching and private tinkering. Brennan was convinced Nate was a genius, and I liked that. I thought, at last, somebody outside the family sees it.'

'You didn't think he was given his due where he was?'

'Oh, they loved him as a professor – they wanted to keep him and they gave him as many goodies as they could afford. But he wasn't doing the really challenging work that I knew he was capable of. The Minnesota job offered him a chance to make his mark.'

'So no regrets about the move?'

'Oh, I can't claim that – I miss the job I had before. But I made up my mind to make the move for Nate's sake, and a deal's a deal.' Something about that phrase brought a look to her face that I hadn't seen before – a hawk-like intensity that made me wonder what she was going to say next. But she took a deep breath, then the look was gone and her magisterial calm was back – the look, I guessed, that had struck Rosie as glacial.

Ray had been quietly twitching for a while, and it was certainly his turn, so I asked him, 'Ray, do you have any questions?'

'Yes.' He cleared his throat. 'The genetic modification Doctor Gold was doing – was he mostly using biolistic methods or agrobacteria?' He had turned to face her, looking as if he expected to have a warm, intimate chat with the doctor about how she liked her GMOs. Turning sideways would also, I thought, prevent his seeing my face while he trotted out the results of all the study he had been doing.

Naomi gave him one of her trademark rueful smiles and said, 'I'm afraid I'm not the right person to ask about Nate's work, Sergeant. We both worked hard at our jobs all day, and the last thing we wanted to do at night was talk about them anymore.'

'So you don't know where he was in the process—'

'I know he was quite excited, and optimistic they were getting close to having faster-growing . . . *something*.'

'But you don't know what?'

'It never was clear to me which product they intended to put the smarty into once they had him built. They may not have decided yet.' She spread her hands. 'Ask Dan. He's been talking it up for a while, I think.'

'But Doctor Gold was still happy and optimistic? His attitude hadn't changed recently? You hadn't noticed any signs of discouragement?'

'No.' No stopping to ponder, no soul-searching. This grieving widow had no need to chat. He wasn't discouraged, and that was that.

I decided to wind things up, so I asked her, 'What do you think killed him?' Maybe it was an unfair question, but I thought her opinion was worth having.

She settled into an analytical pose, head cocked a little, consulting herself. Naomi Gold, I realized, thought her opinion was worth having, too.

'It's puzzling,' she said. 'There were no precursor signs. I asked our family practitioner to contact the coroner, to make sure he understands that Nate was in supremely good health.'

'Any history of sudden death in his family?'

'No. In fact, they have a reputation for longevity. His father is taking a turn right now, at nearly seventy, with Doctors Without Borders, and his grandfather died at ninety-five.'

'Did your husband have any enemies?'

The rueful little smile came back. 'Quiet professors of biochemistry don't have enemies, Captain. At most, an inter-departmental spat – but Nate didn't even have those. He had a very . . . accommodating personality. Everybody loved Nathan Gold.'

Clint led her out and waited with her for the elevator. He made sure she had his card. There was nothing we needed to do for her, I heard her tell him, 'But thank you, Detective, you've been very kind.'

'If you think of anything you need,' Clint said, 'you just call me.'

Clint is no flirt. A happily married man with good instincts honed over many years on the streets, he had decided, he told me when he came back in, that 'That is one of the finest ladies I've ever met, I believe.' He looked at the two of us, still sitting there as if we were waiting for something, and said, 'Isn't she?'

'She is,' I said.

Ray said, 'For sure.'

'Funny, though,' I said, 'she has a somewhat different version of his morning from the one the office manager told you the day they found the body.'

'She does? I'll have to review those notes,' Clint said. 'People always think they can tell you exactly what happened, but they always forget something.'

After Clint was gone, I said, 'She *is* a fine lady but there's something hinky about that morning, isn't there?'

'Yup,' Ray said. 'Something there she didn't want to talk about.'

'Or can't stand to remember. I wonder why everybody loved Nathan Gold? He sounds kind of . . . disengaged, to me.'

'Hard to tell without being around him a while, I suppose.'

'Well, we've missed that so we have to keep talking to people. Who's next?'

'The Aardvark engineers are coming in later. I'm hoping Bo gets here first. Damn, I wish Pokey would find a nice old-fashioned heart attack and we could turn that body loose to the grieving widow.'

Bo Dooley passed my door coming back from the autopsy, moving with that quiet air of caution he has, like a man who just heard a twig snap behind him in a forest when he thought he was alone.

'Ah,' I said, 'you're back.' I can be as obvious as the next guy when I want to stop somebody from passing my door.

'Yeah, I'm just' – he paused uneasily – 'looking for . . . uh,' and nodded his head sideways toward Ray's office.

He had been working for Ray for a little over a year, and was uneasily aware that he still made his new boss a little nervous. Bo was a narc in bigger cities downriver before he came to us, trailing a rep as a hard man. He got recruited onto the Rutherford force mainly to do drug interdictions, working autonomously and often undercover. The feds took most of that action out of our hands last year, and just as his job was getting phased out, his coke-addicted wife almost derailed his career entirely before she left him and their child. He was not a man who expressed emotion easily but I knew he was fiercely focused, now, on staying put in Rutherford and raising his daughter in peace.

Not wanting to interfere with Bo's effort to observe strict protocol, I got up and walked along with him. We found Ray Bailey curled like a pretzel in front of his screen, surfing plant science blogs. His thousand-yard stare took a couple of seconds to fade before he rejoined us earthlings. Then he jumped up, saying, 'Ah, here you are. Come in. Sit down. Tell me about it.'

We pulled up chairs, and Bo opened the long detective's notebook he still likes to use. Most of the crew has moved onto some form of electronic tablet, but Bo's personality is an odd mix of dauntless courage and fussbudget Luddite. He rides a Harley almost as old as he is and collects long-playing vinyl records of jazz standards.

'The victim's primary care doc came and watched the whole autopsy – Jackson, his name is. Seems like a good man. He cleared his schedule for the day because he said he'd have sworn Gold was the least likely of all his patients to suffer sudden death. He wanted to see for himself whether he'd missed something.

'He and Pokey agreed that Nathan Gold's appearance didn't suggest any catastrophic event. There was a small bruise and kind of a pimple or maybe pinprick on the back of his arm. They considered anaphylactic shock from a bee sting, but the red spot didn't look at all troubled and he hadn't complained to his office manager about dizziness or nausea when he came in. She said he seemed his usual self while he was sending her off on her errands. The only thing out of the ordinary – Pokey had noticed it too – was that his clothes looked as if he'd been sweating, although the room was a comfortable temperature.

'After they opened him up they took turns saying stuff like "Look at this heart, beautiful," and once Pokey said, "Woods is fulla guys would like to trade him for that liver, by crackey." I don't always understand everything docs say during autopsies, you know—'

'Who does?' Ray said. 'I usually read the autopsy and then call Pokey with about a dozen questions.'

'Yeah. But I did hear Jackson say something about taking a close look at that pancreas, in view of the sweat-stained shirt. So they did a lot of slicing and dicing of Gold's pancreas, and carried on about something just perfect that he had in there. I finally asked them what that funny name was they kept saying and Jackson wrote it out for me: *Islets of Langerhans.*'

Ray said, 'And that cleared it right up for you?'

'Shee, not hardly. I just thought it was interesting so I wrote it down. We need lots of those little islets to get our insulin and other good stuff from the pancreas, the docs told me. And what they wanted me to remember is that Doctor Gold had plenty of islets in very good shape.'

'So he wasn't diabetic.'

'Wasn't diabetic, had no heart disease, nothing wrong with his kidneys or liver. I have a long list here of things Doctor Gold did not have wrong with him.' Shrugging, Bo turned to a fresh page, scanned his notes for a few more seconds and said, 'Also, Jackson kept saying there was no way this man was suicidal. "He was probably the most self-motivated man I ever met," he said, "and careful to a fault." Said he once prescribed an antibiotic when the doc had a bad case of flu, and Gold insisted on reviewing every possible side effect till Jackson was sorry he'd suggested it.'

Bo read another sentence and looked up, grinning. 'Pokey got bored with Jackson after he'd described that scene for a while. He said something in Polish and then, "Yah, Crissake, I get it – he was careful."'

'So then Jackson got all humble, said he didn't mean to get pushy, just wanted to be sure everybody . . . He kind of glared at me here to spread the blame out a little – isn't it funny how people will always do that? They paint themselves into a little corner and pretty soon start to blame the cop. Everybody's always ready to do *that*.'

'Uh-huh.' Ray's got a little Joe Friday twitch himself about just-give-me-the-facts – he gets restless during colorful asides. 'What next?'

'Jackson said, 'I just want to be sure you know you're looking at a damn strange event if a super careful and very knowledgeable scientist like this one ingested a fatal dose of some poisonous substance.'

'And then Pokey said, "Yah," in that funny flat way he has: "Yah, or some clever sumbitch offed this guy. But which was it?"'

'Sounds like both the docs were quite . . . invested,' Ray said.

'Oh, you better believe it. They weren't ever really fighting, though – just two very smart guys getting frustrated because they couldn't find the answers to hard questions. Kind of fun to watch, if you want to know the truth.

'They went over all the evidence again, and sometimes it was almost like they were cussing out Gold's insides for being so perfect.' He grinned happily again. 'Funny kind of a complaint to hear from two doctors.'

'Bo,' I said, getting restless myself, 'didn't they speculate at all about which poisonous substance they thought did the damage?'

'Well, yes, sure, but Jackson got going for a while with some anecdotal stuff about insect bites one of his colleagues got in a jungle once, then Pokey cut him off. Said, "We don't have all day in this lab." That surprised me. You'd think . . . two experienced doctors . . . they'd have some ideas to swap. But Pokey said, "There's so many possibilities, if you start guessing you could be here all week."

'Finally Pokey decided to send a lot of tissue samples of Gold's pancreas and small intestine to BCA. And blood – he sent lots of blood. I couldn't quite follow the conversation about that – for a while all I've got in my notes is they were asking questions about questions.'

'What?'

'They spent some time trying to decide which questions were appropriate to ask.'

'Appropriate? Wouldn't anything be appropriate if you don't know the answer?'

'Jake, all I know is I wrote down what they said. They didn't even want me to do that. Pokey said, "Hell, you don't need to make notes of things we wonder – makes us sound like first-year med students." But I said, "Pokey, you keep your notes and I'll keep mine." After that he didn't talk to me at all for some time.'

'Doctors hate to have civilians argue. They

say we don't know enough and just waste their time.'

'They're probably right, but I still don't need him telling me how to do my job. Anyway, in the end the queries they sent to St Paul were mostly about hard-to-detect poisons. Oh, and something called C-peptides.'

'C-peptides?' Ray said. 'What're they?'

'Beats the shit outta me,' Bo said. 'I guess we'll find out when that report from the BCA comes back.'

'Which will be at some future time that nobody cares to predict,' Ray said. 'Isn't that just peachy?'

Bo turned his hands over in a gesture that said, *Nothing we can do about the crime lab.*

'Bo,' I said, 'what's your take on this?'

'Jackson's sure it couldn't have been an accident. Pokey's thinking was more along the lines of, "Unless BCA identifies something that couldn't possibly be self-administered, I may never be able to call this one a homicide."'

'You've seen more of this case close up than any of the rest of us,' I said. 'Where do you come down?'

'I'm inclined to agree with Doctor Jackson. He knew his patient well and thinks he was too smart and careful to get killed by accident.' He put a hand up, like a traffic cop. 'Remember, that's just a hunch.'

'Damn,' Ray said, 'where does that leave us? Don't get me wrong, Bo, I respect your instincts. But' – he looked at me – 'we start investigating hunches, pretty soon we're getting yelled at for unreasonable searches and seizures, right?'

'Well . . .' I pulled on an earlobe while I thought how to say it. 'Sometimes if you sniff discreetly around the edges of a hunch for a while you turn up some nice reasonable doubt that will keep you from getting yelled at.'

'That sounds wise,' Ray said. 'What does it mean?'

'It means I haven't heard about guys out there in his grow fields, finding out what he's been growing this summer. I know the fields are all frosted now but they've still got greenhouses working in some of the small plots. And what were the neighbors growing in surrounding areas, and what fertilizers and weed killers were *they* using?'

'Well, we haven't covered all of that, but Clint and Andy are both working on it, any time they can spare from other jobs. And we're getting phone calls from everybody who ever took Biology 101, didn't I tell you that? All the people who've been saying all along that modified crops are dangerous and that nobody knows what's in these weed killers, now they all want to tell me what they think they know about those crops, and I'm writing it all down. You never know,' he said, 'it might not all be total horseshit.'

'Good for you. Why don't you get in touch with the county extension agent? See if they'll send some guys along with ours to help identify what they're looking at? Might save some time.'

'I'm working on that. One of our cold-case guys, when he's not working part-time here, is a partner in a small farm over by Eyota. He knows a guy in that department and I asked him to reach out.'

'Good. Also, Rosie expressed some rather strong opinions about Naomi Gold's mother. Why not have her set up a real interview with the mother, see if she still feels the same? Because I have a question about Mama – how come she followed her daughter out here? Does she follow wherever her daughter goes? Why? Tell Rosie to see if she can chat up a clue or two about the marriage – was it happy? Any chance Naomi's got a lover? Could that be why she's so glacial now her husband's dead?

'While we're at it, whatever became of all that schmoozing with the hockey players that Andy was doing? I never heard a follow-up report.'

'Oh, he came up bland on Nathan Gold – not many remembered him, but the ones that did said something like, "Swell guy, not a great player." Andy did turn up one other little bit of hockey lore – that youngest architect, Diebencorn, the one they call the colonel? Andy said the guys all say you have to watch out for him on the ice as he likes to make the dirty hit.'

'There's something about hockey that brings out the little secret twitches, isn't there? Is he the one who goes to paramilitary camp on weekends?'

'Is he? First I've heard of it.'

'Marilyn told me he does. I thought that seemed completely out of character for him. He's such a smiley little guy. But dirty hits on the ice too? Maybe we need to take another look at Diebencorn.'

'What time is it? Getting pretty late. The

architects were supposed to come talk to me this afternoon but I guess they got too busy.'

'Let's be sure we see them tomorrow, hmm? The weekends in the woods might not be as funny as his partners think. And just keep all your people walking around this possible homicide, kicking the tires, looking for dents and scratches.'

'OK,' Ray said, rubbing the spot by his right eyebrow that always gets punished while he thinks. 'Fine. We can do that.'

'Good. I'll go see how Kevin's crew is doing on the break-ins.'

Bo walked out with me. As he turned to go into his cubicle, he said, 'Remind me not to ask you what anything means, huh?'

Kevin was just hanging up his phone when I stuck my head in his door. He waved me in with the other hand, saying, 'That was Amos Deaver at BCA. He's my favorite guy in fingerprints up there – he never gets all huffy if you ask how your search is coming. But so far, alas,' he rested his head on the top of his chairback and scowled at the ceiling, 'he says they haven't found a single print on any of those messages.'

'I was afraid of that. Stands to reason somebody so careful with the locks wouldn't leave any evidence.'

'Careful eco-warriors wearing gloves while they spread the gospel. Damn.' He beat a thoughtful march tempo on his desk with a pencil.

'DNA, maybe,' I said, 'but it takes so bloody long.'

'Even after they get started. Right now my

messages are still near the tail of a long queue.' He sighed. 'Anyway, think about it. These break-ins were all done at night, in October. Probably no sweat.'

'Have you talked to any other jurisdictions?'

'Several. My colleagues are enjoying my strange story. A couple of them seem to think I'm making it up. I just put out a BOLO to the five-state area, but I'm not optimistic.'

'Have the handwriting people had a look yet?'

'Oh, you bet, they hopped right on it. They're living for the day they can crack a case, get some ink.'

'So?'

'So the good news is that all the messages were written by the same person.' Kevin made an umpire's *you're out* gesture. 'Bad news, they have no idea who that is. Is that Lulu bellowing out there?'

Lulu Breske, the chief's secretary, is not a beloved figure in the department. She serves McCafferty loyally and bullies everybody else in the building. Right now she was calling my name.

'Damn, she's paging me,' I said. 'I gotta go.'

Interrupting my job to answer a summons to a chore I didn't have time for and probably wouldn't want to do anyway, my brain went into flat-out rebel mode. And into that red-hot knot of rage, unbidden, jumped an ancient memory. I was angry for years after I got carried kicking and screaming out of Maxine's house, and for a while I'd tried hard to become a thug. Luckily I'd got some help and reformed before I wrecked my life, but sometimes now, when I'm ticked off, I start to remember how much fun it was to indulge in bad behavior.

Lulu's page set me off. In a blink, I remembered a time in fourth grade when a Miss Peabody – colorless, humorless and earnest – taught the remedial reading classes I always had to take. Hating the practice sessions I was kept after school for, I teamed up with some other scruffy losers to get the only revenge available to us. We began inventing obscene versions of Miss Peabody's name, whispering hilariously before class, 'Heads up! Here comes Miss Pissbody!'

We actually increased our vocabularies (as Miss Peabody was always urging us to do) after Bud Perry got his mom to show him how to use the dictionary. Mama Perry was thrilled – at last her boy was Showing An Interest. She never saw us rolling on the floor in the boys' bathroom, helpless with laughter as we called out, 'Miss Crapchassis! Miss Sewagebutt!' And as our labors with the doorstop-sized *Merriam Webster's Collegiate* paid off, 'Miss Fecalframe! Miss Urineass!'

Kevin and I disrupted the peace of Government Center the day we discovered that we shared this memory. He was a few years behind me but he'd taken the same class with the same teacher and the tradition, I guess, had been passed down among fourth-grade boys. Stolid Property Crimes investigators stared open-mouthed as we faced each other across Kevin's desk, crying happily, 'Miss Shitstack! Miss Fartbody!'

And on this hectic afternoon years later, suddenly filled with the boyish hedonism with which I once tipped over mailboxes and climbed barns to steal the roosters off wind vanes, I stepped back into Kevin's office to say, 'You know, what you really ought to do is show one of those messages to Miss Peabody.'

Kevin laughed and said, 'Hey, yeah, wouldn't that be a kick in the pants?' When he saw I wasn't smiling, his expression changed quickly to surprise, and then to some crumpled version of *Are you crazy?* But as I turned back toward the hall, I saw his eyes brighten with delight and he called after me, as I walked toward Lulu's desk, 'That's so off the wall I just might do it!'

I entered Frank's office smiling brightly, cheered by remembering my favorite of all the nicknames, Miss Tinkletorso.

'Jake?' The chief eyed my antic expression curiously for a couple of seconds before he gestured toward the well-groomed man in his visitor's chair. 'This is Gordon French. He's an attorney for Minnaska.'

Attorney French was, as Kevin had said, elegantly pinstriped. Also three-piece-suited, wing-tipped, cuff-linked and tie-tacked. His assurance was way beyond arrogance. Obviously French was used to getting what he asked for, and right now he was getting ready to ask for a lot.

He reminded me, as if I needed reminding, that his company's lab had been broken into the same day as SmartSeeds. From an iPod Mini that he pulled from its own clever nest on the side of his briefcase, he read off to me the message that had been left for Minnaska, putting a fine rhetorical flourish on the final phrase, 'Retribution will be swift and sure!'

'Retribution, if you please,' he said, flaring his nostrils. 'So of course we're alarmed to hear that another company that got a similar message that day has lost a scientist.'

'Yes. We haven't established that his death is a homicide.'

'Mmm. The cause of his death is unknown, the paper said.' He sat back and gave me the demanding stare again. 'Unknown. You don't hear that a whole lot these days. It's not going to stay unknown, is it? Can you give me some idea what's going on?'

'I only know a little more than what you read. The medical examiner did an autopsy on Doctor Gold today. He wasn't able to determine what killed him.'

'Dear me.' A disappointed frown started between his eyebrows and spread across his sleekly barbered face. 'So what happens next?'

'Well. I can't share all the details of an ongoing investigation, but since the initial results of the autopsy were inconclusive, blood and tissue samples have been sent to the Bureau of Criminal Apprehension in St Paul. The scientists there will continue the investigation. And while we're waiting for those results, down here in Rutherford we're checking everything else.'

Gordon French re-crossed his legs. 'That certainly sounds wise. What does it mean?'

I blinked. Had Ray Bailey crept into the room? What was it about this day that made a simple declarative sentence cause for a fight?

But as I watched his smooth face grow pink and puffy with annoyance, I thought, *Declarative hell, he knows damn well I'm tap-dancing*. And sometimes, when I'm caught like that in the act of being diplomatic, I find a straight shot of truth can do wonders.

I turned in my chair till we were looking into each other's eyes, and said, 'It means this is starting to look like a tough case. We don't have enough information yet to decide what killed Nathan Gold. And even when we find out what killed him, we may not know how. And if you think that makes you impatient, Mr French, believe me, everybody in this department is just about busting a gut over it.'

'Uh-huh. Doing what?'

I ran down a partial list of the chores I'd given Ray. When his eyes started to glaze I decided on a new tack to hold his attention. 'Also, I'd like to get a copy of your mission statement for this year.'

'What? I couldn't possibly—'

'And we'll need a complete list of all your experimental scientists, and the jobs they're currently working on.'

'Well, I'll consult my clients, but I'm afraid they'll be very reluctant to divulge any of that information.'

'Will they? Then you'll save us all a lot of time and trouble if you remind them that this is a possible homicide investigation, and in that case we can subpoena any records we need.'

'Well, now,' his eyes swung away from me and fastened on Frank, 'Chief McCafferty, is this the standard practice in Rutherford? You train your detectives to go on the attack when a tax-paying citizen asks a reasonable question?'

'We pretty much do what we have to do to close cases,' Frank said. 'But we certainly don't mean to bully anybody, and I'm sorry if you feel our answers here today have been in any way offensive. Remind me, what reasonable question did you not get an answer to?'

'How soon,' French said, glaring at him over the beautiful Italian leather of his briefcase, 'can we expect you to get off the dime and find the little sneak who broke in and left those messages?'

'Well—' The question caught Frank flat-footed. Ever since we got news of the smart scientist dead at his desk, we'd been talking about Gold's company and his family, waiting for the autopsy results – I think he'd completely forgotten about the nutty-sounding notes that started the whole case. So he looked up at me with naked appeal in his face and said, 'How's that part coming along, Jake?'

'The handwriting experts at BCA have confirmed that all the notes were written by the same person,' I said.

'Well,' French said, 'that's something. I guess.'

'Yes. But so far they haven't matched the writing to anyone in their databases, so' – French was sitting there, waiting for the next good news, and I couldn't seem to stop myself – 'we're developing a two-pronged approach to that part of the puzzle,' I said. 'One member of our team did extensive research into handwriting analysis in school, and he's going to reach out to people he knows from those days to see if they can help.'

Thinking about Miss Peabody, I think my face must have brightened, because both men were watching me with something like fascination. 'Kind of a long shot, maybe,' I said, 'but it can't hurt to try.'

'No,' French said, getting a little bit interested in spite of himself. 'Well. That sounds . . . enterprising.' He stood up, gave a little shake that magically straightened all the folds in his beautiful suit and hoisted the black briefcase that must surely be stuffed with records of wealth. 'We'll be in touch then, eh?'

When he was gone, Frank said, 'I'd completely forgotten those crazy notes.' Looking at me sideways, he asked, 'Have you really got something going, or—'

I made a little hand-wave, low down, and he said, 'OK. Nice save, anyway.'

That night when I got home from work, I put Benny in a tattered old playpen that I kept out by the garden, so he could watch me work but couldn't eat bugs or dirt, or impale himself on a nail or run away. Everything I did with him had to be calibrated that way – enough amusement to keep him contented, but not enough freedom so he could destroy himself by mistake. We yelled words at each other – 'Bird! Flower! Car!' while I dug up the last of the carrots.

After supper, when the dishes were done and Ben was in bed, I brought in the sack of carrots. I put them in the sink carefully, trying not to make a mess on the floor, and Trudy cut off the tops and washed them. By the end of the evening we had a sack full of messy carrot tops to go in the compost heap, and a box full of clean carrots ready for me to take out and bury in sand in the root cellar.

While we worked I told Trudy about the mysterious case we were working on: the scientist who seemed to have nothing wrong with him except he was dead. She gave me a couple of email addresses – one for a biologist and one for a chemist. After I wrote them down, I asked her, 'You think you ever flashed any cleavage at a guy without knowing it?'

Standing over the sink, cutting the tops off the last of the carrots, she put the knife down with a little clink and stared at me. 'What kind of a question is that?'

'The kind that needs an answer. A peek at the store is an invitation to sample the goods, isn't it?'

'You been standing a little too close to one of your detectives, Jake?'

'No, no, please. Not in a million years – God, haven't I told you enough times, never? No, I'm talking about a *witness*.'

'Oh. And you're trying to decide how to feel about her?'

'I don't feel anything about her. I'm trying to

decide how much of what she says is worth putting in the case notes.'

'Oh, in that case, throw it all out – the wretch is a whore.'

I looked at her, surprised, and she laughed and threw her arms around me, getting shreds of wet carrot tops on my shirt. 'Come on, silly, I don't know the whole truth about all women any more than you do about men! But just to be on the safe side,' she snuggled a little closer, and then a little closer still, 'let's make it a firm rule that you don't let that witness into your office again without several other witnesses present, OK?'

Did I mention that I'm just putty in this woman's hands? It was a whole day later before I got those carrots put away in the root cellar.

Six

Rosie Doyle climbed the stairs onto the second floor the next morning just as I stepped out of the chief's office. She'd been out in the bright and breezy fall weather, obviously – she was pink-cheeked and tousled, her hair standing up in wiry red corkscrews all over her head.

I fell in step with her and said, 'You look supercharged. Tell me what you've been doing.'

'Talking to Grandmother Bedford.'

'Who is, remind me . . .?'

'Naomi Gold's mother.'

'Oh, yeah, the classy mama.'

She gave me a little ironic nod and then said quietly, 'Naomi and her mother are both strong, impressive women, Jake. But that's a family with a lot of problems.'

Quiet speeches are not Rosie's usual style. Impressed and curious, I asked her, 'You on your way to tell Ray about it?'

'Yeah, if he's got time.'

It puzzled me that she was so favorably impressed by a granny who followed her daughter from place to place, so I said, 'I think I'll tag along.' This weird little office-invasion case kept turning into a big, fast-growing storm of calamities. I was trying to stay on top of details without going over anything twice, and Rosie was good at delivering full reports right off the street.

Rosie was the first female recruited into the Rutherford PD detective division. She'd had to climb a high brick wall of resistance put up by otherwise reasonable men in the department. They thought of themselves as the elite corps of the RPD and were not prepared to believe a woman could handle the job.

I admired the way she dealt with the problem by ignoring it. Most of the men in her family are in law enforcement, and she grew up among brothers, getting and giving no favors. Nothing about the behavior of begrudging city cops surprised her – she just worked harder than everybody else and kept her head down till she won acceptance.

Since she never tried to become one of the

guys, she became the colleague who brought something extra to the table. She's noisy and feisty and sometimes drives me up the wall defending her point of view, but she's becoming the paradigm for the tough, capable female investigator. The chief always uses her as an example when he's trying to get qualified women into the training classes.

Ray Bailey was the only one home in People Crimes section. He was coiled in front of his computer again, learning more ways to improve the plants that thrive in good black Minnesota dirt. He switched gears quickly this time, pulling up his extra chair, telling us both, 'Sit, sit. You interviewed the dead man's mother-in-law?'

'And the widow too, Naomi Gold.'

'I thought you went to see the mother.'

'I did. But after she agreed to see me she persuaded her daughter to clear a half-hour on her schedule. And as soon as she gave me some background, we walked across the hall to Naomi's home office so I could talk to the two of them together.'

'Why?'

'Mrs Bedford was afraid she might forget something. Her response to the stress of Nathan's death has been to start losing things – her car keys and her wallet, in just the last two days, she said – so she concluded she must be starting the slide toward Alzheimer's. I told her she shouldn't worry – it happens to me whenever I fight with my mother.'

A look of rare delight grew on Ray's face. 'Is that true?'

'No, I just said that to make her feel better. I can fight with my mother without turning a hair – I only lose things when I fight with Bo.'

Rosie and Bo had started a passionate romance last year, as soon as his divorce was final. She had loved him secretly, devotedly, for a long time before his wife left him. When they finally felt free to express the attraction they'd both been suppressing, I guess Rosie thought, with some justice, that her time for happiness had come. But Bo was concerned that his young daughter, Nelly, jerked around for so long by his wife's addiction, deserved some settling time before she accepted a new woman in the house.

Rosie said she saw the need for adjustment, but lately I thought she was getting snappish. Rosie Doyle losing patience was not a prospect I looked forward to dealing with. I felt for their predicament, but I felt for mine even more. They were both good detectives. If they started a ruckus in the section I might lose one or even both of them.

Ray asked her, 'Did you get anything new from seeing the two of them together?'

'Some. Naomi had her dream job in New Jersey – head of internal medicine in a big-city hospital with a top salary, slated to be appointed to the board soon. The job she's got here pays less than half of what she was making there. But more importantly, she's lost a lot of ground in terms of career advancement.'

'So Naomi had plenty of reason to be totally pissed, is that what you're saying?' Ray was making notes in his tiny script. 'Mad as hell at the beloved Nathan?'

'No, I didn't get that impression. It was more like she was in kind of a slow burn, aware the balance was a little out of whack in the relationship and wondering how to fix it. Then he died and right now she doesn't know what to feel. There's another big issue, too – the couple's second child, a son named Zachariah, suffers from Down Syndrome. He'll always need special care and education. She had a perfect setup in New Jersey, a wonderful private school for him and another for the daughter, who's exceptional in her own way and has a very high IQ. She'll soon be ready for one of those prep schools that zip them right into Harvard.

'And she gave all that up to follow her husband to the Midwest so he could – wait, I want to get this quote right, it's a real pip' – Rosie whirled through her notebook till she found the spot – '"pursue his dream of creating new crops that would fare better in the uncertain weather of the twenty-first century." Honest to God, that's what she said – these people are wicked idealistic. She said it was hard to give up her job but decided it was a sacrifice worth making. She insists that Nathan was a brilliant scientist and she still believes he would have found the crops that the world's population is going to need.'

'That sounds a little . . . Walt Disney, to me,' Ray said.

'I know, I know. But this woman's the real deal, Ray. You don't often hear a wife praise a husband the way she did today.'

'Jesus, no,' Ray said. 'Not unless they're feverish.'

'Poke fun if you like but take my word for it – Naomi was sincere. But now, suddenly, he's dead. And his partner is already talking about moving the firm they started to Alaska.'

'He is?' Ray said. 'First I heard of that.'

'Me, too. But both Naomi and her mother mentioned it. Looks like the partner talks more out there in his office than he does in here.'

'Probably so. What else?'

'Naomi's mother doesn't follow her everywhere she goes. This is the first time she's followed her anywhere. *She* gave up plenty too – a part-time job she loved, librarian in her local junior college – to come out here and help with Zack. She said it was a big sacrifice, "But Nathan was a good husband and a fine scientist, and I felt my daughter was lucky to be happily married to such a man."'

'She said that? About them being happily married?'

'Yes. Kind of made a point of it. Like maybe she wanted to be sure of it herself? I don't know. It's a very stressful time and I think they're both feeling kind of . . . left high and dry.'

'I don't know, Rosie,' Ray said, frowning. 'This feels like a description out of Horatio Alger. The doctor is a faithful mate, her mother is a helpful heroine, and the husband was a brilliant scientist but now he's dead and the ladies are in a pickle.'

There was a short silence, during which Rosie's cheeks got pinker.

'Seems to me we should be thinking that

maybe,' Ray said, warming to the analysis, 'they both got mad as hell, decided they weren't going to take it anymore and found some clever way to off the guy so they could escape back to New Jersey, a well-known Paradise on the eastern shore.'

Rosie cleared her throat and said softly, 'Golly, Ray, I bet you got A-plus in summing-up class, didn't you?' Her eyes were like two frozen blue marbles.

'Just trying to get clear on where we stand,' Ray said. 'First time you came back from talking to the widow, you said she was glacial. Now she seems to be turning into Mother Teresa. Which is it?'

'Usually neither and sometimes both,' she said, slapping her electronic tablet shut and jamming pencils into her chaotic hair. 'People aren't robots, Ray. I'm sorry they don't deliver cookie-cutter emotions so you can keep your forms neat. Those two women are living through a tragic family event, they're grieving and conflicted as reasonable people sometimes are. And you and your staff are going to look like idiots if you treat them with anything but the utmost respect and sympathy.'

She stomped out and across the hall to her own workspace, where she sat down, turned her chair so her back was to her boss, and began typing her report into the case file.

Ray looked up at me with his saddest Bailey face and said, 'When did I ever—'

'Never,' I said. 'You treat everybody with respect. But we sent her to sort out a very emotional scene, and she's analyzing it as fast as she can.'

'Well, that's no reason to bite my head off.'

'Sure it is. When frustration strikes, people always bite off the head that's closest. Maybe you should make a note to have somebody else interview Doctor Gold, when there's time? By the way, what did you think about Marilyn?'

'Who? Oh, that pricey-looking office manager Kevin was strutting around here with? What comes over him sometimes? He walked in here and presented her like I was supposed to decide win, place or show.'

'Which did you decide?'

'Nothing. I was busy. I waited while she poured compliments over me like syrup over a waffle and they finally left.'

'OK. Where are you – what's next?'

'I'm waiting for reports from Abeo. She's supposed to bring me everything else she's learned about Gold's contacts and work history. And Winnie's still working on Brennan's career in start-ups – last I heard she hadn't found any sheriffs sniffing on his trail. Clint's interviewing the neighbors in that office complex with SmartSeeds. Let's see, what else? Oh, yeah, somewhere in this town, Andy Pittman is working his way through many cups of coffee with hockey players. He'll turn up when he's got something else or he knows there's nothing more to get.'

'Sure,' I said. 'No need to worry about Andy.'

Ray's phone rang and as he reached for it I eased out the door. I'd gone ten steps toward my office when I heard him call my name.

I turned back. He was standing in his doorway. Even for Ray, his face looked unusually grim. I hurried back so he could tell me quietly, 'The head of the experimental science team at Minnaska just got attacked. I'm going there now. I'll take Rosie with me since she's the only one here.' He pulled his ear; it helps him think. 'Will you call the crew and get them headed over there? Not the store, now, the lab on First Avenue.'

'Gotcha,' I said. 'Go.'

I watched him step into the opening of Rosie's cubicle. She looked up in surprise, listened as he said one short sentence and was on her feet. Without a word, she slid her tablet into its bag and hung it on her left shoulder, dropped her cell phone into her purse and draped that on her right. In less than a minute they were at the top of the stairs, headed down. Looking as if she'd never exchanged a cross word with Ray Bailey, Rosie had her head tilted toward him, listening intently to the few facts he had to share.

'His name is Mark Hoving,' Ray told me half an hour later. 'He's not hurt at all. He was parking his boss's car, for some reason, and he'd just pulled into the parking spot when the right headlight exploded. When he got out and looked, he decided the car must have been shot at. So naturally he's a little unnerved.'

'You agree the car's been shot?'

'Looks like it to me. I've got a crime scene tech underneath it now, taking off the right front tire. He thinks he can see where the bullet went in.'

'Is the driver calm enough to answer questions?'

'Pretty soon, I think. He got scared when he saw he was being shot at, so he dived under the car and hid there for a few minutes. When nothing more happened he crawled out and ran into the building yelling bloody murder. So now he and the entire company are out in the parking lot having a shit fit. Any of my crew got back there yet?'

'No. But I reached everybody except Abeo, and told them to go straight there. You haven't seen anyone yet?'

'Clint and Bo are here. Oh, now I see Andy pulling in. So if either Winnie or Abeo stop in there, will you have them bring me a laser pointer? Nobody told me this attack was from a firearm. I think the shot must have come from one of the higher buildings in the area. If I had a laser pointer I might be able to figure out the angle.'

'Good idea. Let's see, what's near there?'

'I'm guessing maybe the parking garage on Third Avenue? That'd be the easiest place to get in and out of, the best command of the area with the least hassle over windows. If I could find the location fast enough we might still get some DNA. I got a couple of lab techs coming, in case we find the right spot.'

'Hell, Ray, I'll bring you a pointer. Wait, though, here's Abeo just walking in. Tell you what, it'll be faster if I bring both her and the pointer – that way I don't have to waste time on directions and I can explain the attack on the way.'

'Do it,' Ray said. 'This place is crazy – we need to show them some leg.' It was the chief's expression for when the client needed convincing. Ray doesn't cave easily to pressure, but he apparently thought this was one of those times.

I stepped into the hall and said, 'Don't go in your workspace, Abeo. Come with me.' I scooped her up, if you can be said to scoop up a woman who's looking down at the top of your head. Too new to the detective unit to argue, she just opened her dark eyes very wide and strode along beside me, down the stairs and out to my pickup. She climbed nimbly into the passenger's seat, trailing billows of fine gray fabric.

Once under way I told her the little I knew. She was sorry but not contrite about having her phone turned off. 'I was in the library, and you know they won't tolerate any ringing . . . well, understandably. I left a note on my desk saying where I was going, but I suppose nobody thought to . . . well.'

'There's a rule that we never turn our cell phones off when we're out of the office,' I said. 'But to be honest we all get in situations like that from time to time, so next time set it on vibrate and step outside to answer. But never mind, we're here now.'

Finding the crime scene at Minnaska was not a problem. We followed a shrill hum of voices to the crowd milling around a shiny black Cadillac Escalade, gleaming like a big luxurious jewel except for the right headlight cluster, much of which lay shattered and crumpled on the tarmac.

The group was just as Kevin had described it: lab guys in blue smocks and lawyers in hand-tailored suits. They all wore good watches and several were talking fast into smart phones. They all spoke well, but as far as I could tell nobody was listening. There was a sprinkling of private secretaries in four-inch heels and that strange warped hair you usually only see on TV. A couple of them had wept and wrecked their mascara.

Ray was in the center of the crowd, pretty much penned up against the damaged Caddy by the two most aggressive question-hurlers, one in pinstripes and one in perfect navy. The damaged light was being periodically covered up by the bodies of Minnaska employees pushing in to see it.

I forced my way through the crowd and handed the laser pointer to Ray. Then I seized the right hand of the pinstriped man and shook it while I told him I was Jake Hines, chief of investigations for the Rutherford Police Department.

'And the first thing we need to do,' I said, 'is get all these people inside.'

'Well, they all wanted to see—'

'I know, but you don't know for certain that the shooter is gone, do you? So let's get all your people under shelter and then we can talk.' I made a grand, sweeping gesture toward the side of the building, where double doors and a big gleaming window were shaded by a broad overhang.

The pinstripe and several other suits, a little off-balance for once, actually followed me toward the door, and several smock-clad scientists followed them, bringing their secretaries along. Abeo acted as sweep, urging the laggards along. They obeyed her mostly because they had no idea who she was, and on a day when someone was shooting at the boss's car, anybody who seemed authoritative was reassuring.

Once inside I introduced myself and then Abeo. She took them so aback they all fell silent for half a minute. While the peace held, I suggested she talk to 'one group here,' waving vaguely at the two keen-looking scientists nearby. 'And I'll take the other half over here,' I said, herding my two apparent execs ahead of me to the other side of the room. As I knew they would, the group self-sorted, the scientists clustering around Abeo like iron filings around a magnet, and the attorneys mostly drifting to my side of the room.

Abeo pulled a small electronic device out of her woolen folds and began directing short soft questions down toward the hairlines of the nearest scholarly men and women, typing their wordy answers without a glance at her keyboard. They gazed up at her, mesmerized, plainly hoping she would think of many more questions to ask so they could go on watching her and decide if they were dreaming.

As soon as she had that group's attention I launched into a flurry of questions with the suits, starting with: how many shots did they hear? Most of them hadn't heard any. They had run outside in response to all the yelling inside the building.

I asked if anybody had seen the shooter. Nobody had. Was this the first hostile act they were aware of since the break-in, when the message was left? It was. I may have duplicated some questions that had already been asked by Ray, but I didn't begrudge the effort because the suits kept edging further into my circle, adding their own questions and answers. I wasn't sure we were uncovering any useful leads, but they were staying off Ray's back so he had room to work.

They all exclaimed about the lucky timing – Mark had just parked Mr Gordon's car in its designated spot and come to a full stop, they said, so he wasn't hurt. Navy worsted, the chief question hurler, turned out to be Mr Gordon, the CEO. It took me some time to learn that his first name was Alan, because all the others called him Mr Gordon or sir.

'Why was he parking your car?' I asked him.

'Because somebody else was in my spot when I came to work,' Alan Gordon said. His expression told us all what a grave infraction that was. 'So I left the car by the door then went in and told Hastings to find out whose car it was, get it moved and get mine put away.' Hastings was an older secretary with gray hair in a short bob, apparently a trusted retainer. She nodded gravely from the back of the group.

'Is your parking spot labelled?'

'No. Everybody knows I use the corner space nearest the door. But a new lab technician started today and someone forgot to tell him.' Gordon cast an offended glance across the room, where the offender sheltered among the smocks.

'So then,' I said, digging through the chaff in search of kernels, 'the shooter may not have known that Mark Hoving was driving your car, is that right?'

All the heads turned toward me. For once, they were all listening.

Nobody answered my question, so I plowed on. 'We were called over here to investigate an attack on one of your scientists – that's how it was reported to me. Is that what you said, or not? Who reported this attack, by the way?'

'I did,' Hastings said, quietly, from the back row.

'Did you call nine-one-one?'

'Yes. I don't know the number at the station so I just—'

'Quite right, that's what it's there for.'

'A person answered and I said, "Please help us, one of our scientists has been attacked." I guess I should have said his car's been shot at, but you know, it wasn't his car, and rather than get into all that I just asked for help.'

'You did fine. I'm just trying to establish what actually went on here. A person shot at Mr Gordon's car. Mr Hoving doesn't normally drive that car, does he?'

'Certainly not,' Gordon said. 'Why would I trust my Escalade in the hands of anyone who drives a heap like his?'

Instead of looking embarrassed about a bitter insult aimed at a colleague, everybody in the group had a nice laugh, the kind of comfortable haw-haw you enjoy when somebody says, 'That Uncle Pete, ain't he a card?' I looked around at them and said, 'Hoving's car is funny?'

'Here,' the pinstripe suit named Neal said, 'step over to the window for a minute.'

When we stood where I had told all of them not to stand, he pointed. 'That's Hoving's heap, right there.'

It was parked three spaces east of Gordon's Escalade, a battered Chevrolet pickup, its faded blue finish blistered and peeling. It would have been noticeably rundown anywhere, but in this parking lot crowded with top-dollar SUVs and European sports cars, it made a statement. Since it wasn't saying, 'I belong to the long-term unemployed group,' it must be, 'I am a member of the working poor.'

But that certainly didn't describe any of the power players in Minnaska's science section. I asked Neal, 'Why is he driving such an ancient vehicle?'

He shrugged, and said, 'I think it's one of his experiments. He's always trying to prove something.'

'Like what?'

'Something about power, I think. He thinks Minnaska's not doing all it could on behalf of the' – he gave an embarrassed laugh – '*earth* and all that. So he's always running some experiment of his own on the side.' He shrugged and rolled his eyes up. 'He's a geek, what more do I need to tell you?'

We went back to the group, where a discussion of sorts was taking place. The attacker must have used a high-powered long gun of some sort, and the company lawyers, in defiance of reason, kept zeroing in on the idea that the shot had been intended for their lead scientist. Maybe it was a defense. It allowed them not to suppose the obvious: that it must have been intended for their CEO.

What they really wanted to know was whether the attack was part of the same conspiracy behind the messages.

'Because if they're coming around again,' they began saying, 'the people who killed Nathan Gold must be ready to start on us.'

'We still haven't proved anybody killed him,' I reminded them. This drew cynical shrugs and eye-rolls. *Look what's happening*, their faces seemed to say. *Of course somebody killed him.*

Assuming the shooter was the same person who'd left the warnings, they all began to wonder why he'd changed his MO from whatever it was that killed Nathan. Why would he switch to firearms? (They were proud of themselves for knowing about MOs – loved using the term.)

But actually, if today's attack came from some new person or group, Alan Gordon said, that would be even scarier, wouldn't it? He had a long face and was given to slow, grave speeches. He gave one now, that concluded, 'Because then, don't you see, instead of a generalized attack on anybody involved with GMOs, we'd be looking at a new outbreak of hostile behavior directed *specifically* at Minnaska.'

Heads nodded all around him after he said this. I thought his reasoning had more holes in it than Swiss cheese, but he was obviously the Number One Serious Guy in this group, so they nodded.

I asked them a lot more questions then, like, how many people had each of them told about the message scroll? Any chance somebody in that informed group might be holding a grudge? And was this the first time their parking lot had ever been attacked? 'Going back to when?' somebody asked.

'To whenever the last time was,' I said. 'Are you accustomed to getting attacked in this parking lot at regular intervals?'

'Absolutely not,' Alan Gordon said. 'Where'd you get that idea?'

Many of these questions were random and even inane, but our time wasn't being wasted, because while these execs were busy showing me how smart they were, Ray and his helpers had positioned the laser pointer within the wound track that the bullet had left in the Cadillac. Presently they had an almost steady red beam directed at the north end of the Third Avenue parking garage, midway between the fifth and sixth floor. Ray and his crew began waving and speculating then, deciding where to start searching up there.

Hastings walked quietly out to Ray when I wasn't watching her. I was alarmed when I saw her out there, but I soon realized that she was telling him she had a laser device like his, and asked if he'd like to have it. Ray gave her one of his rare smiles and she trotted back in and got it out of her desk.

Before long I saw four heads moving along the railings of the parking garage: Rosie and Clint on the sixth floor, Winnie and Bo on the fifth. We could hear their voices faintly calling to one another, but not what they said. Bo had the second laser pointer, I saw, and every few feet he stopped and, taking pains not to touch anything, shot a beam over the railing at the Escalade.

Andy, I knew, was at his vehicle, nearby but out of sight, loading a satchel with crime scene tape, evidence bags, labels – all the tools they'd need to use if they got lucky and found a place that looked promising.

Just before I'd left my desk I'd pulled a pair of binoculars out of my console and hung them around my neck. I took the caps off the lenses now, asked the lawyers to please stay where they were, and stepped over to the window where I could watch the detectives work.

Four heads appeared and disappeared in the distant parking garage. Rosie's head popped out of the gloom on the sixth floor, into sunlight that set her ringlets afire. She leaned over the railing, being careful not to touch it as she called down some new factoid. A few seconds later I saw what she was talking about – the two red beams were lining up left to right, but the one reaching up from the Caddy was a little above the one Bo was sending down from the fifth floor.

I saw Bo dial his cell, and then Ray's phone rang. I put my hand up like a traffic cop to hold the people inside where they were, and said,

'Abeo, you're in charge in here. Make sure nobody leaves this room.' She had demonstrated great people skills so I knew she could do it, and I needed to get outside. I slid out the door and hurried toward Ray, who was having a short conversation with Bo that ended just as I reached his side.

Ray closed his phone and told me, 'The beams are lined up left and right. We could probably get them to mesh up and down too but I'm reluctant to meddle with the pointer in the Caddy. The metal in that housing is all shot to hell. If I fool around in there maybe it'll collapse and then we've got nothing to work with.'

'But as it stands now the shooter could have stood on either floor,' I said.

'Yeah. We'll have to search both floors for trace evidence. I'm going to send Andy up now.' He dialed again, got Andy and told him, 'Take the techs up with you, but have them wait in the aisle till we decide which area to test first. Go first to where Bo's searching on fifth and then to Rosie one floor up. Tape off both areas, keep everybody but our guys out. Somebody wants to get a car, tell 'em tough cheese, they just have to wait.'

I trained my binoculars on Bo, who was just inside the gloom working his careful way right along the railing. Winnie was twelve feet away, using the same strategy in reverse – shine a flashlight over every inch of railing, top to bottom, then move three careful inches to the left.

When they were still maybe ten feet apart, Bo turned his head toward Winnie and said something. She stuck a marker where she left off and moved over beside Bo. Just the top of her head was visible above the railing, but I could see between the rails that she was holding both flashlights now. Above them, Clint and Rosie had adopted the same strategy. Rosie held both Streamlight beams steady, while Clint moved slowly, an inch at a time, scrutinizing every inch of railing and floor.

Bo disappeared, briefly, and then I saw him again, crouched in the circle of light from the flashlights, peering down. He took a couple of pictures with his phone then picked up something and stood, holding it out in his gloved right hand, showing her.

He dropped whatever it was into an evidence bag, handed the bag to Winnie and dialed his phone again. Ray answered on the first half of the ring, listened for a few seconds and gave a grunt of satisfaction. When he closed his phone he told me, 'Bo just found a casing.'

I said, 'How do we know this casing is the one from the bullet that hit Gordon's car?'

'Bo said it looks fresh,' he said. 'And it's a thirty-ought-six, so the caliber's right for the distance. But I told the other team to keep searching on the sixth floor, just in case. Hang on—' He dialed his phone again, and I now heard a guttural answer. Ray said into the phone, 'Andy, Bo found a casing – we think it's the right one. So tell the techs to go find Bo and Winnie on the fifth floor. Tell them to swab the hell out of that area and then try for prints.'

I privately thought the chances for a good

DNA sample were slim to none on that surface. And I knew there wasn't much chance that pebbled concrete would hold an impression of body oils. But the tops of the rails looked pretty smooth. Maybe we'd get lucky and lift a print there.

Ray and I began the phoning and texting marathon that inevitably directs the after-action at a crime scene. At one point I asked him, 'Shouldn't we be getting Kevin over here to look at this?'

'I've called him and left messages three times,' Ray said. 'It seems to be a bad day for cell phones.'

I called the chief then, to settle the question of how to get the casing to BCA as fast as possible. A flurry of phone calls later, he came back with the answer – a two-way shuttle of evidence that had been scheduled for tomorrow could be moved up to today. And the chief was talking to Admin about getting moved up a bit in the queue, since we were so hot on the trail and had corporate clients in jeopardy. Department policy at these times could be summarized as, 'Since human life is not yet perfect, be prepared to grab somebody else's share.'

The rest of the drudgery at the scene was for the specialists, so I got ready to slide out of a crime scene that really wasn't on my jobs list. Before I left, though, I made a date for an interview with Mark Hoving.

'Tomorrow morning,' I said. 'Let's make it around nine.'

Hoving didn't want to leave his nice cocoon at

Minnaska to come downtown and talk to cops. He did his best to squirm out of it, saying he had 'samples ripe for testing every day this week.' Maybe at a later date, he suggested. I got ready to bump chests but was saved from confrontation by Alan Gordon, who gravely delivered his opinion that an attack with a high-powered firearm tended to crowd out routine matters like leaf analysis, and 'Probably we have enough scientists in this building to look after your samples for one day, Mark.'

'Whatever you say, sir,' Mark Hoving said.

Alan Gordon nodded with a little glint and said, 'Exactly.'

So that was that, and I took the shiny brass casing back to the station, signed it into the evidence room and then out again and got it wrapped by Pete Schroeder, two years retired and now double-dipping on the evidence desk. Nobody begrudged him the money, since hardly anybody can tolerate the boredom of communing all day with a row of stolen bikes. He did a nice job on the wrapping and had it ready by the time the shuttle arrived.

I was in the chief's office, meanwhile, giving him the quick-and-dirty before I wrote it up. On my way back to my office, though, I saw a light on in Kevin's office, went in and said, 'Hey,' to his back, which was just visible behind his desk. He rose up, looking pink-cheeked – the way Rosie had earlier.

'Wrecked a good pair of suede oxfords out there,' he said.

'Been in the fields, huh?' I watched him getting

ready to say something flip about how shrewd I was to realize he probably had not wrecked his shoes on the bone-dry streets of Rutherford, but before he got the perfect sarcasm formulated I added, 'Cell phones don't work around the soy beans?'

'What do you mean? I haven't had—' He grabbed his phone off his belt and looked at it. 'Low power! Damn!' He found the cord and plugged it in.

Tossing a dirty pair of shoes into the box his new ones had just come out of, he said, 'Why are you needling me about this? Did you try to call me about something?'

I told him about the attack at Minnaska. 'It started out looking like a crime against a person, and maybe the shooter meant it to be. But his aim wasn't quite good enough so in the end it's just a damaged Escalade.'

'But a Minnaska Cadillac, shee-it,' Kevin said. 'I bet the suits don't think of it as "just a damaged Escalade," do they?' He grew a little sneaky-gleeful look. 'Are they climbing all over poor old Ray?'

'He seems to be holding his own. Are you done tying those new shoes? Because it might be very good PR for the department if you hustled over there right now and showed concern.'

'You think?' He rubbed his face, suffered, shook his head and got over it. 'You're right, I know you're right – this is our chance to show them our righteous stuff, isn't it?' He studied the ceiling light, muttered something.

'What?'

'I said I'm never going to eat another GMO as long as I live.'

'If you can tell the difference. The headman there seems to be Alan Gordon – you know him? Older guy. Serious.'

'God, isn't he?' He rose to his full height, dropped his voice three notches and intoned, 'I am Alan Gordon, more eminent than most persons.' He took a deep breath and began strapping on tools – spare smart phone, recorder, Glock.

'Make sure your phone's turned on,' I said, driving in the needle. I wanted him to stay over there and be solicitous, showing everybody how much we cared. Ray's a good detective but he can get very focused and dour and forget about the emotional fragility of victims. To keep them off the chief's back, Minnaska needed a big dose of Kevin Evjan charm.

When he was gone I went back in my office and pulled up the case file for Minnaska. I entered the information about the casing, including the number of the shuttle that took it to St Paul. Then I did what I always do now in quiet moments, and opened my email. How did we all manage before this invention made it so easy to bedevil each other? I was a cop before email existed and I remember we made arrests and put people in jail. Why does that seem impossible now?

I was on the next to last message when my phone rang and Sorenson said, from the Dispatch desk, 'Jake, are you the only live body in your section? I'm showing everybody else out of the building.'

'Yeah, we're having kind of a busy day.' Understating the case like that makes me feel stoic. 'Whaddya got?'

'Apparent second break-in at an office on South Broadway, a firm called Portal. No message left this time but the owner thinks they sabotaged her desk chair. It was fine yesterday, but today, when she sat in it, it collapsed and she hurt her arm, shoulder, stuff like that.'

'And her name is?' I said, writing.

'Mrs Margaret Ross. She's the owner and about half the staff, I guess. Seeing her can wait – she's in the hospital right now. But you'll need to have a detective contact the office downtown . . .' He gave me an address and two phone numbers. 'See the junior partner, name's Lily Trask. And Officer Casey, he answered the call and he's waiting there, says the chair leg does look like it might have been tampered with. So one of your heroes better hustle on over there and get the story from him.'

Sorenson has tested twice for detective division and failed both times, so he is prone to making little snide remarks like that. He pisses everybody off, but I've told my crew to remember we have to work with this man, so keep smiling and be grateful stupidity isn't catching. I filled out a telephone message slip and put it on Ray's desk. By the time I got back to my desk my phone was ringing again.

The chief said, 'Jake, did you get the word on Maggy Ross's accident?'

'Just now, yes. I left a message for Ray—'

'Her husband is Mortimer Ross. He's one of

the partners in Enfield & Ross – the law firm that defended the Rhoady twins. Remember them?'

'Remember the case, sure.' Enfield & Ross had been a synonym for evil around here while we were trying to convict the Rhoadys of Murder One and Ross's team did its best to plead it down to manslaughter. Luckily their best wasn't quite good enough, so the Rhoadys got Murder Two and a good stiff sentence. We called it a win even though we wanted them gone, off the planet forever.

The chief seemed to be ready to forgive those lawyers now. 'I served on a committee with Mort Ross last year,' he said. 'He's a sensible man and he's very worried about his wife. He says she's the last person in the world to imagine trouble where it isn't. She's not a hysterical type and right now she's very busy and focused on growing her new firm. He asked me to make sure we take her claim seriously. Says if she thinks the chair was jiggered, it probably was.'

'We'll take it seriously,' I said. 'Don't we always? But everybody's out right now working on the Minnaska attack – you know about that?'

'Yes. What about that – somebody took a shot at one of their scientists?'

'Looks like it. Sure as hell hit their Cadillac, anyway. It could be some kid shooting out headlights, but—'

'Well, Minnaska's one of the firms that got broken into, so it figures, doesn't it, that this is what the message threatened? The retribution sure and swift or whatever?'

'Yes. And Portal got one of those, too.'

'That's what Mort said. Damn, it always seems to come in bunches, doesn't it?' He made windy noises into the phone for a few seconds, then got down to it. 'The thing is, Jake, Mort Ross called me personally to ask me to meet him at his wife's shop so we could look at the chair together.'

'Chief, come on,' I said. 'You know we can't—'

'Of course I know that, and I explained how completely he would jeopardize his wife's case if he started investigating it himself.'

'But what?' I said, because I could feel the protocol-bending special favor coming.

'Well, he's just frantic with worry because his wife told him whoever left that nutty message must have broken in again and turned her desk chair into a death trap. So to get him to calm down I said we'd have somebody look into it right away.'

'Ah.'

'So do you think you can detach somebody from Ray's team to get over to Portal and take a look?'

'I was just going to call Ray and ask. Tell your friend not to worry, Chief; we'll hop right on the case.'

'Appreciate it, Jake. Thanks.'

I picked up my cell and started to call Ray, but before I got to the end of the numbers I thought about that crazy scene at Minnaska, how much he had going on there, people pulling at him on all sides. I stopped dialing and thought, *How hard could it be to look at a chair leg?*

I thought about reclassifying it as a property crime and sending one of Kevin's crew to check it out. But they were all out in fields looking at frosted soy beans and cornstalks, and I had just sent Kevin to Minnaska.

So I stepped into the hall and asked LeeAnn to let the desk know she was taking all the calls for both sections till further notice. Then I got in my red pickup and drove a few blocks south to the formerly empty block on South Broadway, where in the last year a gaggle of enterprising citizens had begun filling old buildings with new ideas.

Seven

I spotted a squad car parked on Second Avenue, found an open space nearby and pulled in. I couldn't see any signs for Portal so I walked around the block, checking foyers. Finally I noticed a sign by an inside elevator that listed Portal along with several other businesses. It was on the third floor, a tiny foyer with a desk and two offices behind, both with closed doors.

A young officer I didn't know, whose name tag read 'Casey' was standing in front of one of the doors, talking on his cell. I nodded and he nodded back without pausing in his conversation.

I approached the desk, where a receptionist with many freckles sat behind a name plate that said her name was Doris Ganz. She blinked through her round wire-rims while she studied my badge. Satisfied at last, she pressed a button. A phone rang behind the second closed door and in about two seconds a young woman with the lively gait of an athlete opened the door and came out, smiling. She said she was very glad to see me – not a greeting police detectives hear often enough – and added, 'I'm Lily Trask. The other half of Portal.'

'Jake Hines,' I said. 'Let me just see if the officer here can spare a moment to bring me up to speed and then I'll come in your office and we'll talk, OK?'

I went and stood in front of Casey, made the squelch sign, and heard him say, 'Yeah, well, a detective's here now so I guess I better . . . hmmm?' He stood listening to a torrent of words coming out of the phone from an excited young woman. I reached across him, took the phone out of his hand, said 'Officer Casey has to work now,' and poked OFF.

He got all red-faced and chesty and said, 'Now wait a minute—'

'No, you wait a minute. I'm Jake Hines, the chief of the detective division, and I do not have time to listen to the personal conversation you should not be having while you're on a call.' I pulled on gloves. 'Now show me the chair that collapsed.'

The wind went out of his balloon fast. 'It's in there.' He pointed at the door behind him. 'The door's not locked – there isn't any lock – and I don't have any more gloves on me. Will you open it?'

I handed him a pair of fresh gloves along with a little sneer as I went past him and opened the door.

Mrs Ross had a standard office, no frills – a desk, two computers and a lot of other electronic gear, one window over the console. There were two straight chairs for visitors and one black padded swivel chair lying on its side behind the desk. Lying on both its sides, actually – the legs seemed to be facing one way and the seat and arms another. I stood beside it, looking down, thinking, *I am not a chair expert.*

But then, who is? Only the manufacturer and they're probably in China. *So suck up and soldier on*. I squatted beside the chair and used the experienced detective's favorite ploy: put the responsibility on some other poor sod.

I turned to Casey and said, 'Show me why you think somebody messed with this chair.'

'Well, see, the thing that makes this chair work is this central cylinder with the air suspension, agreed?'

'I guess so, yes.'

'This handle allows you to adjust it up or down. The wheel assembly bolts onto the bottom of the cylinder. On top it's attached to a metal plate that supports the seat and arms.'

'Which seems to have come loose. I've never seen a chair come apart this way. Isn't this just the standard office chair we all wear out every couple of years?'

'Looks like it. Right off the floor at some office supply store.'

'Maybe not thrilling, but they're usually pretty

sturdy. But this . . . The seat and arms just slid off the base. Support plate and all.'

'Yes. Because of these.' He fished an envelope out of an inside pocket and shook out half-a-dozen short bolts. Metal bolts painted black to match the chair, but now that I looked again, they were really quite short.

'Ah. They do look a little short, don't they?'

'Yes. See' – he shoved one though the flange – 'they're just long enough to catch the support plate. Barely.'

'You found them scattered around the floor here?'

'Yup. I think whoever replaced the original bolts knew these would fasten the top back on so the chair would look the same as always, but when she sat down – she's a pretty big woman – the top just flew off and down she went.'

'She wasn't all that far off the floor, though.'

'Fifteen inches,' Casey said, showing me with the ruler on his Leatherman. He sensed we were putting the telephone thing behind us, and now he was enjoying this chance to show me he hadn't wasted all the time he'd spent waiting.

I said, 'So why's she in the hospital?'

'Well, it wasn't a pretty fall. She got tangled up in the chair legs and sustained some bad scratches in' – he cleared his throat – 'sensitive spots. And she was scared, and flailed around some, getting up. The way she was holding onto her shoulder, it looked like she might have sprained it.'

'You called the ambulance?'

'No, the partner had already done that before

I got here. Mrs Ross didn't have to wait long at all, which was good because she was in great distress. Partly from pain but mostly from fear, I think. She said it was her second break-in this month and I could see that it really unnerved her.'

'Understandably. Will you stand by here a few minutes longer while I see if I can get an evidence tech in here? Then I'll interview Ms Trask and you can go.'

'Sure. You want the bolts?'

'Yeah, I guess I'll need them for pictures. I'll mention in my report that you found them, though.'

'Thanks. I'm sorry about that business with the phone earlier. My fiancée's planning our wedding and sometimes she doesn't understand that I can't just drop everything and help her make decisions.'

'Better have her talk to one of our counselors.' I was personally betting on a short first marriage for Sean Casey. I could relate because my own initial try at family life had ended in a screaming debacle. It's hard enough to be a cop's mate even when you both know the score and agree on priorities, which we certainly did not. I was trying to build a career as a detective and Nancy thought young, attractive wives had a right to expect plenty of attention and fun on weekends.

I hope to live long enough to forget the last months of that marriage. I know my luck went off the charts when I got a second chance with Trudy Hanson. It took persistence, but I finally enticed her into bed and eventually into marriage. Besides being a blonde beauty who turns my ticker on every time I look at her, she turned out to be a great cook and a devoted mother. As soon as she stops getting mad at me for reading the Sports page when I should be listening to her, she'll be perfect.

Lily Trask said no, she wasn't afraid to stay in the office alone. 'There are people all around me and I have the janitor's assurance he'll come at once if I call him,' she said. 'Whoever this wacko is, he seems to like to work alone at night.'

'That's very reasonable,' I said. 'But if for any reason you do start feeling alarmed, will you call this number?' I gave her the card with my cell number. I don't do that often but the chief said to spread some comfort, and I'm his man. How else do I get to be him some day?

'I pulled up the report from your first break-in before I came over,' I said. 'It said Mrs Ross had decided the first floor was too accessible and she intended to move to the third floor.'

'Which, as you can see, she did. And we can't see anything wrong with the lock.'

The front door had the usual panic bar on the inside, and a good deadbolt lock on the outside, working perfectly with not a mark on it.

'So we're looking for a busybody who wants to tell everybody how to live, and who's also good at going through locked doors,' I said. 'You got any candidates in mind?'

'No,' Lily said. 'An environmentalist preacher who's also very tech-savvy? I don't think I know anybody like that.'

'Your employer has no ideas either?'

'Mrs Ross kept saying, after the first break-in, "I thought we'd be perfectly safe in this nice, quiet old building." Finally Mr Ross said, "Maggy, it is what it is. Move to the third floor and get a better lock." So she did. The last thing she said before they rolled her out on the gurney today was, "But I moved to the third floor and changed the lock!"'

We went back in Lily's office. It was even smaller and plainer than Mrs Ross's – one straight chair in front of the desk and no window – so it didn't take long to inspect. Lily's desk chair was the exact duplicate of her employer's, but seemed to be holding up fine. She stood up so I could inspect it. I jiggled it some, keeping my face solemn. The support plate showed no tendency to come loose, and the bolts were unmarked. Having shown her all the chair expertise I could muster, I sat down for a visit.

She had the clean-and-breezy look of your best gal pal in high school, the one you still think about sometimes and wish you'd asked to the Senior Prom. My first question was, 'How'd you find this out-of-the-way job?'

'I didn't. Mrs Ross found me. I was working for dog's wages in an office full of young attorneys who were living on scraps themselves. She came in looking for a cheap lawyer to help with a couple of details about setting up her business.'

'And there you were, ready to make a change.'

'Boy, was I. My job there was to type a lot, keep the coffee fresh and answer the phone. I was the only female in an office with eight young, randy men. Even the married guys kept trying to cop a feel.'

Jotting notes, I wrote 'steno @ att'y firm.' Details like 'cop a feel' went without saying, I thought, for her good looks and age group.

'My folks had no money for college so I was just doing what I could, using what I had – good computer skills from high school and math aptitude. I applied to all the architects' firms in town, hoping to apprentice, but nobody was building anything. Most of my classmates were flipping burgers and making beds, so they thought I was lucky to get the job I did.

'But before long I started getting this desperate feeling. A dead-end job is like being trapped in an exercise wheel – two or three years of this and I'd marry one of the guys trying to get in my pants. And then I'd get pregnant and the whole thing could start over for another generation – what the hell?

'So I was trying to save enough for accounting classes at night school, and when Mrs Ross offered me some weekend work I jumped at it.'

'What did you do to impress her so fast?'

'She noticed my speed on the keyboard. She's pretty creaky herself' – Lily grew the condescending expression all people under twenty-five have for their elders' computer skills – 'and she knew there would be a lot of spreadsheets and online forms and hours and hours of revising and formatting Word docs.'

'Portal does what again? Write grant applications?'

'Yes. Technically we're just advisors to the grant writers, but most of them need a lot of help. They supply the ideas; we help them find the funding. We'll work on any kind of grant at this stage but we specialize in those SBIR grants from the departments of Agriculture and Education. There's lots of folks doing agricultural research around here.'

'My tribe doesn't know SBIR.'

'Small Business Innovation Research. Means just what it says. So where do I fit in? Well, I started with more dog work on the keyboard. But after I talked her into letting me try some background research for her, we both saw I could make a difference here. She's a smart lady but she can't Google her way out of a paper bag. Always uses the most complex search terms. Simple ones and patience get the job done so much faster.'

'I'm kind of a doofus myself. Try to keep my email answered and stop there.'

'US standard for your age group, right? As soon as Mrs R sold one big job she offered me full time and I took it without thinking twice. It was the right move for both of us. She's growing her business fast and I've had two raises since I started.'

'So the job's all you hoped for?'

'Yes; even better than I thought.'

'Tell me about this morning.'

'I still come in first, open the calendar and type up our schedules for the day. Still make the coffee!' She gave me the big good-natured grin again – I couldn't see any malice behind it.

'Surprised you don't have Doris do that.'

'She doesn't start till ten. We're still in frugality mode. We never see more than two or three clients a day so we don't schedule any appointments before ten. Doris still gets only thirty hours a week. But soon we'll be bigger and all our arrangements will change again. We haven't had two whole months without major changes since I started.' Her face said it was the only way to fly.

'But for now you open at what, nine?'

'Yes.'

'And Mrs Ross comes in when?'

'Depends – she travels some, contacting clients, and she does a lot of phoning from home. But usually between nine-thirty and ten.'

'This morning?'

'Not till a few minutes before eleven. She got tied up on a long phone call with a prospective client. She came in my office first, all excited, to tell me about him. He's got pots of money – can't seem to say exactly what he wants to do but is very sure he wants to do it. "He keeps trying to get me to say what the project is," she said. "He thinks I'm Google."'

Lily giggled. 'I told her that sometimes I think that too.' She liked that moment a lot and glowed at the memory. Lily Trask aglow made the day seem brighter. 'Then we talked a few minutes about the big project we're working on: a grant application for funds to support more field testing for SmartSeeds.'

'Oh, you're working for SmartSeeds? Is that why you got the message warning you to cease and desist?'

'I suppose so. The only other major project we have going right now is a proposal to build a teaching tool for the Hempstead County school system. I don't think even a loony could find anything objectionable about that.'

'But SmartSeeds – that's been up and running longer than Portal, hasn't it?'

'That's right – we didn't help get any of the initial funding. But SmartSeeds is the kind of project that will require several rounds of financing and will always be looking for more funding for special projects and more research. SmartSeeds could be a recurring customer for the next several years. Especially if their project breaks out.'

'I've never thought about this money source before. It's actually lucrative enough so entrepreneurs can pay somebody to write the proposals?'

'Well, nobody's getting rich off it, but grants from foundations and governments are important funding sources that allow innovations to get tested. And the SBIR ones are particularly nice because the government gives you the money but you get to keep all the IP.'

'Eye Pee?'

'Intellectual property. If you take private funding you either have to pay back a loan or you owe the investor part of what you build. And some kinds of grants have strings attached about making the results public or even open source. SBIR just gives you the money and lets you keep what you create.'

'And the proposals are so complicated it takes a pro to get them right?'

'Pretty much. Some folks do write their own but getting professional help can up your chances from, say, one in ten to one in two. And then, longer term, we try to sell them some help managing the contract. Because the paperwork if you get the contract can be worse than writing the proposal.'

'Catch twenty-two, huh?'

'Yeah. This teaching proposal we're doing now is for a very clever game to teach math to slow learners. In order to do the grant application we've had to help the client design parts of the game and illustrate it. There are time constraints, and we're not the only ones trying for the account. So it's kind of like building the boat you're sailing in – better be quick or you'll sink.'

'Sounds like nervous work.'

'Well, Mrs Ross gets pretty stressed sometimes.'

'But not you?'

'No, I'm pretty much like this morning's client. All my life I knew I could be good at something, I just couldn't say what it was. Now I've found it and I'm having the time of my life. I mean, today I feel bad about Mrs Ross's accident, but normally I'm about the happiest grant writer in town.'

Her phone rang. She answered and then said, 'Oh, hi! How're you doing? Yes, the detective's here, we're just discussing – hmm? OK, hold on.' She handed me the phone, saying, 'Mrs Ross wants to talk to you.'

The voice that greeted me was a firm, strong contralto with no hint of confusion. If this was

Margaret Ross on tranquilizers, I thought, we'd all better bring our best game when the drugs wore off.

She liked having the full attention of Rutherford's finest. She wanted to talk.

'My injuries are not serious; I could probably go home,' she said. 'But my blood pressure spiked when I fell off that stupid chair. The doctors here suggested I stay on the monitor till I prove I'm stabilized, and Mort's begging me to take advice for once. So here I sit, all trussed up like a turkey, but I'm having a hard time calming down because I should be at work – there's so much to do!'

'Probably the work will wait for one day.'

'Have you been talking to my husband? That's what he said.'

'No, believe it or not I made up that original thought all by myself.'

'Just got the knack for wise sayings, huh? You must be married. Have you seen my chair yet?'

'Yes. All the bolts fell out of the support plate.'

'Why?'

'They look too short to be the originals. You got any enemies that you know of?'

'Just this nut who writes notes telling me what I have to do to please him. Why do you suppose he thinks I care?'

'I have no idea. Soon as I'm through here I'm going to turn your chair bolts in as evidence and get them sent to BCA.' I didn't have to explain; she knew about the crime lab from the first break-in. 'Are you really all right? No broken bones?'

'Not even a bloody nose. Just a few scratches and, you know, I just keep getting so *angry*. I put a small, discreet sign on my place, just the name and something about grant applications, and I got broken into anyway, just as if I'd advertised loose diamonds inside. So I moved to the third floor and changed the locks, and got broken into again. What do I have to do, set up my consulting business in a cave? Where do I go to file a complaint about damn nuisances who ruin my concentration?'

'Right here. I'm writing it down as we speak.' I was beginning to like Mrs Ross. 'I want you to know we're all just as sick of this craziness as you are, Mrs Ross, and our whole crew is working on it, every minute.' I didn't tell her they were mostly working on Minnaska and SmartSeeds. But they were all part of the same problem. Weren't they? I stared at the wall a minute, wondering, and didn't catch the next thing she said. 'I'm sorry. Will you say that again?'

'I said I know you are but I'm beginning to think there's something obvious here that we're all missing. Where's the quid pro quo in all this? Who stands to benefit?'

'Who stood to benefit from the Unibomber? Or the Colorado shooter in the theater? Sometimes there's just a crazy guy loose and running around. The trouble with this one is he's leaving so few traces . . .'

'So few? I haven't heard about any. What do you know that I don't?'

'I better not answer that on the grounds that it

might make me look foolish.' I was trying to divert her with humor but she wasn't amused.

'I could move my office again,' she said. 'But what's the use? I have this obscure little enterprise on the third floor of a stodgy old office building; if he found me there he can find me anywhere. I feel like I've got a scarlet letter on my chest – and all I do, for God's sake, is write grant proposals. How bizarre is that?' She did some heavy breathing for a few seconds and asked me, 'Can you come here and talk to me?'

'Mrs Ross, I'm the head of the detective division – I've got no business even being out of the office. I came to look at your chair because everybody else is out on cases right now and your husband was so anxious he called the chief—'

'Oh, my,' she said, 'Mort pulled one of his power plays, did he? Say no more, dear, I understand.' She laughed a big, Duchess-y laugh. 'Oh, excuse me, I didn't mean to disrespect – should I be calling you Sergeant?'

'Captain, actually. But Jake will do.'

'Please accept my apology, Jake. I'm a little bit rattled today.'

'Of course you are, and it's not a problem.'

'Good,' she said. 'When I get out of this network of wires I'm entrapped in here – when I'm back in my office, will you come and see me? You sound like a sensible fellow and that's exactly what I need right now.'

'Somebody will come to see you, for sure,' I said. 'It probably won't be me because I don't get off my chain very often.' I made a note to send Clint – his Goldilocks personality is usually the best soother we've got.

As soon as I hung up the phone it rang again. Lily answered and told me, 'Man's here from your department, says he got called to test for prints?'

I went out and found Norman Dahlke standing by the receptionist's desk in his neat blue shirt, holding his canister of supplies and smiling at Doris as if he'd never seen a freckled girl with round glasses before. To be fair, the smile she was sending back at him suggested that a medium-sized evidence technician with plastic gloves and a funny walk was exactly what she'd been looking for all her life.

'Morning, Norman,' I said. 'You two know each other?'

'Not yet,' he said. 'But I'm working on it.' Doris's smile grew wider.

'Probably better stop working on it for now,' I said, 'and start doing careful DNA swabs on the front door and Mrs Ross's door – that's the one over there behind Officer Casey. And then dust for prints on all three doors.' I asked Doris, 'That's all we've got here, right? Just these three doors?'

'Guess so,' she said absently, still smiling at Norman. 'All I've ever seen.'

I stuck my head back inside Lily's office and asked her, 'You got any back doors to this place? Any other way for people to get in and out?'

'No. But I was just thinking: maybe if you're checking for fingerprints you ought to have him dust the coffee console too.'

'The coffee con— You mean, you have one of those companies come in and set up the coffee service?'

'Yes.'

'What's the name of the company?'

'It's right there on the sign.'

I turned and looked. 'I don't see any sign.'

'It's right there on the—' She got up and came out. 'Oh, well, all the supplies are in front of it.' She pushed aside plastic cups and spoons and showed me a small sign bolted to the back of the cabinet. 'Inn-House Coffee,' it said. A couple of lines told me the coffee was the best, and gave me a number to call if I needed more before the usual re-supply date.

I took a picture and copied the number, asking Lily, 'These folks have a key to this office?'

'Don't think so. They always come in office hours when we're open. But if you're eliminating prints . . . That's what you're going to do, isn't it, take our prints and then check for matches?'

'You've been through this before?'

'No, but I read a lot of mysteries.' She flashed her Great Pal smile. 'So I'm an expert at police procedures.'

'Terrific. We'll consult you whenever we get confused.' I am not a great kidder, but something about Lily's good-natured grin invited chaffing. 'Is it always the same person who brings the coffee?'

'Yes; always the same sweet lady named Lois.'

'Last name?'

'The embroidery on her shirt only says Lois. I

think maybe she's like a whaddyacallit, franchisee? She does all the work herself and seems very motivated. Except lately she has a young man driving the truck for her, and sometimes he carries up some of the supplies. She told me he's her nephew – he's helping her out for a while because she sprained her knee.'

'So we can expect to find some of the nephew's prints too?'

'Maybe on some of the boxes. But he never helps with the stocking. He brings supplies up to the doorway and leaves them there. Then he waits in the truck while Lois cleans up the console and re-stocks. She's a demon cleaner and neatener.'

'You like Lois, huh?'

'She's just the dearest person. So tidy and cheerful.'

I got all the relevant phone numbers and email addresses from Lily, told her we'd be in touch and hurried back to the station. Norman stayed behind, dusting for prints as slowly as possible. Doris watched him, still smiling.

LeeAnn was having no trouble covering my department, which was silent and empty. She gave me my phone messages, saying, 'Hey, Jake, from now on why don't you send all your guys out on the street every Wednesday? I could have a clean desk once a week!'

I opened the case files for Minnaska, SmartSeeds and Portal, and confirmed what I suspected: most of the information collected in the last two days was still riding around in the notebooks of busy detectives. Ready or not, I thought, the world had better be left to cool it for a day while we caught up to ourselves.

I got LeeAnn to produce a one-page flyer with a lot of caps and exclamation points, telling every detective in the department to come to the big meeting room at eight tomorrow morning, any and all excuses flatly rejected. Warming to the task, I added, 'You call in sick tomorrow, be ready to die and prove it.'

She put it on bright orange paper and trotted around, humming a cheery little tune while she put it in a prominent place on every desk. About time, I thought, that the good guys got to be the ones leaving messages.

On a fresh page, I started drawing up an agenda. By the time I reached number fifteen, the march of question marks down the page was beginning to make me queasy. Wasn't there anything we knew for sure about this case? To begin with, was it even all one case? And if it was, did it include a murder?

We still hadn't proved Dr Gold's death was not accidental. Maybe he just happened to die while we were investigating a string of break-ins. A string of break-ins into offices, including his, where people were in one way or another involved in the genetic modification of crops, just like he was.

Sure. And my mother was the Queen of Romania.

Which, come to think of it, I couldn't disprove either.

Damn! I hit SAVE and turned to my phone messages. Maybe throwing a few of those pink slips into the trash would clear my mind. I worked my way through three meeting notices, a reminder that the OSHA report was due in three days and a request for a ride-along from the new police reporter at the local daily.

Holding the last pink slip in my hand, I looked past it to my notebook, lying open on my desk. A happy thought blossomed: there was one thing I could know for sure, right now. All I had to do was call that number from the coffee console.

The phone was picked up in the middle of the first ring, but nobody answered. I heard, I thought, some breathing. After a couple of seconds I said, 'Hello? Is this Inn-House Coffee?' A funny little soft commotion started, then a soft grunt and some harsher breathing. I figured I must have dialed one number wrong, gotten a child somewhere, and was reaching to press OFF and start over when a quiet female voice said, 'Inn-House Coffee, this is Lois. How may I help you?'

'Oh, Lois, hello. This is Captain Jake Hines. I'm calling from the Rutherford Police Department . . .' I explained about her client, the company named Portal, which as she probably knew had suffered a break-in recently . . .

'Yes,' she said. 'Such a shame. Mrs Ross was very upset. She told me they didn't take anything, though.'

'Do you know Mrs Ross pretty well?'

'Only as a customer.'

'Did she tell you about the note they left?'

'No, she didn't, but I saw something in the paper. Somebody's leaving messages?'

'That's right. At quite a few places. So, I'm sorry to bother you about this, but we have a few questions to ask of everybody who contacts these places.'

'Oh? What kind of questions?'

'Well, for instance, do you by any chance also deliver coffee to a firm called SmartSeeds? In that new start-up place—'

'I know where it is,' she said. 'SmartSeeds is a customer of mine. Did they get a message too?'

'Yes. How about Minnaska?'

'Minnaska's the biggest customer I have,' Lois said. 'They have that big lab building with two coffee stations. And then they have another one in the manager's office in back of their store in the shopping center.'

'Good big account, huh? Did the company set that up for you?'

'You kidding? The company doesn't do squat, except supply the product. I've built this business up all by myself.'

'You have to sell the accounts and then service them? I bet that keeps you busy. But Lily said your nephew works with you sometimes to help out?'

There was a little silence and then Lois said, in a voice that was noticeably less friendly than before, 'What are all these questions about, young man? I can't see your badge – how do I know I'm even talking to the police?'

'I'm sorry, I can understand why you might feel like that. Why don't I get your address so I can send one of my detectives to talk to you? Then you can see his badge, and you'll know—'

'I do not want you people coming to my house,' she said. 'I can't have that.'

'Well, Lois, I'm just trying to save you a trip here. Because we have to talk, so if we can't come to you, you'll have to come in to the station and talk to us.' I made the HELP sign to LeeAnn across the hall.

'I don't have time to do that,' Lois said. 'I work all day servicing my accounts and then I have to get ready for the next day's orders and take care of my house . . . I'm sorry, I don't have any spare time at all.' Her quiet voice had grown firmer – the voice of a lady accustomed to calling the shots in her life and not expecting to yield to the demands of a stranger.

LeeAnn came and stood by my desk. I handed her a slip with the phone number I was talking to and a note: 'Find the address for this.'

'I know it's not easy for the people we contact to help us out. But we have to get the cooperation we need, so . . . let me have that address now and we'll—'

The line had gone dead. I was talking to myself.

Ray walked back on the floor while I was still listening to my dial tone. He was trailed by five detectives who all walked into their work spaces and began calling to each other, as soon as they found their orange notices, wanting to know what was up.

LeeAnn came over with the address I wanted and I asked her, 'You got a last name to go with this?'

'You didn't ask me for—' She whirled to go back to her desk and collided with a small herd of detectives coming to quiz me.

By the time I had persuaded Ray and his crew that the meeting was about nothing more ominous than the need to get everybody on the same page, LeeAnn was standing behind them, looking puzzled. When they had all filed out and gone back to their own spaces, she said, 'There isn't any name but Inn-House Coffee.'

'Nothing listed for Lois?'

'No. Did you ask her?'

'Just coming to that when she hung up.'

'Oh. Was she mad about something?'

'Seemed like she didn't want us at her house.'

'So I suppose that's where you gotta go, huh?'

'Yup. Looks that way.'

I walked into Ray's office, which had a heap of evidence growing on the floor by his desk – two laser pointers and baggies full of broken glass and shards of metal. He had his notebook open and was already typing notes into the Minnaska case file. I waited while he finished a sentence, marked the spot in his notebook and said, 'What?'

I told him about Mrs Ross's broken chair and my visit to Portal, about the coffee service that appeared to link the three places that had been attacked, and the fact that Lois, the 'dear, cheery person' Lily had described, had just hung up on me. I would not have been surprised if he'd launched into a rant about being too busy to listen to all this, but instead the information lit him up.

'God damn, Jake,' he said, 'it's the first break we've had, isn't it?'

'I think so. I don't see yet how it works, but it's too neat to be a coincidence.'

'Especially if . . . let's find out how many more of those she . . .' He didn't even wait to finish the thought, just walked across the hall into the pod of workstations his detectives occupied. In two minutes he had doled out the names and locations of a dozen other break-ins. Soon the area was a hive of sound as five detectives dialed numbers and asked questions about coffee service.

While we waited, I told him the little I knew about the nephew. Ten minutes later, Andy Pittman thumped across the hall to Ray's doorway. With Rosie and Winnie grinning over his shoulders, he stood there, smiled his sad crocodile smile and said, 'Bingo.'

Eight

Clint brought her in, sitting up very straight in the backseat of his department car. Rosie rode beside her.

She had not behaved like a dear person when they showed up at her house. When she'd seen Clint's badge, she'd made one small sound of distress and done the best she could to close the tiny crack she'd opened in the door. But Clint already had a leg against it, and went on pushing gently but firmly till he was all the way in her incredibly messy living room.

Looking at the floor, she said, just above a whisper, 'I can't have you here. The neighbors—'

Clint said if she didn't want to talk at her house he had 'orders to bring her to the station.'

Lois said, 'No, no, I can't go there. I can't go anywhere.' She put her hands on either side of her head, closed her eyes and hissed, 'How can I make you understand? I can't leave this house!'

Clint turned toward Rosie and shrugged. She stepped around him, stood directly in front of the trembling woman, and said, in her strict-Mom voice, 'Lois, listen to me.'

Surprised by a female voice, Lois opened her eyes. 'We need to ask you some questions now, but first I want you to understand what your rights are.' She pulled a card out of her shirt pocket and read off the Miranda rights. 'You have the right to remain silent—'

Lois began to nod – it sounded just like TV, she said later. Clint asked her if she wanted to lock up her house. She said, 'Well, yes,' and then, 'but where's my purse?'

'Just like my mom when she gets rattled,' he said. 'She asked me if we had to put handcuffs on her and I said, "Can I trust you not to try any rough stuff on Detective Doyle?" Rosie stood there with her hand on her pepper spray, giving her that "Make my day," look – and Lois got all like this—' He did an imitation cringe, which looked hilarious on his strong, confident form. 'I don't think this woman's ever been arrested before, Ray. She really didn't know what to do.'

'Why'd you bring the nephew?'

'Lois said we had to take him along – he

couldn't stay in the house alone. "That's what I've been trying to tell you," she said. So I put him in the squad car with Casey and Melville. I didn't want to argue about what he was charged with – I just sent the two uniforms in his room to get him. He came out of that pigsty space already making a speech. When he saw nobody wanted to listen he got mad and started to fight. So we put cuffs and belly chains and a mask on him and Mirandized him. In some perverse way I think he kind of enjoyed all that. The guys said he got in the car without a struggle and rode in nice and quiet.'

Ray asked Andy to take the nephew through fingerprinting and establish his identity. His wallet held ID in the name of Carl Arthur Twiggs, with an address in Sioux City, Iowa, 'And damn little else,' Andy said. 'Are we sure this is legal? What's he done?'

'Don't know yet,' Ray said. 'But his aunt says he can't be on his own, and he's safer with you than anyplace else I know to put him.'

'OK,' Andy said. 'We'll have a visit.' He attached himself like a mother duck to the spindly nephew and led him away.

Ray and I decided to talk to Lois in my office. It doesn't have sophisticated recording equipment, but I thought if we kept the setting simple she might start connecting the dots for us. All the evidence against her was circumstantial, so we were all rolling our eyes sideways at each other, trying to see if anybody had an idea how to sew this up.

Rosie was still there, helping Lois into a chair.

It looked as if Lois and Rosie had kind of bonded on the trip in. So I said, 'Let's find a chair for Detective Doyle,' and when Clint brought one I put Rosie and Clint on either side of Lois, with Ray behind my desk with me.

Ray asked her to state her full name.

'Lois Andrea Phelps,' she said. Lily Trask was right: once she'd recovered her poise Lois had a nice voice, quiet and clear.

'And you're the proprietor of Inn-House Coffee – is that right?'

'Yes, of course.' She looked at him, beginning to show a little spunk. 'That's no secret,' she said. 'I *advertise* it.'

'I understand that. And three of the firms you service are Minnaska, SmartSeeds and Portal – is that also right?'

'Yes, indeed.'

'And do you also take coffee to . . .' He rattled off a list of other firms and she kept nodding, yes, yes, as a suspicious frown grew between her eyebrows.

'And all those firms were broken into last month, weren't they? And got messages left on their premises, telling them the work they do is evil and they must desist?'

'I don't know about all. I heard some did.'

'Every one of those firms suffered a break-in, Ms Phelps.'

'Well, what if . . .' Lois's lips parted in a little round, '. . . oh.' Her head tilted a little sideways and rotated around the room. Bird-like, she focused on each of the detectives around her. 'Is that what this is all about? You think I had something to do with . . .' She grew a little smile and took a breath. 'But see, I don't have keys to any of those places! I only deliver coffee to my clients when they're open! I wouldn't have a clue how to get in any of those places at night!'

'I never said the break-ins happened at night,' Ray said. His voice grew ominous, which suited his face. He looked around at us, doing his tricky-detective shtick. 'You guys hear me say anything about night?'

'Maybe not, but the paper did.' Lois didn't wait to hear what the rest of us had to say. Her voice was very firm now – this lady knew what she knew. 'More than once I read that, "These mysterious invaders seem to like to strike at night." Once they said something like, "Whoever these lawless note-writers are, they apparently do their best composing in the dark." Sort of making a joke out of it – and the next day there was a letter to the editor that said, "The places that got broken into don't think this is funny."'

She paid attention to the local news – she was nobody's fool and she was looking at Ray Bailey the way a mother looks at her son when she catches him in the jam jar. Beside her, Clint shuffled his feet and cleared his throat.

'Lois,' I said, 'if you didn't have anything to do with the break-ins, why have you been so evasive about talking to us? Why wouldn't you let us come to your house?'

'I thought somebody must have complained about Artie again. My nephew.'

'People complain about him?'

'Sometimes, if he gets to ranting. He stands on street corners and warns them about poisoning the earth. People don't want to get advice from a young person who can't even hold a job. Which he can't because he's always ranting, you see.'

'That must make life so hard for you,' Rosie said. This was the new Rosie, sensitized to the special hardships of women.

'Tell me about it,' Lois said. 'And you were in my house – you saw the ungodly mess he's made out of it. So you know he isn't exactly . . . normal.' Lois's voice was not so pleasant now; she was getting wound up. 'See, I promised my sister I could keep him out of trouble for the winter so she could go to Colorado where her daughter really needs her, but I had no idea how much he's deteriorated since I saw him last.'

She was going to cry. I reached for the tissue box to hand it to her but then all the pain that she'd been hiding from customers boiled up to the surface and she began to wail.

'I can watch him all day but I have to sleep! I mean, I work hard at my job and I have to get a good night's sleep or I can't go on!' Tears were rolling down her cheeks. I pushed the box across my desk toward her. She grabbed three tissues and disappeared into the linty heap. Sounds of nose-blowing came out.

She surfaced briefly, crying, 'He doesn't listen to a word I say!' and went back into her soggy retreat. I pushed the wastebasket closer too. She felt it touch her knee, raised her head and discarded the whole wad, grabbed more and resumed her lament. 'I think he's figured out a way to get in and out of the house without keys. I'm pretty sure he's going out at night—'

My desk phone rang, surprising me – I had told LeeAnn to hold all our calls. When I picked it up, Andy said at once, 'I think we got something here, Jake.'

'Oh? What?'

'Better come to meeting room two, mooshtoosh.'

I have no idea where Andy got that expression, but I know when he says it he means don't argue – move the flab. I looked around at my three detectives, whose reactions ran the gamut from seriously irritated to downright pissed. Why was I allowing this interruption just when things were moving along?

I said, 'I have to . . .' and got up and left.

Muffled sounds were coming out of meeting room two. More weeping? Andy's not a roughneck unless somebody jumps him; then he's a pile-driver. People who get crosswise with Andy do not cry softly. If they still can, they scream.

I opened the door and went in. Andy sat quietly on one side of the small plastic table, looking as immoveable as a stone barn. Lois's nephew was in a chair across from him, curled up into himself and sobbing. I made a small gesture toward the door and raised one eyebrow. Andy got up and followed me out.

I said, 'Artie's unhappy?'

'Artie's guilty.'

'Of what?'

'Fuck, don't you even remember what you brought him in for?'

'We never meant to bring him in. We went after the aunt and she said we couldn't leave him.'

'She's right. Artie's a full-blown paranoid schizophrenic with delusions of grandeur, in my utterly worthless opinion. And he just confessed to doing all those break-ins.'

'No shit!'

Andy nodded.

'You believe him?'

'Seems to know a lot about locations and stuff. Why are you surprised?'

'Because I didn't even know he existed until today. Andy, how did he happen to tell you this?' I've never heard anyone accuse Andy of needless brutality, but he exudes self-confidence and is always sure he's right. I can remember being young and testing the boundaries, and I know if I'd ever been Andy's prisoner, I'd have been scared.

'I asked him if he knew why he was here and he said he supposed it was because he was in his aunt's house when the stupid cops came to arrest her for something she didn't do. I said, "Why would they do that?" and he said something like, "I suppose they finally noticed how many of her customers got broken into." And then he kind of snickered and said, "I told Billy that was bound to happen."' Andy did a contented upper-body stretch, re-settled his shirt and smiled. 'So then we did some Q and A.'

'Jesus.' I shook my head, thinking about all the detectives out in the distant grow plots, looking for any clue. 'This feels too easy. Who's Billy – do you know?'

'His partner.'

'Last name?'

'Haven't got it yet. That's the next round.'

'Just the two of them, you think?'

'Sounds like there's a few more doing the driving and backing them up. Snug little group of eco-terrorists who get together and skank about what swine their fellow Americans are—'

'Hoo boy. Wait till the Tea Party hears about this.'

'Well, it's not just Americans – sometimes it's the whole human race.'

'Ah, that helps. Why's he crying; is he remorseful?'

'No, he's proud of the messages. He's just sorry he got caught – he's starting to think about the consequences. He said just now, "Billy was so sure we'd never get caught!" Artie doesn't seem to realize he caught himself – I didn't know what the hell he was talking about at first, so I just sat here looking wise and he told me all about it.'

'Nice work, Andy. You want me to sit in with you to get Billy's last name?'

'Uh . . . thanks, but I think Artie and I are such good friends now he'll tell me the rest pretty easy. Bring in more cops, he might start to pull back.'

'OK, your call. Let me know as soon as you get the last name. We better pick the guy up ASAP before he gets word off the street. And as many more names as you can get while he's in here crying.'

I went back to my office, where I found Lois drying out after her own storm of weeping and talking fast. She had been alone with her nephew for several weeks, worried and scared. She was getting a little giddy with relief at finding people who would listen and could understand her dilemma.

'My sister Althea has always been a rock,' Lois was saying. 'But it's been so hard for her ever since her husband had that stroke – deep down, I think she feels guilty about his death and has tried to compensate by indulging Artie.'

Ray wore the dour look he gets when he has to listen to people talk about their emotions. Ray would rather walk to Edmonton in flip-flops than hear how people feel deep down.

'And now her sweet daughter's worthless husband leaves her just as Artie gets diagnosed bipolar. Althea says he's supposed to be OK as long as he takes his meds, but you have to watch—'

'Lois,' I said. 'Artie's confessed to doing all the break-ins.'

Reactions varied. Lois gasped and put her hands up to her face. Rosie watched her, concerned. Clint simply waited for the details, his seasoned cop's face saying, 'How'd he manage *that*?'

Ray brightened up at once – we were back to police business and Lois had stopped talking. He said, 'How much have we got on Artie?'

Mostly just a confession, I told them, but Andy had that on his digital recorder and would have it on paper, signed, in a few minutes.

'So a lot more than we had yesterday, but still plenty of blanks to fill.'

'God,' Lois said softly. 'You know, on some level I think I knew.'

'Lois,' Rosie said, 'it might be a good idea if you never said that again.'

'Especially in a police station,' Clint said, 'or around any other cops.'

'Oh, you mean people might think—'

'Aiding and abetting, stuff like that.' Clint tried to look solemn but was having trouble keeping his face straight. Part of his mind was already home, I thought, telling his wife about this day.

My phone rang again. Andy said, 'Last name's McGowan and I've got the address. But Artie says at this hour he's almost certain to be in the Red Rooster Bar on the northeast corner of that block he lives on.'

'If we're going to yank him out of a bar I better have a description.'

'Hang on.' There was some muttering, and then Andy came back on the line. 'Artie says he's a fat loudmouth with very white skin who's always eating and drinking.'

'That probably describes half the guys in that bar.' But I wrote it all down and said, 'Andy, I'll call you back in five, OK?'

I asked Clint and Rosie to take Lois into another meeting room and continue their conversation. 'Get everything she can remember about the date Artie arrived in town, what she knows of where he's gone since he's been living with her. See if she knows the names of any other eco-warriors he's been working with, will you? And any other details we can use.'

When they were gone I gave Ray the name and address of the house and the bar. He got busy with that, getting Dispatch to send two squads to pick up Billy McGowan. Meantime, I called Andy back and said, 'Since Artie has proved he's such a wizard at going through doors, I'd like to get him in a cell and locked down tight. Book him for B and E and criminal trespass, get him a case number and type up the bare bones of a charge. Just what he's already admitted to, and get him to sign it. Tomorrow we can contact that town in Iowa he comes from, Sioux City I think it is, and see if he's got a record there.'

'You're right, there could be more. Although . . .' He did some breathing and thinking.

'What?'

'Well, when I asked him about the dead doctor at SmartSeeds he kind of shit a brick. He claims it's never occurred to him to do bodily harm to anybody. He's shocked we would think he did that. In fact, he flatly denies having anything to do with the attack on the Minnaska scientist or the broken chair at Portal. Says whoever's doing this second round of mischief, it isn't him and his friends. "We just wanted to scare them so they'd stop messing with nature," he said.'

'You believe him?'

'I think *he* believes it. He's kind of hard to get a read on – pompous one minute, whimpering the next. But not at all scary – more of a nut job.'

'And of course he couldn't have done the Minnaska attack, could he? He was with his aunt all day today.'

'True. But Billy could have.'

'Which makes me think we better get a warrant to search Billy's house. If he didn't have brains enough to pick up that casing, maybe he never thought to get rid of that nice big gun. I'll get Winnie working on that.'

Some days the police gods smile on me. The squads found Billy McGowan contentedly yelling at images of football players on the flat-screen TVs at the Red Rooster. He had two schooners of beer in front of him and was smoking a joint. We were booking him half an hour after I signed the warrant.

'We had trouble holding his attention long enough to read him his rights,' Stacy told me in the unloading bay. 'He's pretty well mellowed out. He said, "Aw, come on, it's Happy Hour and this is a good game I'm watching here." You got any more of these terrifying criminals we can bring in for you? This really makes the shift go by quick.'

Billy wasn't a reedy misfit like Artie. In fact, he was already running to blubber – had a gut that hung over his belt and soft white hands. 'Can you believe it? The only thing he made a fuss about was when we told him to take his clothes off,' Ray said. 'I guess he feels bad about how he looks undressed.'

By the time we had him in the interview room in the orange jumpsuit, he was pulling out of his lethargy. He was proud of the break-ins he had done with Artie Twiggs – never even tried to deny trespassing. He said, 'We just do what we gotta do,' and reeled off a lot of statistics about climate change. His information was surprisingly detailed and sounded mostly correct. He didn't give a damn that his methods were illegal. He said, 'Time will show we're in the right.'

He was just as firm as Artie had been in his denial of the second round of attacks. He had certainly not messed with any chairs at Portal, he said. 'I don't even know where it is. What do they do again?'

He became downright indignant when Ray asked him where he was standing when he shot at Minnaska's head scientist. 'Is that what you guys do now?' he asked Ray. 'Throw random charges at people and hope some turn out to be right?'

Asked about a dead scientist at SmartSeeds, he began to look concerned. Drawing his soft body up to its full height, he looked down his nose and said, 'You can't connect us to anything like that. Don't you understand, our mission' – he got a faraway look when he talked about the mission, as if he were reading his lines off a three by five card – 'is to save the earth so that humans can go on living.'

It was frustrating to talk to him because his stated motivation sounded so humane that if I'd believed him I'd have been squarely on his side. But he had shifty eyes and a small, cunning smile that didn't fit with the lofty ideals. When he talked about why they did the break-ins everything he said sounded fake, so before long I just wanted to quit talking to him and get him in a cell. I met Ray's eyes and saw the same impatience there. We nodded, and Ray told the prisoner that would be all for now. He went off with an officer, complaining about losing the beers he had paid for, bargaining for a snack.

'I don't believe a word he says,' Ray said when he was gone. 'There has to be something more.'

Winnie came back with the search warrant I'd ask her to get on his squat, and I asked Ray, 'We're OK to wait until morning to execute this, right? You had Stacy put a crime scene lock on the door?'

'You bet. I told them this is one of the midnight message-leavers, so seal the bejeesus out of all doors and windows.'

'Good. You think we could get some extra drive-bys at his place tonight?'

'That's right; there might be some more eco-terrorists hanging out around there.' For a moment, Ray almost smiled. 'I'll get to work on it right away.'

It was almost four-thirty, and the clock had begun to torture my brain, as it does every workday afternoon now. A chief of detectives should be ready to stick with the job as long as it takes, but I've joined that big coterie of working stiffs with a toddler at a babysitter's house and nobody to fetch him but me.

Secondly and even more important, the Rutherford PD budget is already overstretched. We can't pay detectives overtime for anything short of a massacre. Ready or not, we needed to wind this mess up for the day.

Rosie said she'd give Lois a ride home. They both looked satisfied with that idea, so I didn't hesitate to endorse it. I went back in my office and started the sweaty race to get the essentials dealt with before five. I was heading for my door when Ray stepped into the opening, holding a pair of very dirty jeans.

'Stutz called me from Admitting,' he said. 'Said I might want to see these. And I did and so do you.'

'Why?'

'This is Billy's walking tool box. Looka here.' He began pulling burglary tools out of little zippered pockets and inside seams – a slim jim, a wire-cutter, a hole-puncher and what looked like top-of-the-line lock picks.

I said, 'Who thinks this lad is no amateur?'

'I wondered why he made such a fuss about changing into the jumpsuit. Turns out vanity had nothing to do with it.'

'Do these look like the jeans of a person whose mission is to save the world?'

'More like the jeans of a mope whose mission is to get his hands on other people's stuff. Which is kind of puzzling, really, because I didn't read his partner that way at all.'

'No, Artie just seems like a standard nut job.'

'So now we're getting played by a thug.'

'First time ever, right?'

'Yeah. Tomorrow we'll search his records and see what other games he's been playing.'

'Yes, Ray, but will you please check this

garment into evidence and go home now? I'll add these filthy pants to the list of things we're going to talk about at the meeting.'

'Is that still scheduled for first thing in the morning?'

'Yup.'

'OK. Except I seem to be compiling an even longer list of things that have to get done first thing in the morning.'

'So we *argue* first thing in the morning.' I locked my door. 'But not right now. Goodnight.'

Nine

Arguments don't always take place as scheduled in my shop.

Kevin was waiting at the top of the stairs on Thursday morning, saying, 'Got a bone to pick.'

Standing behind me while I unlocked my door, he read off his list of reasons why the meeting had to wait. Three of his detectives had can't-miss appointments with victims of burglaries unrelated to our case. 'Life goes on, you know. We still have to serve the public,' Kevin said.

'Oh, for sure.' I was waiting to hear what he really wanted.

'Norm's testing today for the K-9 course he put in for. If he misses this test he has to wait six months. And Brady's already out in the field. He had an early appointment to interview a farmer who owns a field next to one of SmartSeeds' plots. He's steaming mad at SmartSeeds for growing weeds next to his cornfield. Brady thinks maybe he's found you a motive for murder. But you know how it is with farmers – hell itself has to wait if one of their cows is calving. You get a chance to talk to a farmer, you better grab it while you can.'

'That's true,' I said, still waiting.

'And I'm expecting Miss Peabody any minute now.'

'Miss Pea— The real one? You're shitting me, right?'

He shook his head, grinning.

'You really found her, honest to God? How?'

He grew a look of modest pride. 'Turns out I'm a detective.'

'I can't believe – I just said it for a joke!'

'I know.'

'She actually agreed to come in and talk to you?'

'She did. She'll talk to you too, if you want to stop over. But listen, Jake, the catch is, she still works, part-time.'

'What? That can't be our Miss Peabody.'

'Yes, it is. She's not that much older than us – she just always seemed old because we were little kids. She's retired from teaching, of course, but now she's a part-time editor at that little free weekly called *The Shopper.* Her shift doesn't start till ten, so she said she'd come see me if I could make it early. So I agreed to eight-fifteen.' He looked contrite. 'I'm sorry, Jake! But I just couldn't let her get away!'

I said, 'Well, for Miss Peabody I guess we can

all flex a little. Let's make it one o'clock for the meeting, huh?'

'You mean it? Hey, thanks, Jake, I appreciate it.'

'You're welcome,' I said.

What Kevin didn't know was that LeeAnn had reached me on my cell ten minutes ago and said, 'A person named Mark Hoving called – wants to know if he could change your appointment from nine to nine-thirty. I said I'd let him know, but I'm wondering about this big meeting we called for this morning – maybe you want to move it to afternoon?'

So my face had been saved by LeeAnn, the shy part-timer I'd plucked out of the steno pool years ago. LeeAnn called Hoving back and I called Ray, who said he was just planning how to beg me for a later time. 'One o'clock will be fine,' he said.

LeeAnn is the pearl beyond price who will never tell anyone I forgot about Hoving. And I'm the dirty sneak who just let Kevin Evjan beg for a favor that I intended to ask him for when I started up the stairs.

As soon as I finished the morning email and phone message sprint that's evidently my punishment for breathing the same air as worthier persons, I went to work on my list for Mark Hoving. It almost wrote itself: 1. Do you have any enemies? 2. If not, why is somebody shooting at you? 3. If not at you, could it be that the CEO of Minnaska has enemies? 4. If yes, explain.

I sat and stared at my shortlist. All my

conjectures seemed to lead back to the company. Unless he said yes to number one – that would throw all my ideas out the window, wouldn't it? I tried to remember what the frightened scientist looked like, got an image of a trembling rabbit, and knew that was wrong. For one thing, I remembered now, I had thought it showed a strong independent streak for the lead scientist of a rich company to drive around in an ancient pickup that didn't look as if it was worth more than a few hundred dollars.

Why did he? I wondered. Surely his perks at Minnaska must include a nice per diem on the vehicle he used to inspect their growing crops? I looked him up on Google and LinkedIn and a couple more people-search sites I use. I found a string of classy graduate degrees – nothing indicating subversive tendencies.

But who shoots at a harmless scientist who's minding his own business?

Unable to think of any additions to my list, I got up and walked over to Kevin's office. I was thinking, Miss Peabody won't recognize me from the scruffy kid I was then, so I guess it's safe to say hello.

A pleasant-looking lady in a blue pantsuit was sitting in front of Kevin, smiling. She looked the same as I remembered, but with white hair, and smaller. Of course, I was bigger now.

'Jake Hines,' she said. 'You haven't changed a bit.'

Her voice was exactly the way I remembered it, firm and precise, but with a tiny slur that softened the hard 'ch' into a sound closer to 'sh.'

For the first time ever, I wondered if she had been required to conquer a lisp in her childhood. Was that why she'd worked so hard on our pronunciation?

I wished I knew her better so I could ask.

I said, 'It's very good of you to come in and help us.'

'Oh, it's a pleasure. And such a nice surprise to find you and Kevin both on the police force. Your folks must be proud.'

'Sometimes,' Kevin said. 'Although my mom's getting pretty sick of talking about cameras at stop lights.' We all laughed politely, not a sound usually heard anywhere near that subject.

'Well,' Miss Peabody said, 'you said you had some handwriting for me to look at?'

'Yes,' Kevin said, 'I know this is a long shot, but just in case . . .' A copy of the long Minnaska message scrolled out of his console in its clear plastic wrap. He laid it across his desk in front of the teacher.

'Well, for heaven's sake,' Miss Peabody said. 'Clifford Mangen.'

'You mean you do—'

'He's three or four years older than you, Jake – you might not remember him from school. I taught remedial reading and writing for eight years. Clifford was in the first class I taught, the nightmare class. I went home and cried every night that year. You were somewhere in the middle, Jake. And Kevin, I'm pretty sure I remember, was in the last one. At the end of that year I went to my superintendent and said, "Give me a regular class or I'm going to quit." He said,

"I was beginning to wonder how much more of that you could take."'

I said, 'I'm sorry we were so dense.'

'Oh, you weren't. You just didn't get started right. It all has to set up and jell in those first two years. If it doesn't, after that it takes a bulldozer.'

'Or Chief Frank McCafferty.' I shuddered, remembering some of the tongue-lashing I took from him in my rookie year.

'Miss Peabody,' Kevin said. 'About Clifford Mangen?'

'A sad case,' she said. 'He didn't belong in that class at all. His handwriting wasn't pretty but it was legible when he took his time. And he could read perfectly well when he chose. But his parents were fighting; they divorced right after Christmas. Clifford was trying to find a way to get some attention.'

'I guess he still is,' Kevin said. 'This time he's going to succeed.'

'Oh? Why, what does this long banner say?' She read it aloud. When she got to the part about retribution she put her small hand up to her mouth and said, 'Oh, dear.'

'You know,' Kevin said, 'I know a guy named Clifford Mangen, and he's just about the right age. But he can't be the one who's leaving these crazy notes.'

'Why not?'

'He's a stodgy guy with a comb-over who wears three-piece suits.'

'Yes,' she said. 'That's Clifford.'

Kevin shook his head. 'The one I know is a

music director in the Rutherford school system.'

'And drives a Prius and belongs to Friends of the Earth and Sierra Club.' She looked at him kindly. 'You're a detective. Surely you know people aren't all of a piece.'

'Of course, but – Friends of Earth . . . you're sure? How do you know that?'

'Because I'm a member too and I see him sometimes at rallies.'

Kevin's mouth hung open for a few seconds, till he realized he was looking uncool and snapped it shut. 'I've always thought of Clifford as a total dweeb,' he said. 'But then I never would have guessed you for a member of Friends of the Earth, either.'

'Well, there you go,' she said.

'You're sure this is his handwriting?'

'I'd know it anywhere. The fat "l" and that crazy hook on the bottom of the "z", I could talk myself blue and he'd never change.'

'Miss Peabody,' I said, getting up. 'I have another meeting now but I want to thank you for your help today. You have saved us a lot of time.' I nodded pleasantly to Kevin and made the finger sign for 'see me after this.' I did have another meeting, but first I needed to make a phone call.

'Ray,' I said when I got him on the phone, 'can you come in here right away? I might have the name of one of the Holy Messengers.' There it was again; despite my best efforts that name kept creeping back into this case.

Ray stood in my door a few seconds later, saying, 'Where'd you get it?'

I told him about my visit with Miss Peabody. He was very dubious about a grade-school teacher as an identifier. I told him, 'This woman dominated two years of my childhood and she seems even more impressive to me now.'

Finally he said, 'OK, it's a better lead than anything else we've had. Let's see if I can get the same name out of Billy McGowan.'

He went back to his office to work on the setup for a Q and A in interview room one. First he asked Winnie to pull up Billy's arrest records and search the Minnesota Criminal Records database and then NCIC for any match. The support staff got the room ready while Ray arranged for Bo to back him up at the interview, and they worked up a list of questions together. I wanted to monitor the conversation from outside, so I asked him not to start till I had finished my appointment with the Minnaska scientist. And before either of those I had a moment with Kevin to say, 'Find Clifford Mangen and get him in here today.'

'Already got him,' Kevin said. 'He's on his way.' He rolled his eyes. 'Still can't believe it.'

Mark Hoving was calm enough when he walked in my office, well-balanced on his feet and comfortable in gray flannel pants and a custom-fitted jacket. But he remembered how he'd felt when he saw me last.

'I'm afraid I was a little unnerved yesterday,' he said. 'I'm not accustomed to being used for target practice.' Clean-shaven and smooth-faced, with an Anywhere USA accent, now that he'd regained his composure he seemed like the kind of man who could go around the world on short notice and be perfectly at ease wherever the plane stopped.

In fact, he had been doing something pretty much like that, he told me when I asked him, 'What *are* you accustomed to?'

'Until lately, pretty much all work and no play,' he said. 'I was in customer service for a big biotech firm for eight years.'

'Good job?'

'Depends what you like. I was the answer man, the travelling geek who stays just long enough to fix the problem and then gets back on the plane. Good way to see the world, I thought, but a lot of what you see is airports, and I got very sick of those. Couple of years ago I struck up a conversation with my seat mate and by the time we landed in Minneapolis I was in love with a buyer for women's sportswear. She had a great job she wouldn't think of leaving, at a large Twin Cities department store. My aim in life changed quickly to "Find work in Minnesota."'

'How's that working out?'

'Blissful. Married nine months. Baby on the way.'

'You learning to fish?'

'God, yes. And I'm into cross-country skiing and birding. This part of the country – you people realize what you've got here?'

'The winters can get a little long, but yeah, it's a pretty good place to raise a future president or two, I figure.'

'You too, huh? I never thought I was cut out for domesticity, but . . .'

'I guess we're not till the right lady comes along.'

'Mmm.' He looked at me out of intelligent gray eyes and said, 'So what are we doing here, Jake?'

'Just kind of kicking the tires till you feel you know me well enough to tell me why somebody's shooting at you.'

'Shit, you really think I know?' He looked at the ceiling for half a minute while he got himself in hand. 'I was hoping you'd say it was your job to find out.'

'It is. But . . . you're pretty sure you have no enemies?'

'Enemies, are you kidding? I'm the handyman with the electronic toolkit, the nerd in the green eyeshade in love with his wife. Between her job and mine and getting a house built, most days I don't even have time for a good argument.'

'Wait till the baby's born,' I said. 'You'll look back on this as the easy part.'

'Hey, thanks, that's good to know.' We chuckled together.

'So I guess,' I said, 'it must be something Minnaska's doing, huh?'

'Oh, come on. You think somebody's trying to murder me because my employer makes weed killer?'

'Well, they did get a big honking warning about making war on Nature—'

'Oh, crap. That's just this year's fad crusade. This country' – the quiet geek was suddenly lit up – 'is feeding and watering some of the laziest brains that have ever walked the earth, you know that? They hate global warming but they can't give up their SUVs! Spouting a lot of hazy optimism about electric cars, never mind they're twice the price anybody can afford, not to mention how much coal you have to burn to make the electricity – shit! But just try doing something useful like putting up a wind farm and everybody gets fainting fits: the noise, the birds, oh please, not in my back yard.'

'You're invested in wind farms?'

'A little. And putting solar panels on my house. Trying to decide which way to jump.'

'But you think people aren't taking global warming seriously enough?' *Maybe I've found my Holy Messenger.*

'I know they're not. Mostly because politicians are messing it up, distracting people with trifles so they won't have to do anything decisive that might lose a vote. Everybody knows we have more people to feed every year on a planet that keeps getting hotter, but what gets all the headlines? Some pig-headed legislators who can't stand to see women have birth control. And now all the book clubbers are getting pious about genetically altered seeds and stronger herbicide? Swell, blame the only people who are trying to help.'

I was watching him with interest – his ears were turning red.

I said, 'Take a breath.'

'Yeah.' He gave a little self-deprecating laugh. 'Turns out I do have time for an argument.' He kicked the legs of his chair for a while. 'Sure it's the bottom line that calls the tune at Minnaska. You know any big, successful companies where it doesn't't? We live in a complicated world now

– it's not all black and white. We don't need more passionate intensity.' He seemed oblivious to the fact that he had just displayed a lot of it. 'What we need is more *science.*'

'Also,' I said, 'we need to figure out why, in this complicated world, somebody is shooting at a busy scientist. Or his boss's glossy SUV.' I watched him while I asked, 'You know any short-tempered grudge-holders who hate Cadillac Escalades?'

His face smoothed out again, he smiled, stretched and re-settled his nice jacket. 'That sounds just crazy enough to fit right into the world today,' he said.

'What's the story on your pickup?'

His handsome face split into a delighted grin. 'It's my stealth planet-saver. My neighbor was getting ready to junk his fishing car so my buddy and I bought it for two hundred dollars. Never mind how it looks – underneath we're turning it into tomorrow's super-Prius.'

He told me how much fun they were having, scavenging junkyards and collision centers to turn an ancient wreck into a high-performance hybrid. 'When we've got it aligned, new tires on and so forth, and we're getting the best mileage we think we can ever get, we're going to tear it all down again and switch it to natural gas – see how well we can do with that. In three or four years,' his eyes got dreamy, 'we might be ready to build our own electric motor.'

'Aren't there some problems with matching the transmission?'

'Sure, you have to change the adapter plate.

But I think we can make it work. By the time my son's in school,' he said, 'we expect to know a lot more about the most efficient way to move people over the ground. Then we'll decide where to stage our part of the fight.'

'The fight?'

'To save the planet. The real one – the one for grown-ups.'

'You're going to build better cars?'

'Or batteries. Or even, who knows, maybe run for the legislature.'

'Or leap tall buildings at a single bound?'

'Why not?' His smile was wry and then faded. 'If you can get this nut job with the gun out of my life so I can go back to being ridiculously happy, anything is possible.'

'I think we're getting close. We've got twenty-four-hour surveillance assigned to Minnaska for the next five days at least. And we hope to have the answer by then because we're all working on this, Mark.'

My phone rang. As I reached for it, he stood up and said, 'I'll let you get at it, then,' and walked out.

In my ear, Ray said, 'OK, I got him in the box.'

Ten

'There's something you should know before we start,' Ray said. 'Winnie's found more stuff on McGowan.'

'Billy's been bad?'

'Bad enough to live the last ten years with no employment record – what does that tell you? He's no kid either. Late thirties, best estimate. He's served time for Grand Theft Auto, aggravated break-in and has two outstanding warrants in Waseca.' Ray frowned at the list. 'Nothing violent, though. A career criminal, all on the soft side.'

'You think he's a poor candidate for the shooting at Minnaska?'

'Yes. But I'm going to show him the arrest records and go after him for all those lies about saving the earth. After I get him a little humble I'll accuse him of the shooting and we'll see what that yields. I think he's been pretty careful to stay non-violent – that's his business plan. My hunch is he'll want to bargain to keep that gun business out of his dossier.'

'If he confirms the name of Clifford Mangen, let's try for the rest of the Holy Messengers.' I was just calling them that now and to hell with political correctness, it was shorthand for the group we hadn't found yet and we were in a hurry.

'Sure.' Bo walked up to us then and stood, as usual, silent but ever vigilant.

Ray said, 'Ready?'

Bo nodded, and they unlocked the door of interview room one and went in.

Billy McGowan was slumped on his seat, not manacled, but with his hands in front of him on the small table. He looked up, frowned and said, 'Well, hey, are you finally ready to start? I'm sitting on the least comfortable stool in the city of Rutherford, so let's not drag this out, guys.' His big butt lopped over the edges.

'Oh, hell, you don't like your seat?' Ray turned to Bo and asked, 'Why didn't we think to bring in a chaise, so Billy could get a decent rest?' He spread his papers in front of him. 'Don't want you getting worn out right at the start, here, Billy, because it looks like you're going to be with us for some time.'

'Why are you so bent on punishing the people who are trying to save—'

'Oh, we're not ready to talk about saving the earth just yet, Billy,' Ray said. 'We need to go back a little bit first. Starting from that time about ten years ago, that first arrest that got you three-to-ten years in Moose Lake.'

'Oh, come on. That's all water under the bridge; what's it got to do with this?'

'Well, it doesn't seem to me, Billy, that you were trying to save the earth when you were breaking into that little Walmart in Wabasha, scooping up all the Oxy and Valium and Elavil like they say you did.'

'As a famous politician once remarked, "When I was young and foolish I was young and foolish." And I paid my debt for that.'

'I see that,' Ray said. 'Two years and sixty-two days of paying. And you learned your lesson, I guess, because there's no other record of conviction here for upwards of five years. I'm curious about the fact that there's no work record either. What did you live on all those years?'

'I kind of flew under the radar for a while. Worked on farms—'

'Oh, farms? Must have been small farms – more like garden patches really. Because what I see here is that you were arrested and questioned twice in the Minneapolis airport. People kept complaining that you'd been hanging around them for half an hour and now their laptop was missing, one said, and another man said his wallet had gone.'

'Mistakes, both of them,' Billy said. 'Dismissed for lack of evidence. Why do they file reports of those things? It's so unfair.'

'Yeah, well, life is,' Ray said. 'And then we come to the biggie, the five-car pile-up in Waseca three months ago. You were driving a stolen Ford Escape – hey, good taste there, Billy, the most stolen SUV—'

'Terrible misunderstanding,' Billy said. 'Looked just like the one I was driving, which was parked nearby.'

'And the keys just happened to be in this vehicle. I still haven't figured out how you did that, unless you had a buddy. Oh, that's right, you're the guy who specializes in working with buddies, aren't you? Just like you're doing here.'

'You criminalizing friendship now?'

'The bad part about that pileup,' Ray said, 'is that you were fleeing an arrest warrant when it happened. Skipping on a past-due payday loan, that's bad business – those folks don't have much sense of humor at all. And then you go and wreck that big pretty Crossover that the bowling alley manager had sitting at the curb—'

'His wife left it running with the keys in it,' Billy said, 'to get out and yell one more insult at him. I came running around the corner and mistook it for my car.'

'Which I'm so far having a hard time finding a rental contract for, but OK. You do have freakish luck sometimes when it counts. How the fuck you managed to slither out from behind those air bags . . . And what did you do? Hitch a ride out of there?'

'Had to. My car was totaled.'

'And you somehow turned up here a few weeks later, where we find you involved in a strange series of break-ins culminating in an even stranger shooting. Why were you gunning for a scientist in the Minnaska parking lot?'

'I had nothing to do with that – you can't hang any shooting on me! Check it out: in my whole life, there's not one time I was ever involved with guns.'

'I want to believe you, Billy, I do. And it's true, there's nothing on your record about firearms. But I don't know. You left a lot of people feeling sore and depressed over there in Waseca, know what I mean? In fact, as soon as I release this story to the press, I'm pretty sure we're going to hear from a large number of people who want to get you and roast you over a slow fire.'

'All right,' Billy McGowan said. He looked at Ray very straight, and said again, 'All right. What do you want to know and what have you got to trade?'

'I can't make a payday loan go away,' Ray said, 'but those folks are hated by a lot of the right people, so if you incentivize me a little I can find you plenty of do-gooder legal help with that. It sounds like you're ready to defend yourself on the SUV, but we can give you some help with that, too. This is a big, complicated case we're working on, so we can keep you here where you're safe and warm and well-fed while you work out the misunderstanding about the Ford. So do you want to please me and do yourself some good?'

'Yes, Detective,' Billy said. 'Let's do that.'

Ray had told me before they started that Bo was going to observe, and that when Bo thought he understood Billy McGowan he would write a plus sign in his notebook. After that, whenever Ray felt it was appropriate, he might turn the questioning over to Bo.

'Bo spent years talking every day to people with drug habits, including his own wife,' Ray said. 'Druggies are the slipperiest bastards on the face of the earth. If there's any truth in this bandit I think Bo can dig it out of him.'

Bo's plus sign had been clearly marked in the upper right-hand corner of his notebook for some time, and now I saw Ray turn to him and nod.

I endorsed this move. Whenever it's feasible, it's a good idea to alternate questioners, since it gives the primary investigator, freed from thinking about his own questions, a better chance to observe and judge the demeanor of the prisoner. It works best, obviously, if there's a high degree of trust between the detectives.

Bo's chameleon face was wearing its blandest

expression when he leaned toward Billy McGowan and said, 'You don't give a shit for the future of Minnesota plant life. Why are you doing these break-ins?'

The rude new questioner set Billy back on his heels a little. He blinked at his clasped hands a couple of times. Twiddled his thumbs, twice. Then he seemed to reach his own version of the plus sign, sighed, and said, 'It's a job.'

'You're working for somebody?'

'Yes.'

'Somebody who wants these messages put around on desks?'

'Yes.'

'Why do they want that?'

'I don't have to know that, so I don't.'

Artie had said it was a group, but I wasn't sure how much Artie really knew. Billy didn't change expression when Bo established his employers as plural, but he was a practiced liar. Still, it looked like there was a group. More than one, anyway.

'OK,' Bo said. 'Time for names.'

'I only know the one who pays me.'

'Let's have it.'

'Clifford Mangen.'

'Spell it,' Ray said, and made a show of writing it down.

Bo said, 'He pay you in cash?'

'Oh, you bet. I wouldn't lift a finger till he did.'

'But you never heard any other names? Come on, you know it's a group, so you must have heard them say *something*.'

'Well . . . maybe a few first names.'

'Let's hear them.'

'There was one named Timmy that talked a lot, and one who never talked at all that they called Noons.'

'Noons. So probably Noonin?'

'I suppose. One guy, young but with a white streak in his hair that I think they called Brag, and one that Artie seemed to like a lot called John.'

Bo turned to Ray and raised his eyebrows. Ray nodded and Bo asked, 'The one with the streak – could his name have been Brad?'

'Coulda been. You know the guy?'

'Maybe. How much did Clifford pay you?'

'Come on,' Billy said, looking at the ceiling. 'You don't need that.'

Bo's pale eyes grew icier. 'We'll find out eventually. You want sincere help, or begrudging?'

'Oh, shit.' He twisted on his little seat. 'Five thousand for the whole rotten job. Fourteen fucking break-ins in five nights – I should have got twice as much. But I needed cash in a hurry.'

'I bet. You have all the tools and the know-how. What did you need Artie for?'

'He's thin. Some of those windows—' He made a despairing gesture at his hips and sighed. 'I just can't seem to take it off.'

I was momentarily distracted by a manic vision of a perky Jenny Craig rep pressing a brochure into the waiting hands of Billy McGowan. When I snapped back in focus, Bo was asking, 'How much did you pay Artie?' When Billy made a pleading face, Bo said sharply, 'Don't waste my time, damn it!'

'Five hundred. Don't tell on me, huh? He thinks he got an even split.' Then to Bo's disgusted look, he said, 'Listen, he'd have done it for nothing! Artie's a believer.'

'Is that how you got the job, because he was one of the—'

'No, Artie is not my buddy.' Billy looked disdainful. 'I didn't even know the little freak until one day I came on that place in the park where people air grievances and shit on Saturday mornings. I heard them airheads ranting about global warming, carrying on like they could see all around the world and really knew something. Right away I knew I'd found some folks I could work with. So I hung around, shared their pain a while, and made a few creative suggestions about how to, uh, make an *impact.*' Billy made a sound, somewhere between a sneer and a chuckle. 'These folks really get their rocks off talking about impact. And what's that other thing? Oh, yeah, branding. These messages we've been leaving, they're gonna create a *brand* for the group.' He shook his head in wonder.

Bo sat back in his chair, very relaxed, and scrutinized Billy for a whole minute. It's a way he has, staring so hard at the front of a guy's head he gets convinced Bo's reading his brain. When Billy began to twitch, Bo said softly, 'There's one more thing, isn't there?'

'What? I don't know what you mean.' But he did, you could see it. And not only that – even though he knew he should keep it to himself, he was longing to tell it.

'Billy,' Bo said, 'you know you're going to jail

for a while now. Why not buy yourself a little insurance? We can look out for you in there.' He gave the man a smile as sweet as a sugar tart and said, 'There was one more thing you were getting out of doing all those office invasions. What was it?'

'Well.' Billy consulted the lamp and the windowsill and finally said, 'Oh, hell, all right. Lotta these offices now, they have these electronic alarms installed. Have a little sign out front that says beware, this place is protected. Booga booga. Very big medicine, right? They all work on a combination of four or five numbers – you poke 'em in the right order, it turns off the alarm.

'So?' Bo was enjoying himself now; his eyes were almost warm.

'So you make a note which ones, go back in the daytime with a pail and window-washing gear, or stuff to trim the plants – any little chore – and talk to the girl, it's always a girl, who tends the reception desk. She's bored out of her skull. Express a little interest in her and admire the alarm system; chances are she'll show you just how it works. Admire her eyes enough, she'll probably give you the damn combination.'

'You're pretty sharp, Billy.'

'It's just this year's thing,' Billy said. 'Next year it'll be something else.'

Ray sent Billy back to his cell, with assurances he would keep in touch.

'Bet you're looking forward to that,' Bo said.

Ray shrugged and said, 'A deal's a deal.' But he stood looking into the corner the way he does, and added, 'That went well in there.'

Looking as if he might breathe a little easier for a while, Bo said, 'You think he could be talking about our straight-arrow Brad Polk, the one we liked at Aardvark Architecture?'

'Stranger things have happened, I guess,' Ray said. 'I just can't think what they were, offhand.'

'Let's give him a call, Ray,' I said. 'Tell him you're sending a squad for him, just routine questions but you need to ask them right away.

'And as soon as you've set that up, come on up to my office, because I see Rosie and Abeo are back.'

We had sent them out to find some information about Marilyn DiSilvio, and from the look on Rosie's face I thought the search had not been disappointing.

Abeo was standing in my office door, looking polite and well-behaved. Rosie, by contrast, was crouched over my desk phone, saying, 'Well, page him, please, because we need to— Oh, there you are.' She put the phone back in its cradle without remembering to cancel the page, so in a few seconds I heard my name being called, distinctly, throughout the building.

'Have a chair, detectives, while I answer this important message.' After I got that noise turned off I went out to LeeAnn's workspace and copped the extra chair she keeps behind her desk for me. 'This is for Ray,' I said, setting it down beside Abeo. 'He'll be here in a minute and I want him to hear what you have to say. Rosie, you look as if you enjoyed the trip.'

'Abeo's been on the street the last five years

while I was cooped up in here,' Rosie said. 'She knows all the new wrinkles out there beyond the Beltway. Our little village is growing fast, Jake.'

'Oh, indeed,' I said. 'Almost big enough for major crimes now. Think of the job security.'

Ray walked in on us, carrying a handful of notes, and said, 'OK, the squad's on its way, be back in half an hour. So, what now?'

'Sit,' I said, 'while we hear about that picture from LeeAnn's phone.'

It started the morning after my conversation with my wife, while I was still a little aglow from our unexpected burst of passion the night before. I kept thinking about Trudy – the wonderful joy in her face when she threw her arms around me, smelling like carrots and dirt.

And then what she said began to bounce around in my brain, 'Throw the whole thing out, the wretch is a whore!' She was kidding when she said it, but it reinforced my feeling that Marilyn's gleaming smile and extreme ability to please everybody were oddly placed in an isolated plant science start-up on the far west side. So I walked over to LeeAnn's desk and asked her if she was pleased with the picture she got with her new phone.

'Gosh, yes,' she said. 'But it's not really a new phone. I just said that because Kevin asked me to, so I'd have an excuse to take his picture with Marilyn. And it does do a nice job. Want to see?' She did that sweeping slash that phone-photo enthusiasts learn to do, pictures flew by and in a couple of blinks there they were, the handsome detective and the office manager, with their gleaming smiles.

'Wow, that's beautiful,' I said. 'Would you mind running off a couple of prints of this? Been trying to talk Trudy into getting a new phone – maybe this will convince her.'

When she had the prints, handsome on glossy paper, I strolled into Kevin's office and dropped them on his desk. I said, 'LeeAnn sure gets good pictures with her phone.'

He glanced at them and said, 'Yes.' And then, 'She's certainly an attractive woman, isn't she?'

'Yes,' I said, 'and if you knew anything about her I should know, you would certainly tell me, wouldn't you?'

'Hey, Jake, what kind of a question is that? I don't know anything, I just met the woman. I just thought, you know, that it was a little . . . surprising . . . for her to be working in a pokey little place like SmartSeeds. So I walked her over so you could have a look. Ray, too—'

'I wondered about that visit.'

'Yeah, well, that's the last time I try to include him in anything; he wouldn't even admit to having time to talk to us. I did kind of expect a comment from you, but I guess you were too busy to think about her, hmm?'

'No, I thought the same thing you did. But good looks are not an indictable offense and we already have several of those to work on, so I thought I'd stick to what I know how to do.'

Kevin nodded and said, 'Well, I suppose you're right.' Which is what *I* always say when somebody says something too dumb to deserve an argument.

A few minutes later that same day – was it only

yesterday? – I began to get a growing itch about the office manager. I found Ray and shared it with him. He said, 'Let's check it out,' so we called Andy in and gave him the locations of the three places Marilyn said she'd gone on Nathan Gold's last morning.

'Start from SmartSeeds,' I said, 'and drive to these places, using any approach a reasonable person might use. Return to SmartSeeds, record the elapsed time, add ten minutes each for the two supply stops and fifteen minutes at the post office. Do it again in the opposite direction and tell us the times you get.'

Andy came back and said, 'Hour and ten minutes one way, five minutes more in reverse.'

So this morning we had cut Kevin's image out of LeeAnn's pictures, given Rosie and Abeo the lopsided images of Marilyn that were left and told them where we wanted them to go.

'Tell us,' I said now, 'what you learned.'

'I took the hotels,' Rosie said. 'Abeo talked to the supply houses. You go first,' she told her partner.

'Bestgro Feed and Seed,' Abeo said, pushing rimless half-glasses up on her long nose, reading from a battery-powered tablet, 'is accustomed to supplying more than one brand of fertilizer to SmartSeeds, but they did not fill an order for any of them on Monday, October the seventh. And similarly with Superior Chemical Supply – they confirmed that SmartSeeds is a good customer, but say they did not sell them anything that Monday.'

'We decided not to try the post office,' Rosie

said. 'Too many employees and why would anyone remember? We'll have to subpoena records if—'

'Agreed,' I said. 'Tell us about the hotels.' I knew from her face that this was the juicy part.

'Three of them in that area: a Day's Inn, a Holiday Inn Express and an indie called Red Roof Motor Inn. I tried the chains first because I thought she'd like the anonymity. Day's Inn has quite a large rotating crop of part-time desk clerks and the manager's new, so the fact that nobody recognized the picture didn't mean much. The manager cooperated, searched the name in the records and found no DiSilvio. The Holiday Inn had a male clerk who works every Monday and didn't recognize the picture. He resisted the name search the way he's supposed to, but I talked to the manager, told her we're working on a homicide so we can get anything we need – why make it difficult? After that she opened the books but found no DiSilvio.

'She picked up the picture and looked at it again, though, and said, kind of puzzled, "It's funny, though, I do know this woman from some place." She said she'd think about it and call if she remembered.

'By then I was beginning to wonder about an assumed name. I didn't think a woman doing nooners would much like an indie – they're too small and intimate. But I tried the one I was near anyway – that Red Roof place. It actually does have red tile roofs, and stucco walls. It looks pretty nice.

'Anyway, I found the owner working the desk.

Angie Blake, what a pip. She frequently works lunch breaks for all her employees – that way she knows everything that goes on. She says there's only one thing Ronald Reagan ever said that she agreed with, and that was "Trust, but verify." She works seven days a week and the place is thriving; she's going to be the richest woman in the cemetery soon.'

'Rosie—'

'OK, I just – we don't get out enough, Jake. It's fun to see how interesting people's lives can be when they're not thinking about half-witted thugs all day. Anyway! Angie recognized Marilyn's picture right away. She reserves a room every Monday using the name Mary Brown. Always the same room on the back side, away from traffic. Some Mondays she uses it, some she doesn't; she pays either way, in cash on checkout. The times she doesn't use the room Angie holds the bill and she pays it the next time she comes in. She's always alone, but Angie, like I told you, works all the jobs in her place sooner or later, so she knows from changing the bed that Marilyn meets a man there.'

'Does she know who it is?'

'Doesn't know or doesn't want to know. What the hay, Angie says, people have all different lives and we're all just trying to get by. Why hassle somebody who's not doing any harm?'

'You don't think she's going to tell us who the partner is?'

'No. "I wouldn't be telling you any of this," Angie said, "but you badged me and I know you can get it the hard way if you have to, so why drag it out?" Angie's a lifer in the innkeeping trade. She tries to fix things so she doesn't get hassled either.'

'Good for Angie,' Ray said. 'But I bet we could get the regular maid on that station to tell us, if we went back with pictures.'

'Maybe. I think I agree with Angie: why should we care?'

'We don't, yet. If it turns out Marilyn's sex life is relevant to a murder investigation, we will.'

'Yeah. Well, you told us to get the quick-and-dirty, and that's what we got.'

'Detectives,' I said, 'you have done a masterful job. What do you say, Ray? Round of applause?'

'Yup,' he said. 'Don't know what it means yet, but put it in the case notes right away and we'll talk about it this afternoon.'

'Are we really going to have that meeting we keep talking about?'

'Of course,' I said. 'Why do you ask?'

'Well, we've put it off so many times—'

'Twice,' I said. 'One o'clock, Rosie. Abeo.' I stood up, nodded and smiled until they filed out.

Then Ray said, 'I been wondering myself – why do we need a meeting?'

'We have all these facts collected, but you just said it yourself – we don't know what anything means. We need to compare information and try to get a bigger picture. Try to see how it all fits together.'

'I don't know,' Ray said. 'I think if we get enough facts we'll see how it all fits. Or doesn't.

We still haven't got a homicide case for sure, remember?'

'Maybe not,' I said. 'But we've got some kind of a case, or why are so many people acting weird and lying to us?'

'We're police,' Ray said. 'People always lie to us.'

'About sex, sure. About fertilizer, not so much. Is that you being paged?'

Eleven

My first thought when I saw Brad Polk was, 'Mama's boy.' He looked tenderly raised, with a soft mouth and trusting grey-blue eyes. If this was the lead architect at Aardvark Architects, I wondered, how young was the rest of the crew? The white streak in the front of his hair only made his boyish handsomeness more striking – a sharp reminder that beauty is fleeting.

Bo and Clint, who answered the call to SmartSeeds that first day, had both said he was helpful and intelligent. But when Ray called him half an hour ago all he'd said was, 'Does it have to be today? We're pretty busy out here right now. Working on a big bid.'

'I just told him, "The squad's on the way," Ray said. 'I said we'll be as quick as we can but it has to be now. Told him we're at an inflection point.'

'A what?'

'I read it someplace,' Ray said. 'Some kind of a bend or a turning point – anyway, it seems to work with almost everybody.'

As soon as Ray had him seated in front of my desk I turned on the recorder and said, 'We have to record all our interviews now. So we have a reminder about what everybody said.'

He shrugged and said, 'Anything's fine with me, Captain, but please can we be brief? This bid's important to us.'

Ray said, 'You got a chance for a good job?'

'A good big job – enough to keep us busy for most of a year, but it's got to be perfect. And wouldn't you know it, today's another one of Travis's sick days.'

'You sound kind of disgusted,' Ray said. 'Is Travis frail or just lazy?'

'He just doesn't take care of himself! Off up there in the north woods on weekends, running himself ragged trying to keep up with those macho vigilante guys, and half the time he forgets to take his meds – then he comes home all messed up and takes two or three days to recover. I said to him, "Travis, you just have to decide what's important – are you an architect or a soldier of fortune?"'

'Which did he decide?'

'Oh, he just said, "I thought I was being a patriot." Those weekend warriors have got him so convinced there's a threat to our border up there.' He shook his head, his nice face all crinkled up with irritation. Then he rubbed his hands together and said, 'Well! What's this about?'

Ray said, 'Tell me everything you know about

Clifford Mangen.' We had agreed to be very businesslike, not cordial, but not do any accusing until we'd established that we had the right man. Now that I'd seen him, I was more dubious than ever that this earnest architect could possibly be involved with Billy McGowan.

'Clifford Mangen?' Brad looked curious but not worried. 'That won't take long. Surprised you don't know him. He's the music director of the whole Rutherford Senior High School system.'

'Friend of yours?'

'Well, colleague really. Wonderful man and a prodigious worker. Supervises the band and chorus programs for four schools and a couple of dozen teachers. In the spare time he doesn't have, he plays the organ and directs the choir at my church, Fourth Street Congregational.'

'You know him well, then.'

'Fairly well. My wife sings in the choir. All three of our kids perform in the choral events at school. I'm sadly untalented so all I do is applaud.'

'Well, that's not quite all, is it? Aren't you a member of his eco-warrior group? What do you call it? Friends of the Earth?'

'Oh,' Brad said. 'Well, yes. It's not his, actually – it's quite a large organization. Couple of dozen teachers, several pastors, and maybe forty or so concerned citizens like me. We sponsor tree plantings, birdwatching excursions . . .' He cleared his throat, a small, glottal sound, and examined the toes of his polished loafers. He didn't seem to want to meet my eyes any more.

'Yes, I know about all that,' Ray said, taking on a dark, Baileyish look. 'But you're a member of an elite little, um, kind of a cabal inside the club, aren't you?'

'Cabal – what a strange word. I never thought of it that way.'

'How did you think of it?'

'Well.' The little 'ahem' sound again. 'We're basically kind of . . . a little discussion group, really.'

'Uh-huh.' Ray leaned over him suddenly and grew a wolfish expression; I could have sworn his teeth got longer. 'And what you basically discuss is breaking into people's offices to butt into their business, right? Leave messages about what they do for a living?'

'Well, now wait a minute.' Brad Polk threw his hands up in front of himself like a shield. 'That's not quite— I have to give you some background.'

'Fine.' Ray sat back and folded his arms. 'Do that.'

'It started out as just a few guys meeting for coffee on Saturday mornings to talk about extreme weather events. Wondering what more we should be doing to prepare our homes and churches and schools for the crazy storms we were having. A lot of us had had big trees fall, roofs blown off, and scientists kept telling us worse weather was coming. We started out talking about storm shelters, what we'd need, how much they would cost.'

'How'd you all find each other?'

'Clifford and I started talking, other people would hear us and add something, and after a while we had this group. All very informal, though.'

'But you decided to do something,' Ray said, 'informally.'

'Well,' he swiped his hand across his mouth, 'we know global warming's causing at least some of the extreme weather – all the serious scientists agree on that. And it's getting worse every year – whole towns blowing away almost, further south, and California burning up. And we could see the government had no firm plans for cleaner power – we sign petitions and we vote, the President expresses concern, Congress makes fun of him because that polls better than a carbon tax, and then they go right back to arguing about abortion and same-sex marriage – they seem to be obsessed with those. It would be funny if it weren't so tragic.'

He looked up then and I guess he saw both of us nodding, because he was right about the situation. He'd described it well. Taking a couple of head bobs as a sign we were on his side, he took on momentum. 'Well, you know, every night on TV for a while there, some population in the Middle East was massing in a public square, yelling slogans and throwing Molotov cocktails, and pretty soon they'd bring down another government. And sometimes – like in Egypt for a while, the crowd pulling the guys with the whips off their camels and all – you couldn't help thinking it seemed kind of *inspiring*. After all, our country started with a revolution too, didn't it?

'So gradually some of the guys started saying,

"Maybe we need to do something like that in this country – you think the Senate would stop ignoring us then?"'

'Kind of hard to get people in Rutherford to pile up tires and set them afire, though, isn't it?' Ray asked him.

'Be pretty hard to do it myself, I realized,' Brad said. 'We all had families, jobs, houses, we were law-abiding citizens, raised to be well-behaved. So for a couple of months we concentrated on going to more hearings, making signs and marching. But then there was news about the West Antarctic ice sheet collapsing, articles speculating about how soon the Florida Keys and the Outer Banks would be under water. Timmy Magruder began quoting a motto he heard somewhere: "All that's needed for evil to triumph is for good men to do nothing." When we got sick of hearing that we all turned on him and said, "Yes, but do what?"'

'Good question,' I said. But just then my cell vibrated and I stepped into the hall to answer it.

Kevin said, 'Well, Clifford's here, and I have to believe it now because he just admitted he's the leader of the Holy Messengers. Can you come over? I'd like to have a witness so I don't start thinking later I must have dreamed this.'

I walked across the hall, went in without knocking and sat down on a chair behind the desk, next to Kevin.

Clifford Mangen wasn't wearing a three-piece suit today – he'd gone one step fustier, with a tan cardigan sweater under a tweed jacket. His tie looked as if it might have been present at the creation of a march by John Philip Sousa. I'd seen him around, I realized, always leading the band or chorus at some function.

Kevin told him who I was and added, 'Clifford's been telling me how the break-in idea started.'

I said, 'I heard some of this story from Brad Polk. So just go right on from where you were, please.'

'Well, by that time,' Clifford said, 'some of the fellas were getting pretty, you know, inspired by all these revolutions abroad, how fast they could change things. They were saying maybe we don't have a big town square like that, but there must be something we could do to make Congress stop ignoring us and only listening to the NRA. And that's when I said, "You know, there's one practical thing we could try, and it's right close by. We could try to stop Minnaska."'

Kevin said, 'What?'

'Stop this move to GMOs and super-crop yields. Altered seeds that nobody really understands, more chemical weed-killers every year, washing into rivers, causing cancer, low sperm counts in men—'

'What's that got to do with global warming?' Kevin said.

'Maybe nothing directly but it's an evil development near to hand that we all felt we understood well enough to tackle. We've all been campaigning against GMOs for some time and getting no traction, no sign at all that the government wants to establish meaningful safeguards.

'Well, think about it: this is the food we feed

our children! And a lot of people agree with us, that's the thing. Many people have agreed with me that nobody knows exactly what will come of altering the genetic makeup of our crops. So if we could attack GMOs in a big way, I told the guys, if we could make enough noise so we got some of these products taken off the market . . .'

He looked at Kevin and then at me, wanting to see some sign we agreed, I guess. When we just stared at him, he took a deep breath and started again. 'We agreed that if we could stop a big, successful corporation from marketing products we don't think are safe, well, that would be very big news. That news could go viral. And then, who knows? People everywhere might see that they could make a difference if they tried.'

'This seems so . . . unlike you, Clifford,' Kevin said. 'I've always thought you were one of the most conservative people I know.'

'But that's exactly what I was trying to do: conserve! Keep this sweet planet earth as it is, for future generations to enjoy! And I thought if ordinary citizens felt empowered to act, take some responsibility for . . . At least, for God's sake, get off their dead behinds and vote in the mid-term elections!'

Clifford's temperature was definitely warming, the scalp that showed through his comb-over was turning pink – and the more emphatic his pronouncements became, the more tears welled up behind his bifocals. His ears got red the same way Mark Hoving's had, I noticed, starting with the tops and working down.

'I mean, just imagine,' Clifford said, his earnest face taking on a blazing glow, 'what this country could be like if all the citizens came together at once and reached consensus on the importance of tackling global warming. If we confronted our government the way people did in that square in Egypt, and just insisted on it.'

'That didn't all turn out so well, though, did it?'

'Well, they haven't had two hundred years to practice democracy like we have – give them time. But we're so lucky to have had the founding fathers we had. Just think what could happen now if we all said, "We don't care about your next damn election, we want some action now!" Why, we could have green power, clear air and clean water, in just a few years! All it takes is the will.'

Kevin said, 'The rest of the world—'

'I know, China won't go along, North Korea won't . . . everybody says that but it's just a lame excuse for doing nothing. Somebody has to start. Do you think those farmers in Concord knew exactly what everybody else was going to do if they fired their guns? They went ahead and defended themselves, and gradually the rest of the country came along.'

Several seconds of silence followed while I pondered the shortest route back to the laws of trespass. Kevin had his mouth open, ready to start the journey, but Clifford Mangen took us there in two short sentences.

'That was our idea when we started. But then I guess it kind of got out of hand.'

Painfully then, looking as if it was literally giving him a belly-ache, he detailed how the idea grew. 'Timmy Magruder started the expansion, saying, "What about all these little start-ups planting experimental crops out there on the west side? Nobody knows exactly what happens when the wind blows, do they? If we don't put some rules on them, before long we might not have any original seeds left."

'And a couple of other guys said, "Well, while we're at it why don't we go after the people getting the grant money that's funding these start-ups? We dry up their cash, that'll stop them faster than anything."

'And suddenly there was this guy named Billy drinking coffee with us on Saturday mornings, listening to everybody and giving our ideas a lot of respect. At first he just listened, then he started bringing a story every week about the latest weather-related disaster – he was one of us, showing concern. And one day he said he had an idea how we could spread enough fear around in this upstart group – that's what he'd taken to calling them, he went from start-up to upstart and it was strange how much more bullying and disruptive it made them sound – he said he thought we could get a lot of them to quit.'

'This rabble-rouser named Billy,' I said, 'would his last name be McGowan?'

'You know him?' Clifford looked startled.

'Just met him.'

'Well' – he went into kind of a shrugging fit, as if he couldn't quite believe his own story any more – 'this Billy person began to suggest the noble messages we could leave, making it clear the mission was public-spirited. And to get attention we should stage a break-in at each place, he said, because that's scary, but then surprise everybody because nothing would be taken or broken. Unforgettable, he said. And it would be perfectly blameless because we wouldn't hurt a soul.

'Everybody liked that idea, even though it wasn't what we had started out to— I mean, we'd said we wanted to stop Minnaska. And while a few of these smaller outfits might get discouraged and quit, nobody really thought a message on a desk was going to stop Minnaska. But by then people were saying, "The message is so dramatic! It will give us a presence, a brand!"

'The idea began to have its own momentum, so we started talking ways and means. Billy said he thought he could "assemble the team" – that's how he put it, and get the job done for ten thousand dollars.'

'Whee,' Kevin said.

'Yes. I told him right away that much money was out of the question. That was almost the deal-breaker right there, and maybe it should have been. But Billy thought about it, came back and said if Artie would help him he'd do the job himself and he thought he could fund the technology—'

Kevin squinted at him in amazement and asked, 'What technology?'

'Tools and stuff. Some electronics to sniff out alarm systems. He said he could do it for five thousand. We had twenty-some people by then, not counting Artie and Billy, so we each put in' – he waved a vague hand – 'something close to two hundred and fifty dollars. Even that much brought pretty sharp questions from some of the wives, including mine. We stick to a tight budget in order to save for college for the kids, and she wasn't happy about giving money to something I wasn't able to fully describe. Because we all agreed on that – in case of any blowback, leave the wives out of this. Anyway, we finally all paid, and the more literate members began crafting the messages.'

I said, 'It didn't bother you that breaking and entering is illegal?'

'Of course it did, but we told each other that George Washington knew the British would hang him if they caught him, but he went ahead anyway.'

'Yeah, well,' Kevin said, 'people do get testy about taxes.'

'But not about destroying the planet? See, that's what drives me crazy when I think about it! Global warming is the biggest threat humans have ever faced, but it's happening slowly so people won't take it seriously.'

'All right,' I said, 'so twenty-some serious guys were driven so berserk by the indifference of their fellow citizens that they convinced themselves breaking and entering in a good cause wasn't really criminal. But now explain to me how you justified wrecking Maggy Ross's chair and shooting out a headlight on Alan Gordon's Cadillac.'

'What? What are you talking about?'

I slammed my fist on Kevin's desk. His lamp jumped and so did Kevin, and a mug full of pencils fell over. 'Don't pull that aggrieved horseshit on me!' I yelled, because I could see it coming, the surprised look and then the same you-can't-hang-that-on-me crap we got from Billy McGowan. 'Because those crimes happened this week – I didn't make them up. Maggy Ross is in the hospital and Alan Gordon's SUV is in shreds on one side. And Mark Hoving is walking around very nervous because he was driving the Caddy and he thinks those shreds were meant to be pieces of him.'

'Captain, please believe me, I don't know anything about any of that!'

'Why should I believe you? You've just admitted you didn't think the law mattered compared to your message.'

'But I never said murder didn't matter!'

'Maybe not to me, but you and your cronies must have said it to each other. Because this department just spent a large pile of municipal funds finding the casing from the bullet that wrecked that SUV. And when we find the gun that fired it we are going to hang those crimes on somebody, no more farting around about it. Now tell me, do you see any reason why I wouldn't think that person might be you?'

I waited while he buried his face in his hands. Then I said quietly, to the backs of his shaking fingers, 'See, Clifford, at the police station guilt is easier to figure out. In here we're not concerned about your noble motives; we just need to determine whether you did the crime.

And if you did and we can prove it, you have to pay for that.'

The words weren't even out of my mouth before I began thinking of all the exceptions I could cite, the different arrest rates and sentencing records we compile in this country depending on home address and skin color. But that was just my lowly origins nudging me again, and I kept the thought to myself, hoping to scare him enough to get full cooperation from this improbable law-breaker.

He continued to tremble in his chair while I read out some hard facts about the particular crimes his group had committed. 'This threat of "retribution sure and swift," that you were all so proud of, that would fall under Minnesota Statute 609.713, terroristic threats . . . Here, I'll read you some of the wording: '"Whoever threatens, directly or indirectly, to commit any crime of violence with purpose to terrorize another—"'

'We didn't mean *we* were going to— My God, isn't it perfectly plain we were talking about the retribution Nature will exact if we don't show respect for the natural order?'

'No, it isn't perfectly plain, and I don't believe anybody took it that way. Our phones have been lit up like a Christmas tree all week, my chief getting one call after another from worried people who got those messages, asking what we're going to do to protect them from these terrorists.'

(I exaggerated a little bit there. Frank didn't actually get any calls until after the shooting in the Minnaska parking lot came out in the paper. Alan's shattered headlight photographed like a freaking disaster – very impressive. Frank's wife finally disconnected the McCafferty home phone that night, after Frank proved himself incapable of letting a call go to voicemail.)

I was beginning to enjoy myself a little, reading the law to Clifford Mangen – I could see how this message-sending business could kind of grab you. 'The breaking and entering, now, this crime appears to fall under the statute 609.582 Burglary . . . and the meat of that is here: "Whoever enters a building without consent . . . commits burglary in the third degree and may be sentenced to imprisonment for not more than five years or to payment of a fine of not more than $10,000,00, or both."'

I let that nice round figure echo around the room for a while before I said, to the top of his bent head, 'That's before we even talk about the penalties for hate crimes. I haven't had time to look up all of that law yet.'

Clifford was crying openly by then and I almost began to feel sorry for him, but not too sorry to assure him that the only way we'd show any consideration for his noble motives was if he gave us a complete list of the other twenty-odd people who had contributed to the break-in fund. He wasted two minutes protesting that he could never betray the sacred bonds of friendship. So I re-opened the book, started reading some more law, and he caved.

'But we still haven't got a good suspect for the shooting. Because you know damn well,' I told Ray and Kevin, after we'd booked Brad and Clifford and their devoted wives came to the station (wives never actually get protected from blowback), and they did a lot of murmuring and funds-juggling so they could make bail, 'as soon as they're out of this building they're going to build airtight alibis for both those attacks.'

'Sure,' Ray said. 'I think I could write them myself. Brad was working on the big bid with his partners when the shooting took place, and his wife will swear he was never out of bed the night Ms Ross's chair got wrecked.'

'That one might even be true,' I said. 'Isn't she a nice lady? And Mrs Mangen will come up with equally good places for Clifford to be. So let's hope this list of names he gave us turns up somebody who fits the profile.'

'Which is what? I don't have a good mental picture of a guy who sets out to save the world and ends up shooting at people from parking garages.'

'Ray, you're the one who said if we get enough facts together the picture will start to make sense. Let's get LeeAnn to type this list of names into the case file and we'll start the interviews on Monday.'

We left it there, went into the break room and pulled our brown-bag lunches out of the refrigerator. The noontime follies were especially quiet that day. Ray had found an almost-new issue of *Car and Driver* on one of the tables and was completely engrossed. My mind was so full of crime and punishment I couldn't concentrate on the crossword, so I pulled out the long list of questions I wanted to get answered at the meeting, and while I ate I added more questions.

I'd filled another whole page by the time Pokey called. After I talked to him I hurried out to LeeAnn's desk to ask her to delay the meeting once again.

Twelve

Pokey said the tox screens were back, 'so I can finish writing the autopsy report tonight. You ain't gonna be very happy when you see it – it's kinda wishy-washy. But all I got to work with is what I got back from the lab. Nothing I can do about those geniuses in the cities.'

I asked him if he could take time to go over it with me if I came to his office.

'I guess. Ain't going to change nothing, Jake.'

'Of course not. When did I ever try that on you? I just want to be sure I understand everything in the report, which I seldom do without an interpreter.'

'Life's a bitch, ain't it? Come in half an hour. I'll take care of this numbskull I got in the chair and we'll cancel the next appointment.'

Hampstead County still has a homicide rate so low it gets by without a full-time M.E. Pokey gets paid piecework rates to be the part-time coroner, and maintains his partnership in a full-time dermatology practice to put food on the table. Mostly all he gets to do as coroner is certify cause of death for people who die of old age.

The services of a state-of-the-art Bureau of

Criminal Apprehension in St Paul make the system work when, as now, we have a questionable death. I have nothing but respect for that beautiful crime lab and would certainly never wish for a higher homicide rate, but I often wish all those criminalists were in Rutherford. Maybe if I picked their brains more often I'd begin to understand medical jargon a little better.

I told my detectives, 'Save time for me at two-thirty. He's only cancelling one appointment so I know I'll be back by then.' Then I hustled out to his new offices in the medical complex that's growing on Second Avenue South.

Pokey met me at the front door and led me through a warren of reclining chairs and gleaming stainless steel work tables to his office in back. He had to bootstrap a long way up from his start as a dirt-poor Ukrainian immigrant to achieve the secure status he enjoys now as county coroner and partner in this topflight medical practice. His English is still a little loosey-goosey, but the rest of his life in Rutherford has a high shine he's rightly proud of.

'That St Paul bunch is thorough, by crackey,' he said, hefting the fresh stack of paper that would soon be attached to the main body of the autopsy report. 'This starts out with a long list of things they tested for but didn't find.' He wrinkled his nose as he scanned the closely printed sheets. 'Our man didn't die of arsenic, strychnine, cyanide, mercury . . . on and on. They can't confirm our diagnosis of hypoglycemia, but can't disprove it either – the blood I sent them was drawn close to thirty hours after death. Blood sugar would have dissipated by then anyway.

'What they did find, though, was a low level, just above trace amounts, of insulin.'

'I thought I read somewhere that insulin would dissipate in a few hours too.'

'The natural kind does – the kind your own body makes. You, or a pig or a cow – all works the same.'

'Wait. I've got the same insulin as a pig?'

'Sure. Damn near the same as a fish. We all came out of the same swamp, kid. Get used to it.'

'OK. But today's insulin doesn't dissipate?'

'The natural kind still does but this insulin they sell people now is almost all manufactured. They take a virus and attach . . . you don't need to know how they do it. What matters is this manufactured kind leaves markers that can be detected on something called an immunoassay test. They ran one of those on Doctor Gold's blood and detected some insulin.'

'And they're sure it wasn't his own?'

'Yes, they are, because they didn't find any C-peptides, which would be present if the insulin was natural.'

'Why?'

Pokey screwed up his foxy face. 'Lessee, can I explain . . .' He pulled on his pointed nose for a while. 'Insulin starts out as a big molecule. Somewhere in the process of getting out of the pancreas and into the blood stream, it splits in two. Both halves stay in the blood stream. First half is still insulin, goes right to work regulating the blood sugar. Other half becomes a C-peptide, and to tell you the truth nobody's ever explained to me what the hell use it is from then on.' He laughed explosively. 'Ain't that keen science data?'

'Gosh, yes. Don't know what I'd have done without it.' When his amusement had died down a little, I asked him, 'Where does this leave us?'

'Doctor Jackson's positive Nathan Gold was not diabetic. And not suicidal. Anyway, the only mark he had on him was that little pimple on the back of his arm. No way he could give himself a shot back there.'

'So . . .?'

'Well, if he died of hypoglycemia like I still say he did . . . low blood sugar is a symptom, it's not a disease. If he was showing that symptom from a dose of insulin that he had no business to take and couldn't have given to himself—'

'Then we're looking at murder.'

'Seems like it.' Pokey rubbed his wise face that had been shock-proofed while he was still in his teens, and smiled. 'But I wouldn't want to be you the day you try to persuade your county attorney he can take this case into court and get a conviction.'

'Oh, I don't have to wait that long to get yelled at,' I said. 'This very afternoon I get to take this into Frank McCafferty's office and explain that after all the noise we made in my part of the building this week, what we have so far is a solid maybe.'

'Poor, poor Jake Hines,' Pokey said. 'Somebody

should do something to make your job a little easier.'

Before I talked to the chief I had a quick meeting with the homicide section. They would all have access to the autopsy report in the case files as soon as Pokey filed it, but I wanted to make sure they understood the tantalizing uncertainty of the verdict. Most of the crew sat silently digesting what I told them, but Ray, with a section to run, got right to the point.

'Well, are we looking for somebody to arrest, or aren't we? If we all suspect a murder, do we just let it sit there and stink, or do we keep it on the front burner?'

'Definitely on the front burner. Yes. Start with the crimes you know you have – divide up the twenty-some interviews with the men from Brad's break-in group. Get them in here, talk to them. Be sure you record every word! Try to pinpoint how it all fits together, how they chose the places that were broken into.

'Then there were three repeat attacks, during one of which Doctor Gold was killed. Why just those three? It's all too neat to be pure coincidence, yet it doesn't seem to make much sense – the three who got the repeats don't seem any different than the others who didn't.

'Everybody I've talked to denies that the break-in group did those second attacks. See if you can break down that wall of denial. It must be the same group, or part of it, but how did they pick the final victims – what was the criteria? Brad may not know as much as he thinks he knows;

there could be other things going on in that group.

'Please start right now making appointments for tomorrow – let's get them all in here talking to us before the news gets around and some of them find urgent reasons to visit their cousins in Nashville.'

'What about that – the news getting around?' Bo said. 'Any chance we can keep that autopsy report to ourselves for a while?'

'Good question. I'm going to see the chief now and I'll ask him. So make the phone calls this afternoon and try to get your desks clear. Starting tomorrow, and all next week, we'll be devoting all our time to this case.'

The crew drifted back into workstations, and soon the air was filled with the soft drone of their voices making dates for tomorrow and Monday. Ray and I went into his office for some private face time.

'One thing we haven't explored,' Ray said, 'is why, after fourteen break-ins close together, there was a quiet time and then three of the group got the second attacks. What was going on during that lull?'

'I suppose they were evaluating products from those firms to decide which three would get the punishment.'

'You'd think they would have done that before they started.'

'But maybe the idea kind of grew as it went along,' I said. 'You know, they broke one law and then started to say, well, what if we did this much more? It works that way sometimes – people rev up a little at a time.'

'That's true,' Ray said. 'I've seen it happen in gangs.'

'Obviously the connecting link between these three companies was research into genetically altered crops, but all the outfits that got the messages shared that interest, one way or another, didn't they? All right, then why would these three be particularly likely to attract more attention? You think you could have somebody start digging for other features in common?'

'Yeah. Bo, I think, he's a good, quiet digger.'

'Also, I keep thinking,' I said, 'of what Mrs Ross asked me. "What's the quid pro quo?" I kind of blew her question off at the time she asked it, but now, this many odd events so close together, all with a spooky mixture of noble intentions and lawlessness. It feels like somebody with a purpose, doesn't it? And every time I get that far, I find myself thinking about the office manager at SmartSeeds.'

'Oh? The fashion-forward babe who meets somebody in town during work hours? She's titillating, but I don't see—'

'She's working in an obscure office on the far edge of town, almost out in the fields. But always so well-turned-out, dressed and groomed like she's ready to go just about anywhere, isn't she?'

'So they say,' Ray said. 'I only saw her that one time. She just seemed like a hot babe to me. Why are we talking about her now?'

'What do you suppose a hot babe's purpose would be?'

'For doing what?'

'For burying herself out in the country in an obscure office but still taking such pains with herself, always looking so good?'

'How long you been married, Jake? You kind of sound like a guy with the seven-year itch.'

'No, Ray, I got very lucky a few years ago and got a major babe to move into my own house, so that itch I do not have. Just . . . listen to me a minute.'

We talked about the office manager for a little longer. Then we sent Rosie on another errand, and I went to see the chief.

Frank McCafferty likes an orderly shop. Despite the malfeasance whirling all around him – this is, after all, a police station, where dreams die every day – Frank usually manages to march in lockstep with his inner drummer. Meetings go off as scheduled, phone calls are returned promptly, his desk is clean before he goes home at night.

He gave me a dubious look when I came in and asked me, 'Have you gone over to the dark side this week? I keep hearing *sobs* down the hall.'

'We've been getting some underbrush cleared away,' I said. I told him the news about the break-in group.

'And this Polk claims Clifford Mangen's the ringleader? I can't believe it. I think you better grill the architect some more, Jake.'

'No, Frank. We've talked to Mangen and he admits it all.'

'I don't understand. Clifford's been a do-gooder

all his life. All my kids have taken his music classes. They just idolize him.'

'Well, that's the sticky part, Frank – these people all insist they were trying to do something good for the country.'

'Oh, bullshit. Even a zealot knows going through locks is illegal.'

'I thought so too but this group seems to have been in denial. Anyway, we're talking to all of them, starting tomorrow. We'll see if we turn up any other motivation.'

'What if you do? Invasion's invasion, unless they can prove they thought they were putting out a fire.'

'Yes, well, see . . .' I told him about the autopsy we would soon receive from the coroner, how even Pokey, who was going to write it, said it was 'wishy-washy.' 'So we decided to pursue the crimes we can prove because we're sure they're connected to the murder somehow. And if we pile up enough evidence, we're hoping something drops out of that . . .' I faded about there. Frank had trained his twin blues on me and I was starting to sweat. Stated out loud in Frank's office, my strategy seemed twisted as a rope.

'I don't think I understand,' he said. 'What's Pokey going to say?'

'Something like, "Appears to be death by misadventure." With some footnotes saying he can't account for the presence of insulin, but the low levels seem inadequate to cause death, but the subject does not appear to have died from natural causes and both physical and anecdotal evidence rules out suicide.'

'So essentially he drops it right back in our laps.'

'Um. Yes, I guess you could say that.'

'Swell.' He drummed on his desk. He has large hands and feet and when he gets impatient his desk takes a terrible beating. 'It seems to me we've got to do a little better than this for Doctor Gold. I've been reading some of the tributes the paper's printing – people writing and calling to say what a first-rate man and scientist he was. We can't just come along after that and say we think he was murdered but we don't have enough evidence to punish anybody. People aren't going to accept that.'

'I know. So I want to ask you to sit on that autopsy for a couple of days.'

'What good will that do?'

'I feel sure we're close to something. There are some freaky pieces still floating around – a partner we don't entirely trust, for one thing, and an office manager who seems too fancy for her job. I can't promise anything but it feels like the whole thing's ready to explode.'

'Huh.' He thought, punished his chair a while, then sighed. 'All right. You get Pokey to hold onto the autopsy over the weekend and I'll do my best to sit on it till midweek. But Jake,' he gave me his no-horseshit look, 'bear down.'

I went back to my office and phoned Pokey, reminded him he had said someone should find a way to make my job easier, and told him how he could do that.

'I can if you want me to,' he said, 'but what's the use? It ain't gonna make the report any more helpful.'

'I know. But I can feel a lot of people tip-toeing around this crime. Before long I'm hoping somebody's going to trip.'

Pokey made a small snorting noise and said, 'No disrespect or nothing, Babycakes, but from where I sit you don't sound one bit like Sherlock Holmes.'

But after he'd had his fun he agreed to keep the autopsy report until Monday afternoon. I went back to my office and added still more questions to my plan for tomorrow's meeting. And before long Rosie came back in the building and cheered me up.

'It took me a while at the motel,' Rosie said, 'because Angie wouldn't let me go out in the workstations and poll the maids – she made me wait while she looked up the work schedules and brought the right little Honduran lady into her office to look at the picture.'

'Since when do you let innkeepers tell you how to run a homicide investigation?' I have seen Rosie on her high horse and she is nobody to mess with.

'Well, Angie was just pleading with me not to say anything about a murder around her place. She says these women who work for her have seen a lot of trouble and they spook easy. I think that's code for, "got no papers," but I didn't want to spoil our friendship by asking. "I need them all at work tomorrow morning," she said, "so don't you go scaring them off." I put a stupid smile on my face and promised to play nice.

'But once I finally got Maria Louisa in the

chair and showed her the picture, there was no question. Her face just lit right up. 'Such a sweet man,' she said. 'Always a nice tip, and no trouble.'

'Well, he's nothing if not consistent,' I said. 'Everybody loves Nathan Gold.'

'No hesitation at all?' Kevin said. 'Damn, this is hard to believe.' I had called him in to hear Rosie's report – it was his idea to call attention to Marilyn, and I wanted to be sure that Ray acknowledged that and Kevin knew he had done so. They might never be close comrades but I was tired of hearing them snipe at each other, and I wanted it stopped.

But I wasn't going to get that right away, apparently. 'Why is it hard to believe?' Ray said. 'It's right out of the playbook, isn't it? The perfect husband cheats on his wife?' He looked at Rosie thoughtfully. 'I wonder if Naomi knew about it?'

'Oh, please,' Rosie said. 'Don't even think that.'

'Why not?' Ray said. 'It's the best motive for murder that I can imagine.'

'Ray, for God's sake,' Rosie said, getting really angry, 'hasn't that poor woman been through enough without—' She stopped when she saw how we were all looking at her. 'What?'

'I have a problem,' I said. 'There's a woman in my office who looks a lot like Rosie Doyle, a tough, experienced detective on my staff. But she's making statements that sound like she's reading them out of *The Ladies' Home Journal*, so I know this woman has to be an imposter. Should I throw her out?'

Rosie's mouth turned into a round circle and her color grew, well, rosier. After some labored breathing she turned to face the wall for a long moment. The three of us, for once, had the good sense to keep our traps shut and wait. And when she turned back I saw that my good old Rosie, the authentic Ms Don't-pull-that-shit-on-me, was back.

'I'm sorry,' she said. 'Those two women – I just kind of liked them, I guess. They're so . . . decent and hard-working and quiet. But you're right, of course. It's the best motive in the world, isn't it?'

'Classic,' I said. 'And Naomi's a doctor – she's good at giving shots that don't hurt and she can get all the meds she wants.'

'She was at the clinic all morning though,' Rosie said, and then, reversing field, 'but at home with him before that. With plenty of opportunity to be alone, because her mother minds the children in the morning. They both told me that.'

'How would she find out, I wonder?' Kevin said.

'Motel rooms cost money,' Ray said. 'Didn't we hear they gave up much bigger salaries to come here? Maybe they've been sticking to a strict budget and she began to wonder where all his pocket money was going.'

'Or maybe she went to give him a nice hug when he came home for supper and she smelled something new,' I said. 'Anyway, it fits with that first thing you said about her, Rosie, that she was glacial when you told her he was dead.'

'I did say that, didn't I?' Rosie turned a page in her notes and, surprisingly, perked up and smiled a gotcha smile. 'But listen, guys, can we leave the glacial Naomi frozen in place for a minute? Because that's not all the news I brought back.'

Ray said, 'Jesus, what else?'

'Remember what I told you about going to the two chain places first, when I went out with Marilyn's picture? That the manager at the Holiday Inn Express thought she remembered Marilyn's picture but couldn't remember from where? Well, I was going right by there on my way back, so I stopped in. As soon as the manager saw me she said, "Oh, there you are, I've been meaning to call you."

'It seems this woman – her name's Francine Proebe, by the way – has got a sister named Doreen who's an assistant manager at the big Sofitel downtown, and they have the same days off in midweek. So for one of those days, almost every week, they meet at Doreen's hotel and go shopping or to a movie, and eat dinner together somewhere. And more than once, while she was sitting in the lobby waiting for Doreen, she's noticed Marilyn walk in and meet a man in that little bar in the lobby.'

'That doesn't sound like a strikingly unusual event in a hotel lobby,' Kevin said. 'Why did she notice it – did she say?'

'Yes, she said this very good-looking woman, late twenties or early thirties, came in and met a dignified well-dressed man who looked to be twice her age, and she seemed to be doing her best to please him. Francine said you'd think it would be the other way around, but he didn't get up and pull out a chair or anything, just sat there and drank his drink without ordering one for her, and when he was good and ready they walked over to the elevator together and went upstairs.'

'Francine said she asked her sister about them, but Doreen just shrugged and said, "Every Thursday," but she said there was never a registration card and she'd been told not to talk about it.'

'She's nimble, isn't she, our Marilyn?' Kevin said, pleased with himself for having been first to notice her special qualities. 'A Monday date and a Thursday date. I wonder how many more?'

'And why always in the daytime?' Ray said. 'I wonder how she gets so much time off from her job.'

'I suppose,' Rosie said, 'she just asks her Monday date for the favor. Or she did, until recently.' She closed her notebook softly and drummed a quiet little tango on it, looking thoughtful.

'For a detective who just turned in a stellar performance,' I said, 'you're looking strangely unfulfilled, like you just thought of something new. What is it, Rosie?'

'Well I just thought of a good question,' Rosie said. 'Marilyn has lost her Monday date. Doesn't that kind of put a spoke in her wheels out there at SmartSeeds? Wouldn't you think she might be talking about quitting that dead-end job? But instead she's in Jake's office, telling him how bad she feels. Why?'

'Good question,' I said. 'I wish we could put a tracker on her till we figured out what she's up to.'

Rosie shrugged. 'But then maybe she just came in trolling for new customers.'

'Oh, come on, be logical. Was Nathan Gold the sort of man you would expect to start enjoying the services of a prostitute on Monday mornings?'

'Well—' She sat back and thought about it. 'No.'

'That's right, he wasn't. Every word we've heard about the man, all the beloved family of scientists, the devotion to his work . . . Have you found any of the family yet, by the way?'

'Almost all of them. His parents are devastated. His brother cried openly on the phone from a trench in the Olduvai Gorge. These are special people, Jake. That's why I'm so—'

'I understand you're outraged. I'm telling you to put that aside now and do your job. Come on, everybody, get over the titillation and think. From what we know of him, isn't it reasonable to think that Nathan Gold was risking everything to be with Marilyn in a motel room because he thought he was her one and only?'

'I buy that,' Ray said.

'Me too,' Kevin said. 'I think he was just dweeby enough to be hoodwinked that way.'

'Oh, give me a break,' Rosie said. 'You're thinking it was a real romance?'

'For him, anyway.'

'But why would he need to do that when he already had—' Rosie was still determined to get Nathan Gold back on the straight and narrow where he belonged.

'Because she seduced him, because that was her job,' I said, 'and I bet it wasn't all that hard. Think about it: a wife who wasn't really as resigned as she tried to believe she was about the damage this move had done to her career and her children. A mother-in-law who was just being a brick about sacrificing herself, every day? You think it was pure pleasure to go home to that every night? Add in a special needs child who was better off where he was before the move, and it's so achingly obvious that the only one who wants to be here is Nathan. So now, how much pressure is on him to come up with the super seed?'

'And there was Marilyn, being helpful, every day,' Kevin said. 'Awesome.'

'And not just helping, I bet,' Rosie said, getting into the game at last. 'Admiring, too.'

'Of course,' I said. 'Laying it on with a trowel.'

'OK,' Ray said. 'Say for the sake of argument we've got that half of the equation figured out right, who the fuck is the second man?'

'Ah, now there you have the interesting question.'

'You're assuming he's not just one of a horde?' Rosie said. 'She could have a large night-time clientele.'

'No,' Kevin said. 'You keep trying to make her into a street-walker, Rosie, and she isn't. Marilyn spends a lot of time taking care of herself. She doesn't look like rough trade at all.'

For a few seconds, Rosie looked as if she might be going to say, Well, Kevin, you would know. But then she got pulled in by the puzzle-solving, the part of her job she loves. She extended her right hand toward him, with the index finger extended like a teacher about to make a point, and said, 'You know . . .' And after a while she said, 'Now that I think of it, everything Francine told me about how Marilyn and her Thursday date behaved at that meeting in the hotel lobby . . . it sounded like he had the upper hand, didn't it?'

'Sure did,' I said. 'And wasn't one bit interested in being her one and only.'

'He's her something, though.' Rosie was growing the look Trudy gets sometimes when she's digging potatoes, like, *I know there's more down here somewhere.* She looked around at the three of us. 'What kind of a something, do you suppose?'

'Well, for at least the time when she's with him,' Ray said, 'it sounds to me like they both think he's her boss.'

'Uh-huh.' We were all staring at our shoes now, watching the scenario roll past our inward eyes. 'A boss you meet in a hotel lobby around noon on Thursdays. What kind of a business has that kind of a boss?'

'Shady business,' Ray said. With a little side-wise glance at Kevin, he added, 'Noontime follies for very sneaky guys.'

'Yeah,' Kevin said. 'Ordinarily I'd say sexy

business, but somehow this doesn't feel very sexy.'

'If I knew who he was,' Rosie said, 'I bet I could guess what he's up to.'

'Well, we could find that out fast enough,' Ray said. 'Bring in the Sofitel manager who pockets the registration.'

'Or just put Marilyn in the box and ask her what's up with her social life,' Kevin said. 'I read her as much too smart to go to jail to cover for a john.' His assurance faded suddenly and he added, 'Unless he's mafia?'

'In Rutherford? Not that I've heard,' I said. 'And if we do either one of those things, the game will stop. But with all this talk about Marilyn, we haven't had anybody do a background check on her, have we? Why don't we get Winnie to do a little digging there?'

'I can do that,' Ray said, 'right now.' He got up and stretched, and was just about to walk away toward his own office.

'Well, wait a minute,' Rosie said. She laid her index finger between her eyebrows and thought hard. 'Kevin, who's the man you're always groaning about at Minnaska? Because he's so dignified and overbearing?'

'All the suits there are like that,' Kevin said. 'Did I groan about one in particular? Let me think.'

'Yes, come on now, you did this more than once.' She drew her short body up into a mock-supercilious pose, lowered her voice and imitated Kevin's imitation. 'I am Mister So-and-so, more eminent than most persons.'

'Oh, that,' Kevin said. 'That was Alan Gordon.'

'Yes!' I said. 'Good for you, Rosie, that's just how he said it. Alan Gordon. The boss.'

They all stopped whatever they were doing, suddenly, and said at the same time, 'The *boss.*'

'Say that thing again, Ray,' Kevin said. 'What you said before about the way they behaved in the hotel.'

'I said they both seem to think he's her boss.'

'Francine said he was an elderly, well-dressed man twice Marilyn's age,' Rosie said. 'Does that describe Alan Gordon?'

'Yes,' Kevin said, and then, getting doubtful, 'and about a dozen other guys just in that building. To say nothing of—'

Rosie bounced with impatience. 'But I know a woman named Francine Proebe that's actually seen him. Can you get me a picture?' she asked Kevin.

'Of course I can.' He started to reach for a phone, then put his hand down and said, 'Well, but wait, we don't want him to know why we want it, do we? Let me think.' He consulted the ceiling light for a few seconds. Then he smacked his own forehead and said, 'Woodenhead! They've got a website.' He got on a keyboard and brought it up. And there, surrounded by verbiage praising the many virtues of Minnaska, was a handsome portrait of the boss, Alan Gordon.

'Print it,' Rosie said. Kevin did, and she grabbed it and trotted toward the stairs.

Thirteen

The three of us, excited by this new idea but somewhat disoriented by it too, spent what little remained of Thursday deciding what came next if Rosie came back with an ID of Gordon.

Kevin said, 'Somewhere back there before eleven other things happened, I was going over results from the grow-field research my detectives have been doing, hoping they brought me enough info so I could tell whether Nathan Gold was close enough to a viable product to tempt a thief. Turns out I don't know enough to decide, but can't we find somebody who can? Because if he really had something, you know, there's another motive for murder.'

'Sure,' I said. 'It's the quid pro quo Maggy Ross has been asking about. Why would that get *her* attacked, though? She raised some of the funding for the research, but she didn't own a share of the product.'

'I don't know. Add it to the list of questions. What's giving me fits is I think Dan Brennan is the best person to know if he's close enough to a super seed to cash in. He's also the one best qualified to know if anybody's been trying to steal the genetic code. But do we know we can trust him? Last I heard you two hadn't made up your minds about him.'

'To me he seems the most trustworthy person

I've talked to since we started this case,' Ray said. 'But maybe that's just his clothes. What do you think, Jake?'

'On the basis of his record, before I met him I kind of assumed he was a crook. But in person, when I talk to him, I'd trust him with my last nickel.'

'So yes and no? Guess I better not ask him, then.'

'Actually,' I said, 'I think those two research assistants are more familiar with the records than Dan is – they've been doing the day-to-day tracking. But I'm afraid if we ask questions of them they'll tell Marilyn everything we asked, so . . . maybe we should just tap the phone out there and see what shakes out.'

Ray asked me, 'Do we have enough people to monitor a wiretap, even if we could get a court order?'

'Maybe, if we all worked twenty-four/seven and didn't do anything else. Did you ask Winnie to start on the background for Marilyn?'

'Yeah. She said she's done with the Brennan checks so she can get on it right away.'

'OK. What's cooking tomorrow?'

'Ray said he was going to ride herd on his detectives' interviews, listen to what they were getting and decide where to go from there. And Bo's working on your idea, how the three firms that got second attacks line up together, if they do – I'll let you know about that.'

Then Winnie was in my doorway, carrying the little electronic tablet that seemed to be her magic portal to the universe. 'I can't get any interviews till ten o'clock tomorrow,' she said, 'so can we meet early – will that work for you?'

'Sure. Did you find anything worth talking about?'

'Oh, yes,' she said, and gave me her satisfied smile, Inscrutable #2. 'Dan Brennan is a most enterprising man. And I have one or two other things as well.'

Then we all did the final hustle to answer messages and send one last email. By the time Rosie came trotting up the stairs, we were all secretly hoping she would not get back before we left.

That feeling faded as soon as I saw her. She came panting into my office, gave me a radiant smile, and said, 'So now who's your Red Hot Mama? Huh?'

Everything changed in that moment. 'You mean it really is him? The Big Cahuna himself?'

'The eminent Mr Gordon, yes,' she said, grinning all over her face.

'Where's Ray?' I said. 'Grab Bo before he leaves the building, will you? I'll find Kevin.' The five of us huddled, mapping the new territory that surrounded us now that Alan Gordon was a suspect.

'Of what, though?' Rosie said. 'All we know he did was meet a woman.'

'Nathan Gold's woman,' I said. 'We don't know yet how it fits, but we know it has to fit somehow, don't we? Bo, we're going to have to change your assignment for tomorrow. Give your interviews to Clint and Abeo. We need you to be a spy tomorrow.'

'Oh, very well,' Bo said, pleased.

Looking at my crew, I felt a little lift. They had all been halfway out the door; two of them had keys in their hands. But now they all looked like well-tuned race cars, gunning their motors, waiting for the start of the race.

Winnie is just under five feet tall, weighs less than a hundred pounds and is so ridiculously cute that nobody took her seriously when she first applied to the department – she had to show killer grades on every test to even get considered. Fortunately, for Winnie that was not difficult. As for her size, the department was becoming more preoccupied with the problem of overweight applicants than the reverse. Also, there was a directive from the governor's office that police departments should be reaching out to women and minority populations to better reflect the population. So when the chief got a chance for a whip-smart Asian woman, he saw her as that year's two-fer.

When I first saw her in uniform I wanted to go right back to the station and beg the chief to put her someplace safe before some dirty bozo raped her.

She had a little trouble firing the Glock, at first, because her wrists were too soft and the cartridge stove-piped on the exit. But a little physical therapy fixed that, which she proved by saving my life while she was still a pup. Then all she had to overcome was the tendency of smart-ass barflies to say, when she came to break up a fight, something like, 'Is that a cop or a Christmas ornament?'

She had to use a little more mace than the average freshman cop, and deploy her Taser a couple of times, but she rarely needed help to answer the question. She grew fearless and fast on the street, and won the respect of her peers. Now, as an investigator, she was showing us she could be painstakingly methodical and accurate – a detective after Ray Bailey's heart. 'Sometimes I think I designed her,' he told me recently.

'Dan Brennan is forty-seven years of age,' Winnie said in my office Friday morning. She had her tablet open but delivered most of her report with just an occasional glance at the screen. 'He was born and grew up on a farm in Nebraska, in an area that produces mostly corn, wheat and hogs. He is the third of five siblings, the younger of two sons. Very fortunate family placement, by the way, which tends to produce optimistic, happy people. That seems to hold true for Daniel Brennan – friends and colleagues say he has a humorous, outgoing personality, and makes friends easily.'

'A born salesman,' I said.

'Hmm, yes – although he has never directly sold merchandise for a living. What he does is more like . . . he's a promoter, really.'

'Yeah. What else?'

'His father was not rich but seems to have been successful enough to give all his children good educations – two teachers, a doctor and a dentist besides Dan, who got a BS in Agribusiness from the University of Nebraska at Lincoln, and a Master's in agronomy from Ohio Christian

University in Circleville, Ohio.' She stopped and made a prim little throat-clearing noise. 'One of his sisters told me that Dan and his father both expected him to bring this education home to the family farm. But when the time came they discovered they couldn't work together. Dan had strong ideas of his own that didn't match his father's, so they would fight all the time. And the father wasn't ready to quit, so Dan, his sister says, lit out for the territories. Is that some quaint old American expression?'

'Pretty quaint.' I looked at my watch. 'Anything else on the family?'

'Just a little. Dan Brennan married his college sweetheart, Geraldine Riley, almost twenty-three years ago – their anniversary's coming up in November. They have two daughters, and lived in Lincoln, Nebraska, until he started that experimental farm outside Ames, Iowa a little over fifteen years ago. They took up residence on the farm sometime during the period when he established that first company, Hardiwheat.

'They sold the product but not the farm. Geraldine runs a quite successful organic vegetable business there, with a plot or two for the mystery crop Dan always seems to be raising, and she teaches third grade in a nearby suburb of the city.' She cleared her throat again. 'Mr Brennan is gone a good deal for business, but he is a devoted husband and father when he's home.'

'So he's just what he said he is: a hard-working scientist who develops and sells genetically altered seeds.'

'Yes.'

'I wonder why he didn't try out this new idea on the farm he already had.'

'I asked about that. It appears his wife has re-done the house to her satisfaction and was reluctant to turn it back into a dormitory and computer lab full of young, intense ag-freaks.' Winnie shrugged. 'That's what they call themselves.'

'OK. Is that it for Brennan?'

'For his home life, yes. I did turn up one piece of information concerning his living arrangements here.'

'Well, now. I hadn't even thought to ask you for that. Is Brennan doing some of the naughty too?'

'No. But since he's here so much now, he rents a double-wide in one of the new mobile home parks that are springing up out there on the west side.'

'So?'

'So apparently Nathan Gold has had a key to it from the very beginning. He looked after the place whenever Mr Brennan was out of town for extended periods. But this time, while Brennan was in Alaska, Doctor Gold has been living there.'

'What? Why would he— Oh.'

'Apparently there was a domestic . . . um . . . kerfuffle? . . . in the Gold household about two weeks ago. The manager of the park was very clear – she had dates noted. Doctor Gold came to her and declared his intention to stay there for some time – he wasn't sure how long, apparently. But he wanted her to know he was there, that

Mr Brennan knew he was there, and if there was any extra charge he would pay it.'

'So it was all on the up-and-up except kind of . . . temporary.'

'That sounds about right. She said all she saw him bring in was a few clothes and a bag of books.'

'Like when a couple has had one hell of a fight, maybe, and they're not exactly sure what the next moves are. But the Mrs wants him out of the house, and besides being sexy and beloved he's also a scholarly type so he can't go sleep in a strange place without any books.'

'You didn't like him, huh?'

'I've never met him. But I'm beginning to think he was one weird duck.'

Winnie had to run then, to her first appointment with a Holy Messenger. I sat on alone and unoccupied for a few minutes, thinking about the fact that Nathan Gold did not get up at home on the morning of his death, which meant that Naomi Gold and her mother, those two gracious ladies so deeply admired by my staff, had recently fed us a big heap of stinking lies. Why?

It also meant that Naomi had not had easy access to the back of Nathan's arm that morning – so her opportunity score was greatly reduced. But it answered the question: *Did she know about the affair?* Oh, yeah, baby, she knew. So take that red line indicating motive and extend it right to the top.

I placed the two phone calls I unquestionably needed to make, one each to Dan Brennan and Naomi Gold. Brennan's office manager told me, in her cheery way, that Mr Brennan was 'running in and out,' this morning, and she would give him my message without fail the next time he ran in. Naomi Gold's answering tape extended the same invitation.

I was hot to share my discovery of the revised life of our murder victim, but I knew Ray was spending his whole day supervising and monitoring the conversations with the break-in troupe, and Kevin was deep in conversation with his detectives. If I succeeded in getting either Brennan or Gold into my office, I would call them; otherwise, my job description says I expedite. Nowhere does it suggest I interrupt people who are usefully employed. I did put a message on Rosie's phone, and shared the latest information about the Gold family when she answered it. Her next appointment was at the door, so she had no time to discuss the news. 'I'm too shocked to talk anyway,' she said. 'That whole business about losing things was a rotten lie, wasn't it?'

I said, 'Life's a bitch, isn't it?'

But that was all the talk we had time for. To make the time pass while I stayed out of everybody's hair, I applied myself to some of the routine chores I normally procrastinate about. Frank remarked at the end of that October that he had not had to nag me for the OSHA report, the training requests or the vacation schedule for the next quarter, and he hoped that new leaf was going to stay turned over. I did all those reports on that lonely morning while I sat in my office listening to the soft buzz of conversations all around me.

One after another, the normally law-abiding citizens who had banded together to break the law came in to tell my detectives about the week when they had decided they had to do it. How they had seen that the world was headed for disaster and had to change. And since nobody else was tipping over the bus, occupying the square, they had decided that they had to be the ones to start the revolution – right here, right now.

They all behaved perfectly that day. No shots were fired. Frank heard no sobbing down the hall. There were no loud shouts of anger; I never even heard anybody swear. The investigative division hummed with civilized talk, interrupted from time to time by the sounds of people coming and going up and down the tall staircase.

At a quarter to twelve, Naomi Gold called. I told her I had new information pertinent to her husband's death and needed to discuss it most urgently. She said 'Oh?' the way people do who both do and do not want to hear your news, but she agreed to cancel a couple of appointments and be in my office by three. As soon as I put the phone down it rang; Dan Brennan had 'rung in.'

I said, 'I need to see you.'

'I can come right now,' he said. 'Is now good?'

'Make it one o'clock.'

Ray's door opened two minutes later and I heard him tell somebody, 'Nice work.' Then footsteps sounded in the hall. I closed out my email and pulled up the case notes I'd written after

Winnie left. When Ray stood in my doorway with Bo beside him, I said, 'Come in,' and got ready to tell them we'd probably eliminated one suspect.

But I didn't get to do that until much later. Because Ray said, 'Bo just turned up some juicy stuff on Alan Gordon.'

'I figured you must be about due for the noontime follies,' Bo said. 'So I stopped and got myself a sub.' He unwrapped it and opened his long notebook to the page he had marked. The break room was full of noisy street cops that day, so the four of us ate lunch at my desk while Bo delivered the Gordon report. Kevin was there too, a little reluctantly – he hated carry-out. But this case had drawn People Crimes and Property Crimes closer together, and I wanted to encourage that trend, so I insisted he join us.

'Ray said he thought the first place to look for answers about Alan Gordon would be his company,' Bo said. 'I'm not a gardener, I've never paid much attention to Minnaska and I don't use their products. So to get started from nowhere, I looked up the corporate structure first. Turns out Minnaska's just part, a small part actually, of a huge holding company controlled by the Gordon family.'

'I looked at that too,' Kevin said. 'Isn't it sweet at the start? Like one of those Horatio Alger stories.'

'Yeah, all that American Dream stuff,' Bo said. 'Alan Gordon's grandfather Amos started the company, selling farm implements in Iowa.

There's a short biography of Amos on the company website. It doesn't need to be long because all he ever did was work. He built up a chain of farm implement stores, then he added feed and seed and then a grocery chain.'

'Busy Grandpa,' I said.

'People from olden times, don't they make you feel lazy? Amos and his wife had ten children, too. About the time Alan's father joined the firm they formed a construction company and began to build roads. And then they got into financing. From there it really took off because with financing, I'm told, you begin to control the competition, too. By this time Alan's father had two brothers and several cousins in the business, and since then it's traditional that all the Gordon men and now some of the women work in what they call "the company."'

'Maybe we should have them running the country.'

'Maybe they have that in mind – a couple of them have gone into politics. Gorfax – that's the name of the holding corporation – has companies all over the world now. Alan's brother Eliot is president of the board, his cousin Blaine is CEO, and there are more Gordons wherever you look at the top.

'So I started wondering, what's Alan doing out here running the little seed and fertilizer plant? I know it seems big to us, but Minnaska's not one of their bigger companies.

'I decided to work up some background for Alan, tried schools first and hit the jackpot. Alan Gordon's brothers all went to Choate. Alan started out there too – and went on to a whole string of the best prep schools in the country: Groton, Lawrenceville, Phillips Exeter. One right after the other. He had no trouble getting in because his family was very rich and he always seems to have pulled good grades. He was never expelled from any of them, just "resigned," or transferred to the next place for "a better mix of courses."

'I was having fun by then because I smelled a cover-up. I thought about the times – Gordon is fifty-nine. People had more rigid attitudes about sex back then. But I couldn't find a whiff. I decided I needed to find an insider, so I called and made an appointment with one of those attorneys I noticed on the day of the shooting.'

'You did? All I remember from that day is milling groups of fast talkers.'

'Yeah, but remember how the lawyers all clustered around you, and the scientists around Abeo? But I noticed this one youngish guy in a suit, in the crowd around Abeo, just listening. And I thought, "There's one who's more interested in learning something than getting noticed," so I asked somebody his name. James Fielding, they told me, and for some reason I wrote it down. Yesterday I looked up his name and called him.

'Doctor Fielding has the usual string of degrees from classy universities – you can see them in the case file. He's an attorney specializing in' – Bo was reading from his notes now – 'the laws and policies that govern gene modification and therapy.' Something I never even heard of till this case came along, and they're writing laws about it already. So a lot of Fielding's degrees are in science – botany and biochemistry.

'Whatever you think of Minnaska – one of the things I found out is there are plenty of people out there who think that company is dangerous and should be shut down – in my opinion Jim Fielding is the real deal, up to a point.'

'Up to what point?'

'Whatever Minnaska wants, Minnaska gets. Fielding's got skin in the game like everybody else over there.'

'But you think he's basically honest?'

'Just as much as he possibly can be. But I gotta tell you,' Bo said, looking a little stressed, 'a lot of the time I didn't know what the hell he was talking about.'

'Don't worry about it,' I said. 'As long as you get the overview, we don't need every little detail.' Bo Dooley, who has faced down some of the craziest drug-fueled murderers on the continent and never blinked, was getting anxiety twitches over his inability to follow academic jargon. I wanted to reassure him, but anxiety is kind of Bo's native land; he's a hard man to comfort.

'Here's an example of the things he says.' Bo read from his notes, '"I suspect that we're on the verge of a second Cambrian explosion, but this one is going to be human-caused."' He looked at Ray and me. 'What the fuck is a Cambrian explosion?'

'Something about diversification of species, I think. But really, you don't have to—'

'Bo,' Ray said, 'get to the part about Alan Gordon.'

'OK.' He flipped to the second page. 'When I asked Jim why Alan was out here in Minnesota instead of at headquarters with the rest of the tribe, he asked me why the Rutherford police needed to know that. So I told him about Doctor Gold, the dead scientist at SmartSeeds, and the clandestine meetings Alan Gordon was having in the hotel lobby with Nathan Gold's fancy playmate. He thought about that for a minute and decided I should talk to a man named Ira Newman, who's the family power broker. Or enabler, or – what's that Italian word?'

'*Consigliere*?'

'Yeah, that. Like in *The Godfather.* Jim said, "But he won't talk to you unless I do a little explaining first, you understand?" So then he put in a call to this Ira guy. Some of the rituals in this company kind of remind me of the way drug gangs operate – everything so hush-hush, you gotta know the right words to say and the right guy to ask or the whole outfit disappears into the mountains for a while. Makes you wonder what the fuck is Minnaska hiding?'

'Sounds like we might have to find out before we're done,' I said.

'Please say you don't mean that,' Ray said, his face like a Bailey family picnic. 'Bo, will you please just go ahead and spill the beans on Alan Gordon?'

'All right. But you understand I never did get to talk to Ira. I had to wait in the anteroom to Jim Fielding's office for fifteen minutes while he held the quietest possible conversation with the big cheese. Fielding's secretary is nervous and determined to please, so I said no thanks to offers for tea, coffee or water about ten times before he opened the door and said we should talk now. By the way, he sent her out for a two-hour lunch while we talked.'

'Jesus,' I said. 'What does Alan do – eat babies?'

'No,' Bo said. 'It's much less serious than that, but I suppose that's why they consider it so humiliating. He's a thief.'

'A what? Bo, he's rich beyond my wildest dreams. Why would he—'

'I'm sorry, I didn't say it right,' Bo said. 'He's a kleptomaniac.' He consulted his notes. 'Here's how Jim explained it to me: it's an urge to steal that has nothing to do with need. A response to some other anxiety or imagined slight, he said.'

'That sounds like a very expensive diagnosis.'

'Probably so. Jim says he's been to a bunch of doctors. And some really helped, evidently, because the' – he consulted his notes – 'the dysfunction went into remission for long periods.' Bo allowed himself a smile. 'See, if you got enough money to throw at it, even swiping the prize money at Scout Camp can be buffed up till it sounds kind of dignified.'

'I see that,' I said, 'and I'm impressed.'

'Yeah, well, you should be, because this family has had to spread a lot of dignity over a long list of infractions. That's the other thing to understand: enough money can make a shameful crime into an infraction.

'All his life, the story goes, Alan Gordon has belonged to a large, active family with the means to get anything they wanted. Except what Alan always wanted was the respect and admiration of his father, and he could never get that because all of his brothers were brighter and more aggressive than he was, so his father liked them more.'

'Any minute I'm going to cry,' Ray said.

'Better take notes, Ray, because this is the company line. They spent a lot of time and money building this story, and anybody they share it with is expected to repeat it verbatim. That was made very clear to me as we went along.'

'I can believe it,' I said. 'Remember the Russian bigwig and the ring he couldn't resist? Several people saw him take it, but when they mentioned it he just ridiculed them. The most perfect crime of all – heist your ring and insult your jewelers at the same time.'

Ray said, 'Did the wise, dignified enabler suggest what Alan might be trying to steal this time?'

'Well, no, of course not. Nobody in charge at Minnaska is going to admit to being anything but the victimized bystander here, the patient fellow who has to pick up the pieces after this family calamity.'

'But you don't quite buy that?'

'Well, being the cynical old narc that I am, it did occur to me to wonder whether Alan might be the cat's-paw – the one they send out to find occasional shortcuts like stealing a piece of genetic code from a slick little company that got to home base ahead of them. I mean, this explanation is pretty convenient, isn't it? If he screws up the assignment they can hang the whole thing on his tormented childhood and he can go back in therapy for a while.'

'Kind of like disappearing into those mountains you were talking about.'

'A little like that, yeah. Be hard to prove, though.'

'One more thing we can't prove. At least we're consistent.'

'You're starting to sound like a crybaby,' Ray said. 'You know, before I came to homicide I chased thieves for almost twenty years. I'm proud to say I caught quite a few of them. But if this guy is a real kleptomaniac – clinically proven, as they say – he'll be the first one I ever met. That I know about. Maybe I should go talk to some of those apes I put in the slammer, ask them about their urges.' Suddenly overtaken by the humor of that idea, he doubled up in laughter, emerged after ten seconds to say, 'Can't you just imagine some of the answers I'd get?' and went back into paroxysms of helpless hilarity.

'Now here's a sight worth all the trouble it cost us to see it,' Kevin said, pleased. 'Ray Bailey going apeshit over his own joke.'

Ray snapped out of it then, rubbed his face and went back to looking into the corner where he always seemed to think more information might be hiding. 'Is there any reason,' he said, 'why a kleptomaniac can't be a murderer?'

'Not that I know of,' I said, 'but if Alan Gordon

is the killer, does that mean he was behind the other two attacks? The Holy Messengers keep saying they didn't do any of that; maybe we should start to believe them.'

Ray frowned. 'Why would Alan Gordon wreck Maggy Ross's chair?'

'Or shoot his own Cadillac?' Bo said. 'In fact, how could he, since he was right there in the building when it happened?'

'He couldn't. Should we detach the second set of attacks from the murder?'

'How can you,' Kevin said, 'when the murder was one of the set?'

'Take it out and make it stand alone. What do we have left?'

'Two attacks that make no sense at all, except as additional scare tactics by the Holy Messengers.'

'But isn't it odd,' I said, 'that while they will gladly tell us all about why and how they made the first fourteen attacks, they all consistently deny doing the last three?'

'Sure it's odd,' Ray said. 'Zealots are always odd. Crazy ranting bastards can't see past the ends of their own noses, always think they know better than everybody else . . . What?'

'You're ranting,' I said. 'And it's almost one o'clock.'

'What happens at one?' Kevin said. 'We turn into pumpkins?'

'Dan Brennan is coming in. Come on, help me clean this mess up and I'll tell you what we're going to talk about.'

Fourteen

Brennan looked surprised to see so many detectives waiting in my office. Bo, since he'd been assigned to spying, didn't have any appointments today, so I suggested he stay, along with Kevin and Ray. The meeting I kept announcing seemed to recede whenever we approached it, so maybe, I decided, we should try a piecemeal approach to climbing this mountain of evidence.

As soon as Brennan sat down I asked him, 'Why didn't you tell us that Nathan Gold had been living in your mobile home?'

He blinked at me while he considered being offended. Then, being the born diplomat he was, he softened his stance to dignified and kindly. 'I never supposed that was any of your business, I guess. Obviously the Golds were going through a difficult period—'

'Especially difficult for him. At the end of it he was dead.'

'I mean before that. They were having some major upheaval in the marriage. Which happens to the best of us, as we know. I thought they had a right to work it out in private, so when he asked me to tell no one, I complied. Then I got the phone call – was it from one of you?'

'From me,' Ray said.

'I'll always remember how compassionate you were on that call,' Brennan said, and Ray actually blushed with pleasure. Dan Brennan was as good as they come at adding the little strokes that got people eating out of his hand.

'But right away I thought about Naomi,' he said. 'She'd be getting the notification too – probably had it already – and if word got out, there lay her beautiful life in ruins, for everybody to pick over. And while she's not a public person, they still had a wide circle of acquaintances between the two of them, and it just seemed to me that everything that's always hard about a death in the family would be that much harder if that last quarrel became public. It was certainly an aberration that would have been resolved if he had lived – you see what I mean?'

We all nodded, our grave faces going up and down together.

'So I put in a call to Naomi, and to my surprise I got right through. I was standing in a kind of mudroom, unheated, next to a hut – God, it was cold, my nose kept running, and I didn't have any tissues so I had to start sniffling. I suppose she thought I was weeping. Well, I almost was. And freezing, so I kept it short. I just said, "Naomi, your children, his family, they don't have to know about this little spat you've been having. Why don't we just keep it to ourselves that he slept at my place that last night?"'

'It was quite a bit more than just the last night,' I said. 'Two weeks, at least.'

'All right, but a little bit of . . . wiggle room, you know, to make everything easier – she's going to have to live with this for the rest of her life. Why not put as mild a face on it as possible?'

'Maybe that helps her but it doesn't help us. Lying to the police is not just a polite little convenience, it's a crime. And it wasn't any little spat they've been having. He's been sleeping with your office manager. Did you know that?'

'He what? *He whaaaat?*' He really hadn't known. We see a lot of reactions in this building, and I've been fooled by some tricky ones, but nobody's good enough to show the utter dismay Dan Brennan had on his face then. He turned sideways in his chair and did a sort of Ray Bailey turn with his lips moving silently, dialoging with the corner. He was trying to absorb the appalling news that Nathan Gold, his ideal man, the paradigm of goodness, had been doing the nasty with the help.

Brennan was a small but effective operator in the field of dreams that is twenty-first-century science. He thought of himself as a sophisticate in global commerce, a true citizen of the world. His number two man had pricked his bubble, big time. When he turned back, he was older and sadder. 'No, Captain,' he said. 'I didn't know that, and I'm very sorry to hear you say it. You're sure?'

'Yes.' I wanted to tell him this was a homicide investigation now, so he'd understand the seriousness of leading us down the primrose path. But I had begged Pokey for the favor of a delay, so I couldn't.

'Will you answer one question?' I asked him. 'Did Nathan Gold achieve significant results before he died? Are you going to go on with his work here?'

'That's two questions, Captain,' he said, 'and the answers are yes and no, in that order.

'In science, you know' – I could almost feel the pointer coming out, the strategic pauses being marshalled – 'it's not just about some wonderful result you got once. It's about whether you've reached an endpoint that you can reproduce over and over, reliably, every time. Nate has definitely built a Smarty, a basic . . . I don't want to name it, understand? . . . Let's say *tweak*, that he was able to insert into three different grains and get spectacular growth results, not just once but several times, in the fields and in the greenhouse. He didn't start from scratch here, you know – this was the proving ground for ideas he'd been tinkering with for years. He just never had anybody who'd furnish him with the support system he needed to really make it work. Given another year, I'm convinced he'd have had it nailed so solid there would have been no question. We were both just on fire when we talked; we knew we were close to the breakthrough, big money.'

He hunched his shoulders, squinted and shuffled his feet. 'But he didn't get that year. And I . . .' His sigh was probably windier than it would have been if he'd been telling me this story about the Smarty before I told him mine about the office manager. 'I'm a little too long in the tooth to go looking for another boy genius to put the finish on this. And I'm running out of money. So, to answer your second question, no, SmartSeeds will not be continuing Doctor Gold's work in this location. In fact, the whole concept has just been sold to Minnaska.'

'Oh, it has? You sold the Smarty?' My detectives and I were looking at each other, wall-eyed. 'This happened pretty fast, huh?'

'We've been talking for a while. I contacted their head office – not the fellow here, he's just a flunky – but the place in New York as soon as I saw how much good work Nate had done since I'd been in Alaska. And saw how complex it was, which killed any notions I had about finishing it myself.' He made a self-denigrating face that I liked a lot. 'I only got the final offer today,' he said. His chuckle, which he tried to make mature and ironic, actually sounded a little giddy. 'The contracts are being FedEx'd as we speak.'

'You're satisfied with the amount, I take it.'

A quiet smile and nod; he was getting comfortable with success again. 'Naomi will be very well compensated for the professional interruption this move has cost her. It's terrible about her loss of Nathan, but now I don't know how to feel about that. Will the puzzle of his death ever be solved, do you think?'

'We certainly hope so. We have no intention of giving up on the investigation.'

'Oh, of course not.' He held his hands out at arm's length, like a man measuring yarn. 'Anything else you need me for here? As you can imagine, I have some things to do.'

'I suppose – a lot of packing?'

'Well, no – the big computers, and all the software, that can stay right where it is and Minnaska can decide when and where they want to move it. For me, it's just some personal items and correspondence – but *a ton* of phoning and emailing to fold everything up. Even so, I can be out of there in a week or so.'

'You're going back to Iowa?'

'Oh, you know about the farm? You people do your homework, don't you? Well, I like it when you're watching someone else, so – there's a lot more stuff of Nate's, and of course Naomi hasn't had time to even . . . I had Marilyn making lists for her, but now that you've told me . . . I'd better get her out of there right away, I think. Dear me, what a muddle.'

He got up, ready to shake my hand. Everybody else got up too, but then I said, 'Mr Brennan, there's something I'd like to do for you – really for my peace of mind.' I described the electronic alarm system I wanted to install in the kneehole of his desk at SmartSeeds. 'It's like a door alarm system, but even simpler. They'll show you when they get it installed – you just push the button if you want some help.'

'You think I'm in danger still? Even though I've sold the Smarty?'

'You just pointed out we haven't solved the riddle of Nate's death. Till we do, humor me, will you?

'Well, sure. When will they, uh—'

'This afternoon.' I had a crew standing by, and I'd been prepared to insist if he balked. We'd been setting up suspects for two days and then crossing them off the list. As the list grew shorter, I felt as if I were standing next to a downed wire that was about to go live – I could almost hear it sizzle.

When Brennan was gone, and while I waited

for Naomi, we talked. Ray would alert Dispatch about the alarm system we were installing, to make sure there were SWAT team members on standby all weekend. And all members of the People Crimes section – plus Kevin, who said, 'I've got skin in this game too, come on' – would keep their cell phones turned on and fastened to their bodies this weekend. We all agreed we had no idea what was going to happen next.

Then the reception desk announced Naomi and everybody scattered. Ray found Rosie and sent her to my office. She knew this woman best, and I was looking for help – I didn't think I could quite fathom the mix of emotions that must be churning through Naomi's brain right now.

I only had a minute to review with Rosie – did she remember about the sleepovers at Brennan's trailer, which meant Naomi had been lying about what Nate did on that last morning of his life?

'How could I forget that?' she said, scowling, and then Naomi was at the door. She sat down in front of my desk, where Rosie, after momentary dithering, had chosen to sit in the chair next to her rather than behind the desk with me.

'My mother wanted to come too,' Naomi said. 'But the children are still out of school, and none of the rest of the family's here yet. Nate's parents, I think, will arrive tomorrow. I don't know if that's going to help, though, or . . . They're very distressed – they sound all broken up.'

'We all feel great sympathy for your situation,

Doctor,' I said. 'But at the risk of being tactless I have to clear something up now, so that we can talk openly about this whole situation.'

She was beginning to give me the look you give the dentist when he says, 'This might sting a little.' It wasn't going to get any easier, so I plunged ahead.

'We know you were lying to us about the morning of your husband's death. We know he'd been living at Dan Brennan's trailer for a couple of weeks. And,' I took a breath, 'we know about the room at the Red Roof Motel.'

'Ah.' She took a breath. We waited. 'Such a quaint little hideaway,' she finally said. Her jaws looked as if they might be going to lock up. 'I suppose you can understand why I didn't want my children to know.'

'Of course, and I understand your wanting to spare his parents,' I said, 'and Rosie and I want to assure you there will be no leaks from this department.'

'I'm glad your mother doesn't really think she's getting Alzheimer's,' Rosie ventured.

Naomi turned to her with her face all changed, to human softness – almost smiling. 'She felt so bad about lying to you after you had shown her so much kindness.' She bent toward Rosie and said, 'I have to tell you, though, she got a little kick out of it after you were gone. She said, "I actually made her believe me, didn't I? I never would have thought I could do that."'

'Most of the people who lie to us are ridiculously obvious,' Rosie said. 'She should be proud of herself.'

'OK, good, everybody's pleased,' I said. 'But there are some things we need to get straight with you now.'

'Looks like you're pretty good at getting the facts straight,' Naomi said, her voice like foot-steps through dry leaves. 'Go ahead.'

'So far as you know, was your husband in fear of his life?'

'No. Absolutely not. Well,' the trademark rueful smile showed for a second, 'only from me for a couple of days after I found that motel receipt.'

'You were plenty mad, huh?'

'I don't think I ever fully understood what "enraged" means till that day. And everything he didn't do made it worse! He didn't apologize, except for being stupid enough to let me find that receipt. Even that I wasn't sure was entirely an accident. There was a corner of him that wanted me to know – because he wanted to be free! He wasn't begging me to take him back, that was the unforgiveable part. This wasn't just a whim with Nate – he wasn't given to whims. Nate was in love.'

'Oh, shit,' Rosie said. Then looked at us both apologetically – it had popped out of her because she understood totally, now, because of Bo, how she would feel. 'After all you gave up,' she said. 'That must have hurt.'

'Tell me about it,' Naomi said.

'But back to the question, now,' I said. 'You never saw any signs he was worried about his safety? He never said anything about somebody having it in for him, or stalking him?'

'Never. Why would anyone?'

'Well, he was developing genetically modified seeds. We understand there were some rather high values attached—'

'Oh, fiddlesticks. These dreamers and schemers – they're like people who're always sure they're going to win the lottery. Once in a blue moon maybe.' She pushed her hair back and gave the devil his due. 'Admittedly in Nate's case the likelihood was a good deal stronger because he was capable of very superior work. And I will realize a handy chunk of change soon, but it won't even equal what this disastrous move has cost me – and that's just the money. I may never get back to where I was professionally.'

'But what about . . . I don't want to alarm you unnecessarily, but we are concerned, since we haven't unraveled this puzzle yet . . . You haven't seen anything going on around you that should make the Gold family feel insecure?'

'Certainly not,' she said. 'The Gold family is a nest of obscure scholars and harmless scribblers. I'm the most down-to-earth one of the lot. Even Nate, who we all thought was our star – if this product had been brought to fruition and broken out of the pack, maybe, he might have enjoyed a moment of prominence, gotten a Nobel or something. But it looks like it's going to earn some dollars and then fold itself quietly into a larger effort.' She took a deep breath, and the essential Naomi Gold, the doctor who saved what could be saved, faced me squarely and said, 'I ask again, Captain, how soon can we have Nate's body?'

'Naomi,' I said, 'when the coroner releases it,

you will be the first to know.' I looked at her, sitting there so reasonable and capable, and wondered if she was capable of murder. I decided, not for the first time, that if the stars line up just right, we all are. It was hard to see when she could have got a shot of insulin into him that last morning, though. We'd keep her on the list, but lower down.

Naomi walked out with her head high, and I sat for a minute listening to the sounds of the dying day. The last of the interviewees had clattered down the stairs, and the buzz of talk was replaced by the soft clacking of computer keys. After what felt like the longest Friday in history, we were checking out.

'Have a nice weekend, guys,' Kevin said. 'Unless the buzzer goes off and Dispatch calls us all.'

'Oh, if Dispatch calls,' I said, 'we'll have a helluva weekend.'

Three minutes later, I turned away from my desk with the keys in my hand and stopped in my tracks. Marilyn DiSilvio was standing in my doorway. She was wearing the same skirt I'd seen before, or one just like it, but this time the top was a soft blue cashmere sweater that clung to her as if it knew it had finally found the one right place in the universe to be.

'I just got fired,' she said. 'I get to go back in on Monday and pack up my stuff. But just now as I was driving by I thought, I bet that nice Jake Hines would like to ask me some questions.'

'I am curious about one or two things,' I said. 'Would you like to come in and sit down?'

'Right here is fine,' she said. 'You're not going to Mirandize me, are you?

'Only if you killed Nathan Gold,' I said. 'But I don't believe you did.'

'No. I had no motivation to do anything like that.'

'And apparently not enough to do what I thought you were doing, which was stealing the Smarty.'

Today's smile was one I'd never seen before – all the sweetness replaced by irony. 'Industrial spies these days are pretty much gone, Jake, like shade tree mechanics. The science has gotten too complicated for that.'

'So you what, just transmit enough information to help the big rich company decide when to buy?'

'Well, probably I shouldn't tell you everything I know, but let's just say you're somewhere in the ball park. Funny thing, though – Dan Brennan isn't the least bit grateful.'

'Well, gratitude – it's not something you can count on, is it? I believe Naomi Gold feels that Nathan came up short in that department, too.'

'Boy, she really called that one right. I see you have your keys in your hand so I'd better let you go. I really just came up to say good-bye and good luck, Captain Hines. I'm sorry there wasn't time to get better acquainted.'

I knew she thought she left me on fire with unrequited lust, thinking, *That Marilyn, such a woman.*

Actually, she gave me chills all the way to the bone – I jogged to my pickup and turned on the heat.

Fifteen

Dispatch didn't call – nobody called. Trudy's Mom came by early Saturday and took Ben away with her to the Farmer's Market in Mirium for four hours. While he was gone we cleaned the last weeds and cornstalks out of the garden and bedded it down for winter under the ripest compost in the bins. We used the excuse of how bad we smelled after that job to hop in the shower together, with the usual result. When Ella brought Ben back gurgling and crowing in a heap of fresh vegetables, we had just finished changing the bed and Ben had learned to say carrot (Kay-*rut*!).

Ella brought Trudy up to date with every scrap of gossip she'd heard in Mirium while the two of them fixed a huge lunch of Trudy's bean soup and piles of Ella's veggies. Then it was nap time; Ella went home for hers, Ben went into his crib and Trudy and I awarded ourselves a reading break. In my house, that means get comfortable on a favorite couch with a book, preferably a paperback, so it won't hurt your face when you fall asleep and drop it.

The whole weekend went like that, a country idyll. We spent a lot of time outside in perfect weather, sometimes letting Ben run free and then chasing him through the bright leaves drifting to earth all around us. I ventured one quick garbage run to town late Saturday, making sure my cell phone was turned on and clipped to my belt. Trudy did a grocery run early Sunday, while Ben and I stayed home and did manly things like fix a hinge on the pasture gate and drink a bottle of Imperial Pilsner, my latest guilty pleasure. Actually he had milk and a cookie while he watched me drink the ale that Trudy keeps suggesting I might like to give up if I don't want to keep adding three or four pounds a year to my fine brown frame.

By Sunday night I was so blissed out I had to think hard to remember what I had been so anxious about on Friday.

Monday morning it came droning back in all its tiresome complexity as I drove to work. Face it, I told myself, Dispatch didn't call because now that Nathan Gold is gone there's nothing going on out there. Marilyn can pack up her notebooks and go wherever she goes to rest between jobs. Dan Brennan will make a thousand phone calls, leave Nathan's algorithms for the next clever scientist and go back to Iowa with his new pile of money. Minnaska will no doubt recall Alan Gordon and, as for Naomi Gold, will anybody in this community have anything but kind words to offer when she decides to go back where she came from and rebuild her shattered life?

And sure, the planes fly both ways; if I find enough evidence I can always get any one of them back. But my best chance of getting the goods on this murderer has been here, while we're all together and the chances of goading a killer into a misstep are best. Instead of which, I reflected, me and my keen-eyed investigators are sitting on our tushies, waiting for some magical bot to do our job.

It wasn't true – we'd all been working hard. But it all felt so futile! I wanted to take control of this investigation, shake it up. I grew a red-hot mental picture of me putting Alan Gordon in the box, taunting him about his meetings with Marilyn. What a pleasure to yell rude questions at the bespoke suit – *How's it going with the pretty prossie, you getting your ashes hauled all right?* In his whole life, he'd probably never been spoken to like that. Maybe he'd get so mad he'd tell me the truth, for once. That's what I was longing for – somebody to emerge out of this fog bank of facts we'd been drifting in for weeks and say a simple truth in plain English. *Yes, I did it and here's why, dammit.*

By the time I'd opened my email, though, the reality of life inside a bureaucracy had reasserted itself. Many people had, as Bo had said, skin in the game confronting us, and the job of my agency was to see they were all protected in a just and courteous way until they gave us reason to get rougher. Also, I had dreamed up the buzzer idea, cleared it with the chief and begged tech support to get it installed right away. I couldn't very well disclaim it now without even a week's trial.

Besides which, we were finally going to have the big meeting I had announced so many times. I'd called Ray and Kevin at home late yesterday, to assure them it was on and they should remind their detectives to be in the big meeting room at ten o'clock. And first thing this morning I called Dispatch and modified the order for a simultaneous ring for all my People Crimes detectives, in case the buzzer rang at SmartSeeds.

It was Henderson on the Dispatch desk that day, and he didn't waste words. 'I hope this isn't going to become standard practice, all this multiple-phone crap. What's it all about, anyway?'

'It was just for this one weekend, Scot. Because we thought there was a window of vulnerability out there. Keep me on your alert list when you go back to standard procedure, will you? If that buzzer rings, two squads go out there and I get called, OK?'

'OK. All this special-order stuff though, Jake – we're busy over here; we can't keep babysitting everybody like this.'

Somehow, angrily half-listening to Henderson's bitching, all by myself on my way to work, I got one new idea – why don't we find out if any of our suspects is diabetic? It was so obvious that as soon as I thought of it I winced with embarrassment. I had been hopelessly focused on trying to figure out how Naomi could have got that shot into her husband's arm when he wasn't even in her house. Suddenly, it was ridiculously obvious that a diabetic person would have a hypodermic needle full of insulin handy. And if he/she had a grudge for some reason . . . nobody on my crew seemed to have thought of it either.

But it was there in my head now, so as soon

as I got upstairs I found Winnie and together we made up the list: Marilyn; Naomi; her mother (I could hear Rosie going *What?* and I pushed back with *Why not?*); Dan Brennan; Alan Gordon; every one of the Holy Messengers; and when I got to Brad Polk I said, yeah, and all the other Aardvark engineers while we're at it; and finally, just to prove I was playing fair, I guess, I added Mark Hoving and Lois Phelps.

Winnie asked me, 'You want me to come to the big meeting or keep working on this?'

'Uh . . . you're pretty much up to speed on everything we've been doing. Better keep going on this.' She nodded, looking as if I'd just given her a nice present.

It was a noisy meeting, chairs scattered around the big table, a lot of coffee cups and talking at first. I found a gavel and banged it, demanded order and got some for a few minutes while we reviewed the first stage of this case – finding the body. Clint described the scene at SmartSeeds, the young architect who found the dead man, the older one who came to help, and then the return of Marilyn, the office manager, and her distress when she learned her employer had died.

'Now,' I said, 'I think we'll skip forward a few days here because I want to let you all understand—'

A hand was raised. One of Kevin's detectives said, 'Can't we go through it all the way in real time first? That's what I thought this meeting was for, to get a timeline.'

An argument broke out behind him; somebody

said, 'He's giving it to us in the order of importance, numb-nuts.'

My phone rang.

An outcry rose up from the Property Crimes crew. 'Hey, phones off, isn't that the rule?' Usually it is, for the short time that we assemble one or the other side of my crew for a quick briefing. Today was different, and I didn't have time to explain why.

I grabbed my phone and said, 'Hines.'

'I just sent two squads to SmartSeeds,' Henderson said. 'So here's your notice, OK?'

'Yep. And start assembling the SWAT team, will you? I'll let you know if we're going to need it when I get out there.' I met Ray's eyes and nodded toward the door. I bent toward Kevin on my other side, handed him my list and the gavel, and said, 'Take over.' I walked briskly as far as the meeting room door and ran the rest of the way.

We took my pickup because it corners better than Ray's department car. We monitored traffic on the radio on the way – a lot of fast chatter about a stand-off.

My phone rang. I punched the button on my steering wheel so I could take it on speakerphone. It was Winnie, saying, 'I got a hit on one of those names you gave me, Jake.'

'Winnie,' I said, 'I can't talk now, I'm on my way out to SmartSeeds, they've got—'

'I know; that's why I called you. It's one of those Aardvark architects that found Doctor Gold's body. Uh, the young one, Travis Diebencorn.'

'Thanks, Winnie. Good work.'

Ray said, 'Shit. Why didn't we know this before?'

'Because your esteemed leader didn't think of it till this morning.' I hit the steering wheel, hurting my hand. 'Damn!'

The parking lot in front of SmartSeeds was busy – two more squads had stopped to offer help and been commandeered to string crime scene tape and keep the curious outside it. I found a spot in the far corner for the pickup and we walked to the street cop with the posse box to sign in.

'Casey?' I said. 'What's going on?'

'One of those architects from the firm next door to SmartSeeds is in there with a very large firearm, they tell me.'

Brad Polk was standing white-faced and shaking beside a uniformed officer who was holding a bullhorn. It was Pete Corning, a guy I'd trained with but seldom see any more. A kind of muffled pandemonium was going on inside, some moaning, some weeping, and now and then a loud voice that commanded, 'Shut *up*! I'll tell you when you can talk!'

I stood beside Brad and said, just above a whisper, 'Is that Travis?'

He looked at me, nodded, sucked in a breath. And whispered back, 'We sent for his mama; she'll fix it if anybody can.'

'What?' I said. 'His *mama?*'

'Travis, listen to me,' Corning said through the bullhorn. Have the inventors of that device ever thought about the fact that it is not conducive to a warm, confidential exchange of ideas?

Travis seemed to feel the same way about it – he answered with a string of profanity that ended with 'Yell at me one more time with that stupid thing and I'm going to shoot this guy just for the hell of it, you hear me, Idiot Boy?'

And then, in a different voice – different that any voice I ever heard come out of a human being, actually, sort of like a cat's growl – he said, 'You come and stand right here by me, honey. Right here where I can touch you, sweet Marilyn, baby. You and I are going to have some great times, hear? Soon as we get these other idiots out of our way.'

Marilyn, sounding a little breathless but doing a brave job of keeping calm, then said, 'Travis, there are some things I need to explain to you, things you don't know. Couldn't you just put that gun down a minute so we can talk?'

'No, babe. I know a lot more than you think,' the strange, growling voice said. 'See, this is starting to be just like it was before with Nate – I never could get anywhere with you because he was always right there in the way. But I got rid of Nate so you and I could be together, didn't I? Only now here's this Brennan, taking over everything, saying do this and do that. And I can't keep on killing all the men you give in to, Marilyn, honey, so now I'm just going to have to take you away from here and talk some sense into you. These men are just using you, Marilyn, baby, what you need is somebody who—'

'Whatever you say, Travis, but you're starting to hurt my arm a little,' she said. 'Just ease up a little there, sweetie—'

'Well, I can't do that,' he said, 'because you might get away from me then. You're such a cute, tricky girl . . .'

There was a small commotion behind us then, back by the tape line. Blue-clad arms were passing someone forward, under the tape and up toward Brad. Head cocked a little to one side, listening to Travis's voice, a small, thin woman in blue canvas sneakers and a print housedress was striding steadily. She wore a blue denim apron over her dress and a red baseball cap pulled low over her gray curls.

When she walked up to Brad, he whispered urgently, 'Hi, Mrs Diebencorn. Thanks for coming.'

She nodded and asked in a conversational tone of voice, 'Sonny in there?' Her voice was dry as wind over old cornstalks, but she wasn't whispering like the rest of us. She sounded matter-of-fact, not frightened at all.

Brad said, 'Yes,' with a little tremor.

'He got the door locked?'

'Yes. We've tried and tried—'

She nodded again and walked up to the door, stood close to it and said, 'Sonny? Open the door.'

There was a pause before Travis's voice, much reformed from the one he'd been using, almost back to the one I knew, said, 'Mama?'

'Yup,' she said. 'Open up.'

'Mama, you don't belong here. I'm sorry they

bothered you to come over here but I wish you'd just go on home now and let me take care of things, OK?'

'I'll be the judge of where I belong, mister,' Mrs Diebencorn said, her voice a little sterner than before. 'And I'll thank you not to start telling me what to do. Now open this door before I get cross.'

'Oh, Mama, for Pete's sake—'

Mrs Diebencorn slid her right hand under the denim apron and reached into the deep side pocket of the cotton dress. When she pulled her skinny hand out of the pocket, it was holding what appeared to be a genuine antique, blue steel Colt revolver with a checkered wooden handle.

She got everybody's attention right away – in a blink, half-a-dozen cops had their Glocks out of their holsters and were moving toward her, saying, 'Wait now,' and 'Stop, ma'am,' but hesitating, looking for a clear shot that just wasn't there. And while everybody else dithered, Mrs Diebencorn cocked the hammer back and fired one shot into the strike plate of the cheap hollow-core door.

Hardware and wood chips flew around as the door swung open a few inches to reveal an extremely pale Dan Brennan swaying uncertainly in soiled trousers. Mrs Diebencorn poked at the door with the barrel of the revolver, and when it swung open a little wider we could see a swaying, agitated Travis Diebencorn, holding tight to the right arm of Marilyn DiSilvia, who looked stunning as usual in a pink sweater with little brilliants at the neckline.

'You been making trouble for these folks?' Mrs Diebencorn asked her son.

'No more than I have to, Mama,' Travis told her. 'I surely wish you wouldn't get mixed up in this.' He was looking a little dizzy now, like he might be going to throw up or faint. But in the hand that wasn't holding Marilyn, he was carrying a Remington model 7400 hunting rifle equipped with a Burris scope. A large, impressive weapon, it looked quite capable of firing the casing we'd found in the parking garage.

His mother reached across the doorsill and grabbed the front of Travis's shirt with her left hand. She hauled him right outside that way, not talking any more, just tugging him along. While Travis was trying to twist away from his mother, Marilyn got free of his other hand and stepped behind Dan Brennan. Travis came through the door carrying the big gun, yelling, 'Mama, now, damn it, cut it out!'

Both the squads went into action then, saying, 'We got this, ma'am,' and 'Let me have him, Mrs . . .' unable to finish the long name they couldn't remember. They grappled her son across the sidewalk, many hands on him, one of them snatching the gun away. His mother watched, wincing, as they hauled Travis Diebencorn toward the squad car with the cage in back. They put him in chains and read him his rights. When he acknowledged that he had heard them, one of them put a hand on top of his head as they shoved him into the cage and locked it.

His mother stepped in front of Pete Corning to say, when he came around the front of the squad car, 'He's going to need a doctor as soon as you get him to town, hear? Looks like he's way past due a shot of insulin.'

'We'll see he gets it, ma'am,' he said. 'You want to ride in with the other officer?'

'No, thanks,' she said. 'I'll be along later. Don't look like he's going to be eligible for no bail anyways.'

Travis yelled at her from the cage, 'Get me out of here, Mama!'

She looked at him, gave her head a sad little shake, and said, 'Oh, honey . . .'

It was a steep climb into the Dodge pickup for her, and she had to sit well forward on the seat to reach the gas pedal. She gunned the motor once, released the hand brake and drove out of the parking lot without another glance at any of us.

Sixteen

'I'm having a hard time believing this,' McCafferty said the following Friday. 'You're absolutely sure it was Clifford Mangen's group that did the break-ins?'

'Chief, they don't even deny it,' I said. 'Most of them still insist it was the right thing to do.'

'And they're probably not going to change that attitude,' Bo said, 'as long as they have friends coming around saying, "Way to go, man." Lotta people think those messages were right on the money.'

'Yeah, now that it's clear they had nothing to do with the murder,' Clint said, flashing his easy smile, 'the break-ins are taking on that little edge people like.'

'Hell you say,' McCafferty said. 'What little edge is that?'

'Well, you know, pushing the boundaries a little, giving the finger to the rules.'

'Except they weren't trying to get rid of rules – they wanted the government to add a few,' I said. My People Crimes crew was gathered around the big table in front of Ray's office, coffee and notes jumbled in with smart phones and print-outs. The chief had come down the hall to sit in while we debriefed from the Gold case.

'Because honestly, I'm still not sure I understand everything that went on here this week,' he said. 'Am I exaggerating or did this get kind of crazy?'

'Definitely crazy as far as I'm concerned,' Winnie said. 'I learned so much about so many people so fast, I felt like my brain was on fire. But it never was clear to me – were those note-writers protesting about genetic modification, or were they concerned about the weather?'

'Both, I guess,' Ray said. 'But in the end the murder turned out to be about sex as usual. Which is a big relief; otherwise I was beginning to think we were headed for a clusterfuck about global warming.'

'Oh, please,' McCafferty said. 'Our workload is heavy enough without getting into that.'

'But see, there we go, pushing it under the

rug like everybody else,' Rosie said. 'That's the one thing those guys said that I bet we all agree with – sooner or later we've all got to face it, so why not now while we can still do something—'

'Rosie,' Bo said, 'not now, OK?' His voice was so quiet it hardly carried to the rest of us, but he reached across the table and touched the side of her hand with the tip of his index finger, and she looked at him and raised one eyebrow just a little, and quit talking.

We all sat still for a few seconds while the planets rearranged themselves around these new polar coordinates. Rosie, backing off? In the shocked silence that followed, McCafferty asked, 'This passion Diebencorn had for the office manager – how come nobody worried about that before?'

'I don't think anybody noticed it, Chief. He was just this talkative kid who kept running in and out. They all thought he was obsessed with Nathan Gold, admiring him the way they all did.'

McCafferty shook his head. 'What a mix-up.'

I said, 'Well, it was, but we've had cases that ended a lot worse than this one. Billy McGowan's going to prison where he can't steal anything much for a while—'

'I *guess* that's good,' McCafferty said. 'Pretty hard to see how he'll ever pay for that nice Ford SUV he wrecked while he's sitting in the slammer, though.'

'Come on,' I said. 'Sitting anywhere on this planet, do you really think Billy McGowan might ever pay off that insurance company for a thirty-two-thousand-dollar automobile?'

'Maybe if he had two lifetimes, which God forbid.'

'Amen. And by a small miracle nobody got killed at SmartSeeds Monday morning, so—'

'Yeah, a small miracle named Mama who I wish I could have been there to see.' McCafferty grew a bemused smile, thinking about the feisty housewife who had featured prominently in newspaper and video clips all week. 'I still can't believe the luck, that none of the cops who were there that morning decided to shoot it out with her – though who could have blamed them?'

'I've been wondering,' I said, 'if you were thinking of issuing a directive.'

'Of course I thought of it, but what would I say? "Every time you exercise good judgment like you did on Monday be sure you're all as lucky as you were that day?" I think I'll just say an extra Hail Mary while I let the dust settle.' He looked around the table. 'Who wants to explain how Travis did it?'

We all did some foot-shuffling and scratching till I finally said, 'Pokey kept saying insulin effects are different for everybody but that one shot of insulin shouldn't have been enough to kill the doctor. Travis looked so smug when he asked him about it, Pokey went back and searched the body some more, and now he's sure he's found a second wound track inside Gold's right nostril.'

'So he went back in and finished the job? Wasn't anybody paying attention to this guy?'

'I guess they were used to him running in and out of the two offices. And Marilyn was gone all morning.'

'There's also the breakfast Gold didn't eat,' Bo said. 'He was already on pretty low blood sugar when he got the first shot, so it took him down fast.'

'I get that,' the chief said. 'But how'd the architect manage that first one?'

'Oh, he told us that, right after he got arrested,' I said. 'When Travis first woke up, all trussed up there in the hospital bed – because, you know, he passed out in the squad car before *he* got *his* shot—'

'Yeah, I know about that part.'

'Well, so they tell me the relief is quite remarkable after you've been that close to death. He felt like he'd been rescued, and Ray and I were there by the bed looking anxious. So for a few minutes he just talked to us like we were all pals together. Told us he felt a lot better now; he was going to be OK.'

Ray smiled, remembering. 'Jake said, "That's good, Travis," and then Travis started to brag about how clever he was. So we just shut up and listened.'

'And heard what?' McCafferty said.

'How he waited in the parking lot for the doctor, because he'd decided this was the day – he couldn't put it off any longer. He was carrying some records in a wooden orange crate, had the syringes ready in his shirt pocket. When he saw the doctor getting out of his car, he stepped up behind him, carrying the box, and swung it so it hit the back of Nathan's arm. He yelled, "Stand still! I think I got it!" and quick gave him a shot.'

'Why'd he hit him with the box?'

'Travis knows a lot about shots,' I said. 'He's a type one diabetic so he's lived with them almost all his life. So he knew the doc would hardly feel the needle going in where he'd just been hit. It's an old trick vets use with horses. Maybe Mama used it a time or two when her sonny-boy wouldn't stand still for his meds.

'Travis pretended he'd just killed a bee back there. He said, "I'm not sure I got him before he bit you, though. Looks like a little blood back here, I'll wipe it off." But the doc said, "Never mind that, it's nothing." Impatient to get inside – like always, Travis said, all the doctor was thinking about was his work. If you could have seen his face when he said that,' I told the chief, 'you would have no doubt how much Travis hated Nathan Gold.'

'That must be some office manager.'

'It wasn't only Marilyn,' I said. 'Nobody gave Travis much respect around there – he was kind of the little new guy they all poked fun at. But they were all very impressed by the brilliant Nathan Gold. So Travis was jealous about that, too. And don't forget, Travis was raised to think he should get whatever he wanted.'

'Why?'

'He was his mother's only child,' Abeo said. She and Andy had been down along the river, talking to Diebencorns all week. 'Alice married late, had her one baby after she feared it was too late – she has always had a profound attachment to her son, I believe.'

'To put it very mildly,' Andy said, with a little snort. 'Alice Diebencorn is kind of like those stage mothers you read about – her whole life has been centered on her child.'

'Also they have this clannish way of life, this group,' Abeo said. 'Have their own church down there, home school their children.'

'To protect them from outside influences, Travis's father explained to me,' Andy said. 'We didn't actually find anybody playing the banjo, Chief, but I kept thinking about that movie, *Deliverance*.'

McCafferty gave Andy a very straight look and said, 'You wouldn't be pulling my leg a little here, would you?'

'No – ask Abeo. She talked to the same folks I did.' He grinned across the table at her. The two of them had bonded over this case and were now becoming the most unlikely pair of buddies in the section.

Abeo cleared her throat and folded her hands neatly around her tablet. 'Their behavior is somewhat outside the mainstream,' she said while the chief watched her with great interest. 'But of course, that is the glory of our democracy, is it not? We have room for a wide variety of behaviors.'

'Uh-huh. Not including murder, of course.'

'Well, of course. And Alice does not condone murder. She merely says Travis is entitled to the best defense he can get and she will see he gets it.'

'Good for her. And we will do our best to see that her defense attorney never succeeds in freeing her son. Jake, have we got the physical evidence we need to nail him?'

'We have the recording Ray made while he was still chatty, before Mama showed up with the lawyer. That should be OK because he was Mirandized before they put him in the car. We have a dozen witnesses who heard him confess to killing Nathan. The gun he was holding fired the ammo we found in the parking garage. And we got some DNA off the bottom of Mrs Ross's chair where she's pretty sure she never touched it; we're hoping that turns out to be his.'

'What was that all about, that second string of nutty crimes?'

'Well, one was the murder—'

'OK, but the other two—'

'For cover. That's one of the things he explained to us as he was coming out of the insulin-deprived coma. How he realized these break-ins had created a kind of a cloud bank that he could hide a murder in. But he thought one crime alone might stand out too much, so he'd better create a cluster like the first.'

'Geez. So complicated.' McCafferty got up, shaking his head. 'Good work, guys. Make sure you keep all the "i"s dotted and the "t"s crossed, please. Mama's lawyer is out there looking for weak spots, and we mustn't let Travis get away. He's too warped to run loose.'

Rosie Doyle came in my office just before five, to ask for a personal day next week.

'Sure,' I said. 'Is anything wrong? You seem pretty quiet today.'

'Wrong? No.' She treated me to a sudden, radiant smile. 'On the contrary. The Gold family just taught me a lesson and now I have some shopping to do.'

'The Gold family? Seems to me all their lessons are tragic.'

'Exactly. I got to thinking about that, how those two women gave up more than they could afford just to please Nathan, and when he got sick of the burden of that he found another place to get his jollies. So after work last night I made Bo and Nelly sit on the couch and I said, "We each need to say what we have to have, so we can decide if we've got a future together or not." And you know Bo, he never wants to *talk* about anything—'

'Right,' I said. 'Not even global warming.'

'Yeah, not even.' She rolled her eyes. 'So right away he said, "Rosie, don't talk like that – of course we have a future." And I said, "Well, Bo, my clock is ticking and I want my future now." And then I asked Nelly, "Be honest with me, please. If I married your dad and tried to make us into a family, would that make you jealous and insecure?" Bo looked like he was going to pass out, but Nelly jumped up off the couch and said, "Oh, boy, are we going to have a wedding? Can I be the bridesmaid?"'

Rosie giggled – the happiest sound I'd heard out of her in some time. 'Nelly's so responsible we forget sometimes that she's only nine years old. All her coloring books have weddings in them. She's gaga about weddings.'

I knew it wasn't all going to be this easy, but I was hoping Rosie would at least get some nice quiet time before anything rained on her parade. Sure there would be plenty of tricky places in this relationship – Bo was a poor communicator and Rosie was certainly volatile. But as Clifford said, did those farmers in Concord know exactly what would happen after they fired their guns? Sometimes you just have to go ahead and take your best shot.